SECRETS UNLOCKED

THE JAMES GANG

C. F. FRANCIS

ISBN: 979-8-9872316-0-9 (ebook)

ISBN: 979-8-9872316-1-6 (print)

 Created with Vellum

PRAISE FOR C. F. FRANCIS

Secrets Unlocked

"An exciting addition to the James Gang series. Full of twists, puzzles, and action sure to delight romantic suspense fans. This was my first C. F. Francis book and now I'm eager for more!. - USA Today bestselling author Rachel Grant.

Lovers Key

"An exciting and dynamic Romantic Suspense novel that is sure to have fans of the genre eager for their next fix." – Toni Anderson, New York Times Bestselling Author

Explosive Touch

"If one likes steam romance mixed with sexy military men and the fiery independent women they love, **Explosive Touch is a must read!**" – InD'Tale Magazine Review.

Run, River, Run

"An enthralling tale mixed with tragedy, treachery, and triumph "Run, River, Run" delivers goosebumps of both the suspenseful and sensuous kind!" ~InD'tale Magazine

PROLOGUE

"Move, damn it," Savannah muttered, demanding her arms and shoulders keep stroking. She glanced at the Sanibel shoreline with each new breath she took. Would she make it? Her body was revolting. The powerful kicks that had propelled her away from the boat were now barely a flutter. The adage, sink or swim, slipped into her head. They were literally her only two choices.

This is what she got for being stupid. She thought she was past being stupid.

Something brushed by her leg, breaking the rhythm she'd been trying so hard to maintain. The instant of panic caused her to slip beneath the surface. She fought her way back. Gasping for air as she treaded water, she checked the surrounding area. There was nothing—nothing but a few lights along Sanibel's shoreline. The boat which had been her temporary jail had either left or had gone dark. The second scenario was terrifying. Just because she couldn't hear or see them didn't mean they weren't drifting nearby.

Did they even know she was gone? She'd picked the

lock on the cabin where they'd stashed her. The three men had been quarreling on the bridge as she slipped over the side.

How the hell had she allowed herself to get sucked into this? Her street smarts should have been flashing red. She'd accepted the last-minute invitation from Tony to join him and a few co-workers on a sunset cruise. As she approached the yacht, though, a chill ran down her spine. She should have listened to her instincts.

Stop thinking and swim. She didn't have the energy to do both. Exhaustion had long ago set in. *You can do this.* Don't let the bad guys win. She was alone, but *she* was in control. She swore she'd never allow anyone to control her again. Swim, damn it.

The decision to head to the island instead of Fort Myers Beach may not have been a wise one. The marina was half the distance, but she'd suspected that would be the first place they would look for her. Besides, one of the few people she considered a friend lived in Sanibel.

Sucking in a deep breath, she forced her aching body to move, but after a few strokes she heard the distant rumble of a boat's engines. Scanning the area, she spotted the outline of the darkened yacht now backlit by the lights of a busy Fort Myers Beach. A single flashlight scanned the waters near the boat. They must have discovered she was missing.

The energy she'd been lacking came roaring back. She had no intention of being found.

1

---

*T*raffic was still light as Rick jogged over the expanse of the Sanibel Causeway. It was early and the tourists who would flock to the island had yet to rise. The visitors who stayed on the island rarely frequented the causeway beaches. Most hotels and condominiums had access to their own private strip of sand. A few bicyclists had passed him on his run toward the toll plaza, but other than that it was quiet. A beautiful morning for a run over the turquoise waters of the bay.

As he reached the plaza he crossed the road for his return trek. Glancing at his watch, he confirmed he'd have plenty of time for a shower before reporting to work. Being the only detective on the Sanibel Police Department, he didn't have to punch a time clock. But there were a couple of burglaries and an attempted break-in he wanted to resolve before the season arrived. Snowbirds tended to relax their guard while they relaxed in the warm temperatures, making them the occasional target—and making things busier for the department.

Cresting the highest point in the span, Rick noted the

small private beach at the southwest end of the causeway. Someone was out early. Actually, it was the first time he remembered seeing anyone on the small strip of sand this time of the morning.

Rick checked the sidewalk in front of him. It was free of bicyclists and joggers, allowing him to return his attention to the lone sunbather. The closer he got, the odder the picture struck him. It wasn't warm out, but it wasn't particularly cool either. The woman was fully clothed. And where the hell was her towel or blanket? She was sprawled facedown across the sand, and she wasn't moving.

Kicking up his pace, he hit the end of the span and made an immediate right, pulling out his identification as he ran. If she was okay, he could startle her. His police credentials would, hopefully, de-escalate the situation. Besides, unless she was one of the few residents with legal access to that beach, she needed to leave.

As he drew closer, he knew neither was the case. Her clothing and hair were visibly caked with salt and sand. What he could see of her skin was pale. Dropping to his knees, he quickly found her pulse—strong and steady. She stirred at his touch. He rolled her onto her back and carefully brushed sand and hair from her face. There were no obvious injuries. That didn't mean something wasn't going on internally.

He pulled his phone from the zipped pocket of his jogging shorts and placed a call to the dispatcher requesting paramedics to his location. Her eyes fluttered, then opened wide. Bronze discs, bordering on copper, locked with his for a second before she scooted away. Man, she was a beauty. A frightened one based on her agitated movements.

"It's okay," Rick said, keeping his distance. "I'm with the Sanibel Police Department. I have medics on the way."

She stopped her awkward crab-like crawl and rested her ass on the sand. Her breathing had ratcheted up to the point he was afraid she'd pass out from hyperventilating.

"Do you have identification?"

Smart woman. He extended his hand with his police badge in it.

"You're not dressed like the police."

"I was jogging when I spotted you from the bridge. How'd you get here? What happened to you?"

She scrutinized the beach including the water behind him. Glancing over his shoulder, he didn't notice any unusual activity on the bay. Then it clicked.

"You were in the water. Did you fall off the bridge? Did you jump?" Had she been trying to kill herself?

"Neither." She was quick to answer. "I was swimming."

"In those clothes?" She was wearing black leggings and a long sleeve cotton top, which fit her like a second skin. She didn't back away as he approached, so he continued toward her until he reached her side. He tried to make himself smaller and less intimidating by crouching next to her. He was a big man. While she was tall, she was slim—willowy. Small next to his large frame.

She was holding herself together, but it was obviously taking a great deal of effort. You didn't need his detective skills to note the continual check of her surroundings. She was definitely afraid of something or someone.

"I didn't have a choice." Her eyes flicked from one boat to another as San Carlos Bay filled with watercraft.

She needed to explain that comment, but her condition was his first priority. "Are you hurt?"

She rolled her shoulders then stretched and rotated her neck. "I'm sore but I think I'm okay."

The woman had a nasty bruise on her jaw. It was recent and must hurt like hell. Was she ignoring it, hoping he wouldn't notice, or the discomfort of her injuries had yet to set in?

"We'll have the medics check you out. What's your name? I'm Rick. Rick Wilcowski."

"Savannah Finch." She padded her hips. "I can't prove it. I don't have my phone or identification." Panic laced her words. "I didn't do anything, I swear."

"Nobody said you did," he countered. "How did you get in the water?"

"I jumped."

"You just said you didn't." His internal radar was pinging so loud it was a wonder she didn't hear it.

"You asked if I jumped off the bridge. I didn't. I jumped off a boat."

"Why?"

"I was afraid they wanted to kill me."

2

"Someone tried to kill you?" he asked, raising the hand that held the phone. He was going to call for additional troops.

"No. Wait. I don't know." Her mind was so scrambled. What if she simply panicked? Locking her in that cabin had been so reminiscent of events from her past. Could she have blown things out of proportion? She didn't think so, but fear could do funny things to the mind. She knew that from experience.

Deep furrows were etched across Wilcowski's forehead. The cop was staring at her as if she had two heads. Savannah would probably do the same in his place. Resting her chin in the palm of one hand, she debated what to tell him. She doubted he'd believe her. After he checked her background, he'd question everything she said.

"We need to find Tony." What if he was a victim, too? When she'd dropped into the water, she'd assumed he was one of the bad guys, but he'd been arguing with the men at the helm. Where was he? Where was the boat?

"We need to start from the beginning," the detective stated. It wasn't a suggestion. "Who's Tony?"

Instead of answering, she looked past him to the approaching EMS unit. "I don't want to see them. I don't have to see them, do I?" Her legs wobbled as she got to her feet. She was quickly steadied as his large, firm hand clasped her elbow. She flinched. A knee-jerk reaction she'd yet to get past. "Please. I promise you I'm all right. I'll be fine."

His intense blue eyes studied her.

"Please," she repeated.

"Okay, Savannah. But don't go anywhere. You wait here for me." He walked toward the paramedics who were now exiting their vehicle.

"Finch," she shouted to his retreating backside. "Everybody calls me Finch."

What made her volunteer that? He flicked a quick look over his broad shoulder then turned to address the medics. There was familiarity in their stance and interactions. They obviously knew one another. She couldn't hear what they were saying, but she didn't need to. They weren't socializing. There were two medics, both looking in her direction. A woman, big enough to heft Savannah over her head, and a young man. Both were silently listening to whatever the cop was telling them. They gave her a second glance before nodding to the detective, then returning to their unit.

He was on his phone again as he walked in her direction. All she caught was "see you in a few" as he disconnected.

"See who?" she asked as he closed the distance. His silver blond hair stood out against his tanned skin. His chest wasn't bare, but a t-shirt emblazoned with the name of a restaurant, *Mama's Italian Food*, stretched across his torso. The man was solid.

"I've called a friend for a ride. If you won't let the medics check you out, then I need to get you to the clinic."

"I don't need a doctor. I need to find Tony." Maybe he could add logic where she couldn't see it, assuming he was okay.

"The sooner you explain to me what happened, the sooner we can look for your friend," he said, guiding her toward a large flat rock.

She leaned away from his touch as soon as she had something solid under her. Hadn't she gotten past her reticence toward the police? Apparently not. She didn't see where she had much choice but to talk to him. They had held her against her will—kidnapping was probably the technical term. And Tony may, or may not be, missing.

She should call work to see if he was there. God, she hoped this was all a big mistake, and she'd spectacularly over reacted. Calling would be the smart thing to do before making an official report. Was she being paranoid about nothing?

"Can I use your phone?" When he hesitated, she explained. "I want to find out if Tony showed up for work and talk to him if he did." And hopefully receive a simple explanation of why she almost drowned last night. Why had he lured her to that boat? Which is exactly what he'd done with the promise there would be co-workers and friends joining them there. The only people on that boat were the two men. Tony's story didn't wash, but that didn't mean her assumption was right, either.

"Who is this Tony? And why are you so worried about him?"

"He was on the boat last night." Her head tilted back

as she glanced at the tall man, shielding her eyes from the sun that had risen behind him.

Wilcowski turned his attention to the water. "What boat? How could they not know you were missing? We didn't get a report of a missing passenger, or anyone lost in the water."

His last statement gave credence to her beliefs. "They were probably hoping I'd wash up on a beach somewhere."

"You did wash up on a beach. This one," he pointed out.

"Alive," she countered.

"You need to explain what happened," he repeated more forcefully. "What men? What boat? Were you threatened?"

"Give me your God damn phone," she was fast losing what patience she had and chipping away at her fear. "If I can reach Tony, then you can go on presuming I'm a nut case and leave me alone." Assuming her co-worker had a reasonable explanation for this nightmare. She was wavering between thinking she was crazy and knowing she wasn't.

"You're going to get checked out before you're rid of me," he scowled. "Whether there was a crime or not."

"Fine." Besides, she may still need a cop, depending on what she heard about Tony—or from him.

She held out her hand. He slapped his phone into it. She didn't know Tony's number, but she could call the spa.

Finch's fingers trembled as she tapped each number on the keypad. She reached the manager, Mrs. Gonzales, and explained she wouldn't be in today because of an accident. She didn't elaborate.

"Great. Now I'm short two staff members." Finch's stomach knotted.

"Who else isn't there?"

"Tony. I called and left messages for both of you. At least you called in."

"I'm sorry. It's a long story but I've lost my purse and phone. I'm headed to a clinic to get checked out now. If I can come in later, I will."

"Not much I can do about it. I've already canceled or rescheduled your appointments. Where are you? What clinic are you going to? Do you need a ride?"

"I'm on Sanibel and I have a ride. Thank you."

"I can send one of the staff to come get you."

"You already said you were shorthanded. I'll call later," Finch thanked her boss again, but the line went dead mid-sentence.

"All right. I've been patient. What is going on?"

"I don't know how to explain it." She handed his phone back to him.

"Try," he said, watching her guardedly.

She briefly recounted the events of the prior night and how she found herself on this beach. His silence and the queer look in his eye suggested he was a bit more than just skeptical.

"A man hit you then locked you in the cabin on a large boat. A friend…"

"Co-worker," she corrected.

"This co-worker stood by and didn't stop it. You picked the lock on the cabin door—not a common skill—and jumped into the bay. Now there's no boat. No report of anyone going overboard and, based on what I deduced from your end of the call, no Tony."

What did she say to that? It was all true.

"Why did you get on a boat in the first place? You say your relationship with this guy wasn't personal, and you didn't know the other men."

"I didn't get on the boat voluntarily. One of the bastards on board grabbed me and dragged me into the cabin—after he smacked me."

"Have you any idea how far-fetched this sounds?"

"I have a friend here on Sanibel. She'll vouch I'm not crazy. We've known each other a long time."

"What's your friend's name?"

A large pickup truck was now coming toward them on the narrow road leading to the beach, distracting them both. A man, as big and tall as the detective, hopped out of the cab. The passenger door opened and a small, short-haired woman slid from the seat.

"I asked you to wait in the truck until I found out what was going on," the driver said, shaking his head as he rounded the front of the vehicle and blocked her passage.

"It's Finch, Troy. Oh, my God," she said, dodging the driver. "What the hell happened to you?"

Finch hugged Shayne tightly. She'd been thrown a life-line she hadn't seen coming. "I don't know. Not exactly."

"You can't get a break, can you?" Shayne asked, rhetorically.

"This is your friend?" Wilcowski asked.

"Finch and I worked together at the same country club in Tampa," Shayne explained.

"The same country club that was blown to bits?"

"That's the one."

"So, this is Savannah Finch?" The driver of the truck wrapped his well-toned arm around Shayne's waist, coaxing her back to his side. Finch looked at the stunningly handsome male specimen sporting a patch over his left eye. Troy McKenzie. While she and Shayne had met for lunch a couple of times, she'd yet to meet her husband. Not the best of circumstances to make his acquaintance. He may have had only one eye, but he took in a lot. His gaze traveled from her messy, salt-stiffened hair to her bare feet and up again. "What happened to you?"

"That's what I intend to find out," Wilcowski said, leading her to McKenzie's truck.

3

———

"Okay, Finch." It felt strange calling her that. Perhaps she didn't like her first name, although he couldn't imagine why. Savannah rolled off the tongue smoothly. It also appeared to suit the mysterious woman.

"I let the EMS go against my better judgment. I should be filing a report right now, but Shayne vouches for you, so I'm giving you a chance to explain. What happened out there? Why you think someone tried to kill you?"

"Somebody tried to kill you?" Shayne asked. It wasn't hard to miss the shock in her voice.

"I said I wasn't certain."

"Yet, you jumped off a boat and barely made it to shore. You were so desperate you were willing to take the chance on drowning."

"Tell him, Finch," Shayne urged her. "He's one of the good guys, I swear."

His mermaid slumped against the seat. Mermaid was a good analogy. She was lithe, tall but curved in all the right places. The sun highlighted the golden tones in her caramel-

14

colored hair. She'd added a magenta streak to a swath that hung closest to her face. Her nose turned up at the tip just a little. Her eyes, though, were her most stunning feature.

Shayne unbuckled her seat belt, turning to reach for Finch's hand. Troy shot his wife a worrisome look, but he kept his thoughts to himself. Troy would always consider himself her protector, even though his petite wife was tough as nails. They'd had a rough and tumble romance, and the two of them had almost been killed because of the fallout from the bombing in Tampa.

"Why didn't you call for help?" Shayne asked.

"Things happened so fast. They took my purse and phone."

"Let's take this from the top," Rick told her. "This time with details."

She inhaled deeply, then let the breath out on a huff. "One of my co-workers, Tony, said a group from work was taking a boat out to watch the sunset. He invited me to go along. It was a spur-of-the-moment thing."

"Where do you work?"

"A spa in Bonita Springs," she replied. "Don't give me that look. It's a spa that caters to upscale clients. Resorts that don't have spas, refer a lot of their guests to us. It's not some sleazy massage brothel."

"Finch was the best massage therapist Copperhead employed before the bombing." Shayne came to her friend's defense. "A lot of people lost their jobs when the clubhouse was destroyed."

"Could this incident be connected to the bombing?"

Troy looked in his rearview mirror at Rick. "I kept in touch with that DEA agent, Gardner, until he left the agency. They closed the book on that investigation."

"Why didn't you ask questions about the invitation?"

"Are you sure he's one of the good guys?" Finch eyed Shayne.

"Honey," Troy interrupted. "Turn around and buckle your seat belt before some idiot comes out of a side street and T-bones us."

"We're almost there," she argued.

"Do it for me, sweetie."

Rick watched Shayne lean over to give her husband a peck on the cheek then did as requested. After Troy's injury in Afghanistan and his subsequent, but brief, battle with alcohol, Rick had feared the man would never be happy again. With Shayne in his life, he'd left all that in the past. He was all work when it came to the investigative and security agency he and their friend, Steve Brody had built. Whenever he was with Shayne, however, the gentleness in the man rose to the surface. They made an odd pair yet were perfect for one another.

"Shayne's right. We'll be there in a minute. Tell me what you can before we hand you over to Kevin."

"Who's Kevin?"

"You ask a lot of questions, but don't answer many." There was fear in her tone, so Rick didn't dwell on the point. "Kevin Slawter. He was our team medic in the Army and a good friend of ours. He volunteers at a clinic once a week. Now tell me what made you take a swim last night."

Her shoulders dropped in resignation. "Except for Shayne, I don't have any friends in South Florida. When Tony invited me to join the group, I figured it was time I tried to make a few friends.

"Obviously, that didn't happen. How well do you know this Tony?"

"I don't know any of my co-workers on a social level, but they've all been nice to me since I started to work there. The boat ride seemed like a good way to get to know them better. I didn't think anything unusual was going on until we got to the boat."

"You rode with Tony to the dock?"

"Yes. He said he'd take me back to get my car after the cruise was over."

"And no one else rode with you to the marina?"

"No." Her eyes narrowed at the corners. She'd picked up on his insinuation that she'd made a poor choice. It was obvious she didn't appreciate him pointing it out.

"Do you know Tony's last name?" Rick leaned forward, opening the console separating the front seats. He didn't have to dig far to find a pen and pad. Troy wouldn't be without either.

"Of course, I do." Sparks flashed from those narrow slits. "Gambino. Anthony Gambino."

Gambino? The same name as one of the most infamous organized crime families—and contrary to popular belief most were still functioning, just with less fanfare. The coincidence was a little too unsettling.

"Okay. What happened when you got to the boat?" he asked, softening his tone. He knew better than to antagonize a witness. They tended to clam up.

"I expected to see others there. Co-workers. The friends he mentioned. But it was only me, Tony and two guys I didn't know. One man was on the main deck. The other on the bridge, I think that's what they call it. I got a creepy feeling."

"I don't blame you," Shayne volunteered.

"I asked where everyone was. Tony said they were on their way. He's either clairvoyant or was lying. He never touched his phone after we got in his car. How could he know where the others were? My instincts said to get the hell out of there. I told Tony I'd wait on the dock for some others to arrive. That's when the guy on deck grabbed me and pulled me onboard."

"Do you remember the name of the vessel?" Troy piped in.

"I didn't see the rear of the boat. That's where they paint the name, isn't it?"

Rick nodded. "Yeah. It's called the stern. What happened next?"

"I tripped. Hit the deck pretty hard. I kicked him in the shin with my heel, but all that did was piss him off. He yanked me off the deck by my shirt, then hit me." She rubbed her chin. "The next thing I remember is coming to in a cabin. The door was locked, the boat was moving, and my purse and phone were gone."

They pulled into the parking lot of an old strip mall. Unlike the attractive businesses that lined Periwinkle Way, this small group of buildings catered to the locals and those who worked on the island. A clinic had been set up in one of the suites by several doctors from Fort Myers and Sanibel. It was funded by grants and donations from many of the businesses on Sanibel.

Shayne jumped out of the vehicle as soon as it came to a stop. "I'll run in and talk to Kevin."

Picking at her cuticles, Finch's thoughts appeared to be directed inward. She no longer appeared frightened of Rick, which was a step in getting her to trust him and open up. It was obvious the woman didn't care for authority figures. He should have reported this already, but she was spooked. Her story had a lot of holes in it but pushing her could also push her away. She was a friend of Shayne's. He'd respect that until he couldn't. A little more clarity would go a long way in deciding if an official inquiry was needed.

"You don't believe me, do you?" She glanced at him as if reading his mind.

"I don't know you, but if Shayne says you're okay, I take her word for it. As for believing you, I can see the bruises on your face and arms." She tugged her sleeves down over her wrists at the comment.

"I don't have any way to pay them or give them insurance information," she said redirecting her attention toward the clinic.

"Don't worry. It's a free clinic. You'll be in good hands," Troy assured her.

"You said you picked the lock on the cabin door," Rick resumed his questioning. "Where did you learn that skill?"

"It's not important."

Rick let the unanswered question ride. He was curious about her background, but right now he was more interested in what happened last night.

"Go on," he encouraged her. "You got out of the cabin. I assume it was below deck?"

"Yes."

"That had to be a good-sized boat." Troy was no longer buckled in. He'd adjusted his position so he could be part of the conversation.

"Bigger than any boat I've ever been on, but I wouldn't call it a yacht. Then, again, I'm not an expert."

"And then what?" Rick asked.

"I paused at the base of the stairs to be sure no one was on deck. I slipped over the rail when I heard Tony arguing with the two men."

"What were they arguing about?"

"Me, I think. I heard my name but couldn't make out what they were saying. Tony sounded angry, but I might have imagined their tone. I was so terrified and in a hurry at that point."

"And then you jumped ship?" Rick asked.

"Self-preservation kicked in. I probably overreacted. I'm sorry I brought you all into this."

"If that's a sample of your imagination, you should write screenplays for Hollywood." Rick glanced up as Shayne was returning to the truck. "When we're done here, you need to go with me to the station for a statement. I'll need a description of the men and the boat—anything you can remember."

Rick wasn't sure how to read her reaction. Was it fear, resignation, or sadness—perhaps a combination of all three? If she was terrified enough to risk drowning, something was definitely going on. But was it real or imagined?

"Kevin says they're busy," Shayne told them, returning to the truck, "but he'll squeeze her in. He asked that I bring her to the rear door so no one in the waiting room notices the express treatment."

"I'll get her to Kevin. I'm with her until we sort this out," Rick said. "Can you guys take a few more minutes out of your day and bring my truck here?"

Rick didn't miss Finch's eyes flick toward Shayne.

"Maybe she'd feel better if a woman stayed with her."

Shit. "Were you sexually assaulted?"

"What? No. No," Finch repeated, a little less forcefully. "No one touched me like that. No rape kit."

The finality in her voice surprised Rick. He didn't press the subject. She was just beginning to trust him. Kevin would tell him if she needed one. They'd cross that bridge if they came to it.

"If she's in any kind of danger, it's best I stick around." He pulled his keys from his pocket and tossed them to Troy. It was obvious Finch was still wary of him but didn't argue. She was excited to see Shayne and had accepted

Troy's presence without objection, but her demeanor toward him remained cold and suspicious.

Rick heard Shayne and Troy pull out of the parking lot but didn't turn to confirm it. He kept his eyes on the woman carefully making her way around the side of the building. As tall and thin as she was, she was also shapely. Her hips swayed smoothly as she maneuvered her bare feet over the sandy soil that ran along the side of the strip mall. He didn't need a distraction. He needed to find out what the hell was going on.

4

———

"Finch sat on an exam table in the tiny room wearing a cotton hospital gown. The medic, Kevin, had insisted that she get out of her snug-fitting clothing so he could check her for injuries. He'd stepped out of the room while she'd changed. It was the first time she was grateful to be in a patient's gown. Her clothing smelled of sea water and had formed a stiff crust. It was like wearing sandpaper. Unfortunately, she'd have to put them on when the medic was done with her.

"They knocked you unconscious?" he asked, examining her eyes. For a big man, he had a calming demeanor.

"For a second or two, I think. A right hook to the jaw did the job."

"You have bruises on your arms. Were you hit anywhere else?" He moved her hair aside to look at her neck.

"The guy didn't hold back when he yanked me onto the boat. Resisting only got me a fist to my jaw." Tony hadn't tried to stop him, at least not physically. She did hear him yell at the man to stop.

"Anything else hurting?"

"I ache, but I did a lot of swimming last night. It's been a while since I spent that much time in the water and then it was in a nice, calm pool. Swimming across the bay wasn't easy."

"You swam from the Fort Myers side of the bay?"

"I could see a hotel close to the boat as I slipped into the water. If they realized I was gone, I figured they'd look for me on the closest beach. So, I headed toward Sanibel."

"You're lucky you made it. That's one hell of a swim," he said, rotating her arm.

"I was on the swim team. It was the only thing I excelled at in high school," she added for no particular reason.

While Kevin examined her, he talked about his friends and their wives. He glowed whenever he mentioned his new bride, River, and the artistic masks she created.

After her brush with death, it appeared Shayne had landed in a happy place with good friends. Finch was glad for her. She'd been hoping to find her own special place. So far, things weren't looking too good.

"I think you have a mild concussion and you're going to ache for a while, but there's nothing I can do for you that you can't do for yourself. Put ice on those bruises." He handed her a travel-size packet of Tylenol. "Take these. It will help with the headache."

She gladly took the pills that dropped from the packet and washed them down with a small cup of water.

"You're a bit dehydrated, so don't skimp on the water today."

Sliding off the exam table, she eyed the bundle of clothing she'd discarded before donning the clinic's gown. She shuddered at the idea of donning the sandy clothing, but she couldn't go anywhere dressed like she was, and

Rick said they were going to the police station when they were finished here. As she reached for the pile of clothing, there was a tap on the door. A nurse or technician in scrubs held out a stack of neatly folded clothes. A pair of flip-flops sat on top. The two spoke briefly before Kevin shut the door.

"Shayne stopped by Josie's and borrowed a few items," he explained. "You and Josie are close to the same height, although you're a bit on the slighter side."

Finch recalled the names Kevin had mentioned earlier. She took the leggings and button-down blouse. Between the two garments was a package of new panties and a bra. She checked the size. Someone had guessed correctly. Why did the kind act make Finch want to cry? Years of practice had taught her how to keep her emotions in check.

"Rick is waiting in the hall." With that, the big, gentle man stepped into the corridor.

The clothing fit well enough and other than a shower, Finch couldn't imagine anything feeling better. She grabbed the dirty clothes, tucked the remaining undies between the two pieces clothing and headed out the door.

As promised, Rick was leaning against the wall across from the exam room, one foot propped against the wall.

"You look better," he said.

"The clean clothes help. I need to thank Josie for lending them to me and Shayne for asking on my behalf. Is she gone?"

"Troy and Shayne had to leave." Rick guided her to the rear exit of the building, then toward a massive pickup truck. "Get in," he said, opening the passenger door. She climbed onto the seat, then tossed her items onto the floor. The door slammed shut. Her rescuer wasn't happy.

"What's wrong?" she asked. Stupid question. If he was a good cop, he'd already checked her history.

"Does Shayne know you have a criminal record?" he asked, jumping into the driver's seat.

"Why does it matter to you one way or another?"

"Because she's a friend."

"I consider her a friend, too. And, yes, she knows. For God's sake, it's a juvenile record. I haven't been in any trouble since my early teens."

"You may be in a lot more trouble now. Tony Gambino appears to be missing."

5

___

"**A**re you sure?"

Rick could normally get a good read on people, but she was a tough one. He twisted in his seat and studied her mesmerizing eyes. Eyes were human lie detectors if you knew how to read them. He'd been trained to do that. He could only guess as far as she was concerned. If he was guessing right, she was scared shitless.

"Let's just say I can't locate him. I requested the Lee County Sheriff's office to do a wellness check while you were at the clinic."

"How did you know where he lives?" she asked, her head tilting to the right.

"DMV. There's no sign he'd been home last night."

"What if he spent the night elsewhere? Maybe he has a girlfriend." She squeezed the fingers of one hand in the other.

"He lured you to the boat, helped kidnap you, then went on a date so hot he was too exhausted to work or even call in?"

Her hands fisted and her eyes blazed as his sarcasm hit its mark. He preferred the heat of anger to nerves and fear.

"Is he involved in anything illegal?"

"How the hell would I know? I told you I didn't know him that well."

"Yet you got in a car with him."

"He's a co-worker. Don't tell me you never hitched a ride with a co-worker? And if I suspected he was trouble, I wouldn't have accepted his invitation, let alone get in the car with him. You can believe what you want, but I don't associate with people who could get me in trouble again."

Rick didn't miss the word she'd tacked on to the end of her answer. He needed to know more about her. He wanted to know more about her. Trouble or not, she was interesting.

Rick escorted her up the stairs to the police station and into his office. He was fortunate to have one. Only he and the captain had a private space. The rest of the staff worked in cubicles.

"Have you eaten?" he asked as she settled into the chair in front of his desk.

"Not since lunch yesterday, but I'm not hungry."

She looked a little underweight in his opinion, but he knew better than to comment on a woman's weight. More importantly, she'd spent a lot of energy getting to shore last night. She needed fuel.

"Wait here. I'll be right back."

He hit the vending machine and grabbed a water from the break room fridge, remembering Kevin's instructions that she stay hydrated. Her chin was almost resting against her chest when he returned to his office. As soon as he closed the door, she snapped to attention. She was exhausted, but he couldn't let her walk, assuming she had a place to go and a way to get there. There were lots of questions that needed answering.

"If you're allergic to peanuts," he said, dropping two cellophane wrapped packages of crackers on the desk, "skip the peanut butter ones." He plopped down the water bottle next to the snacks. "You need to eat. We're going to be here for a while."

It was already late morning. He'd order in lunch to get something more substantial in her.

"This is a police station, right? I assume you have coffee?" She actually smiled. It was a direct hit to his solar plexus. That smile and those eyes were a hell of a distraction.

"Yes. Not great but not as bad as the jokes you hear about station house coffee."

"I could use the caffeine. I need the jolt."

"Drink the water first. Then coffee." He wasn't her caretaker, but he didn't need her passing out on him either.

Her scowl returned as she uncapped the bottle. After chugging a third of it, she attacked one of the pack of crackers.

Her acceptance of food and drink had him relaxing into his chair. He'd been worried about her. Well, of course he was. It was ingrained in him to care for others. It's why he'd served his country and now the local citizenry. No reason to make a big deal out of it. Silently, he waited as she ate the six tiny cheese sandwiches before taking another gulp of water.

"Okay." He grabbed a legal pad out of his desk drawer and began taking notes. The interrogation room had built-in microphones, but his office, didn't have any recording devices. He was good with that. Some conversations were private and needed to stay that way.

"Let's take it slow and start at the beginning. When,

precisely, did Tony approach you about joining him on the boat?"

"Shortly before my last appointment of the day," she answered, taking another sip of water.

"Is that why you didn't speak to anyone else regarding the trip? It would be natural to mention it to your other co-workers, or vice versa."

"After he invited me, I didn't see anyone else. As soon as I prepped the therapy room for the next day, Tony knocked on the door and asked if I was ready to go. The parking lot was empty except for our two cars. It was stupid of me to assume the others were already on their way to the boat. I'm usually more cautious than that."

"How long have you worked at the spa?"

"Eight months, give or take a few days," she said. "While I wasn't physically injured in the bombing, emotionally I was having trouble getting past it. I didn't live far from Copperhead, so I drove by it every day to and from my new job. Knowing I was in that building hours before the explosion—knowing I'd almost lost my closest friend—I was having a hard time. It took a while, but Shayne convinced me to make the move. I applied to several hotels and spas and landed the job I have now."

"Anything odd about your workplace or the people?"

"No. As the saying goes, *same shit, different day*. It's like any job I've had. I have good and bad customers, mostly good ones, though."

"And the other employees? Anybody show any animosity toward you? Did you get along with your boss?" Rick waited while she popped another cracker in her mouth. Despite her claim that she wasn't hungry, she was clearing his desk of the snacks.

"I believe I have a good working relationship with everyone there. No one has said anything contrary toward me. I get along with the other massage therapists and technicians. Some better than others," she answered.

Rick refreshed his computer. He'd been watching to see if anyone reported Tony as missing. Being AWOL from work didn't mean he was in trouble. It hadn't yet been twenty-four hours since Finch had last seen him, so it wasn't surprising there was no report. He was glad to see no dead bodies had been discovered—identified or not.

The Lee County Sheriff's Office wasn't looking into Finch's story—and that's what they'd called it, a story. Like Rick, they'd run a quick check on Finch's background. The detective who had returned his call referenced her troubled past. He didn't come right out and say it, but he'd suggested that perhaps she was acting out or trying to get her co-worker in trouble. They needed more than a skeptical claim and a guy skipping work. Rick had nothing solid to give them.

"What did you and Tony talk about on the way to the marina?"

Her nose scrunched up and her eyes narrowed. He had the sudden urge to kiss the tip of that nose. "You ready for that coffee?" he asked instead.

"Huh?"

"I'll get us some coffee, then we'll go over the events of last night in detail." Despite LCSO's opinion, he senses where on high alert or she was a damned good liar. It might come naturally, considering her history, but Shayne had faith in her. That was enough for Rick until Finch gave him reason to doubt her.

6

———

"Oh, shit!" A different reality slammed into Finch. She needed to get to her apartment complex before the office closed. Her purse was missing along with her keys and phone. The management would have a duplicate key to her place. They'd have to change the locks, assuming her purse didn't miraculously appear. Like the boat and the people on it, she suspected it was long gone.

As soon as the door to Rick's office opened, she was on her feet. "Can I get a ride? I need to get to the office that manages my apartment. I don't have any way to pay for a ride share," she said, she couldn't stop her voice from rising. The enormity of what she'd lost in one evening hit her. Credit cards. Driver's license. What else was in her bag she'd have to stop or replace?

"Maybe I should have gotten you decaf," Rick said, sitting the mug on the desk. "What's got you wired?"

"I need to stop my credit cards. I don't have a phone. Shit. I won't have a place to sleep if I don't get over there while the office is open."

Rick gently pressed down on her shoulders, settling her

back into the chair. "It's still early," he said, looking at his watch. "I'll get you there in plenty of time."

"You don't understand…"

"Trust me. I do," he said, retaking his seat. His stare was direct, and she took some assurance from the steel in his eyes. "We've got a lot to cover, so let's get to it."

The sooner they got this done, the sooner she'd get out of here. It surprised her that her fingers still trembled. She had to hold it together. Take it one step at a time.

"You'd asked about the trip to the marina. Tony and I didn't discuss anything unusual. Work, traffic, snowbirds —that sort of thing. I was nervous but not because of what he said or did. This was going to be my first social event, so to speak, since moving here. Except spending time with Shayne, I don't sit around and bullshit with anyone."

"Why not? You're obviously intelligent. Articulate." His head cocked as if he was truly confused.

She ignored the compliment and avoided the question. "I just don't." There was no point in trying to explain. Besides, it had nothing to do with what happened last night.

"You don't remember the name of the marina or the boat?"

"I wasn't paying enough attention." And how dumb was that? A woman alone with a man she hardly knew. She should have known better.

"Can you find the marina again? You said it was on Fort Myers Beach."

"I think so." She took a sip of her coffee. It was strong, which was good. She could feel the energy draining from her body and the day wasn't half over yet.

"I'll ask Troy or Steve to drive you over that way tomorrow. See if something clicks."

"Fine, but I doubt anyone will be at the marina waiting for me to reappear," she snapped.

"The marina should have information on the boat," Rick said. "Or someone else docked there might have seen you and can verify your story."

"Excuse me?" She forgot about her finances and phone. "Are you suggesting I invented or imagined this?"

"I know something happened to you last night. But right now, I don't have enough information to officially investigate further."

"If you weren't a friend of Shayne's, I'd tell you to fuck off. Are you always this much of a jerk or did it come with the badge?" She knew better than to lump people and professions together. How many times had someone assumed she was in a tawdry line of work because she was a massage therapist?

But he'd also managed a verbal punch to her gut. Social workers and police officers had accused her of making things up—of acting out when she was a kid. Most of her foster homes were good, but there were a few places where she'd needed help. One in particular. No one believed the smart-mouthed loner she'd become. Her stint in juvey turned out to be a blessing in disguise. While it put a huge black mark on her past, it got her out of the wretched system and into the counseling she'd needed for so long. Now Rick was acting as if her swim across the bay was a performance to get attention. Screw it.

"And if you weren't Shayne's friend, we wouldn't be having this conversation. Period. So, sit down and let's get this done so we can get you to your apartment."

Finch dropped into the chair. She had no choice, and it grated on her. "If you don't believe me, why are you wasting your time?"

"I never said I didn't believe you, only that I don't have

enough information to work with. Verifying the events of last evening is going to be impossible unless you give me something to sink my teeth into."

Finch huffed out a breath. She'd let her temper get in the way of logic. "What do you need? If I can answer, I will."

Rick flipped a page on the pad he'd been taking notes on. "How long has Tony worked at the spa? What did he do there?"

"That's easy. He started a day or two after our regular guest services person left. That was a couple of months ago. Tony booked appointments, greeted clients, and kept our rooms stocked. I saw more of him than the other employees. All the therapists stayed busy, so we were mostly in our treatment rooms."

"Do you know what happened to the person he replaced?"

"No. She was a no-show for work one day. I assumed she'd been let go because they had a replacement for her pretty fast. If she'd been sick or taken personal time, they would have brought a temp in or had us take turns."

Rick kept scribbling on his pad. "Describe the boat to me. You said it was big."

"Big by my standards. Boxy looking. More enclosed space than open deck. I think that was one reason I hesitated to get on board. I'd expect a sunset cruise to have deck chairs, coolers—those sorts of things on deck. But the deck was small—not built for a crowd."

"Did you see anything below deck that would give you an idea regarding ownership? Personal items, pictures?"

She mentally visualized her escape from the cabin. "Nothing. The bedroom had nothing personal in it that I noticed. I was more focused on escaping than looking at the decor. After I got out of that room, I pulled open a few drawers in the kitchen area, looking for a weapon. There was nothing in them. Odd, now that I think about it. It was like no one used the boat."

Rick's desk phone rang. "I'll be right out," he said. "Lunch is here," he answered her unasked question. "I ordered it when I got the coffee. You need more than crackers and I'm hungry."

"If we're done with the questions, I need to get going. I have a lot to do." After she got into her apartment and retrieved her second set of car keys, she'd need a ride to her car. Driver's license or not, she needed wheels. There was so damn much to do—and having lunch wasn't one of them.

"Then eat fast," he said as he left the room.

7

———

 ick smiled as he shut the door behind him. Contrary hardly described the woman in his office. She didn't hold back, instead giving voice to her thoughts. She was also hard as nails, which he suspected was a trait she developed to protect herself. He hadn't had the time to dig deep into her history, but what he did see was someone who was on her own from the time she'd been born. She was a survivor. Her death-defying swim across the bay was proof of that.

It was odd picturing Finch and Shayne as friends, but then Shayne had stood up to Troy and held her own against a crazy-ass bomber. They were both survivors.

Rick paid for the delivery—two sandwiches and a salad because he hadn't asked what she wanted—and made his way to his office.

"I'm not hungry," she said as he placed the food in the center of his desk.

The comment wasn't unexpected. Like a racehorse at the starting gate, she was ready to go.

"Well, I am. Watch me eat or join in."

She gave him an icy stare before glancing at the food he'd laid out. He did his best not to grin when her stomach growled.

"What type of sandwiches?" she grumbled, unwrapping one. She ate half the club sandwich and picked at the salad. He considered it a win.

"Can I use your computer?" she asked, wiping her mouth on the napkin provided with the lunch. "I need to check my bank account and credit cards."

"I can't let you use the department's computer, but you can use my phone." He slid it across the desk after clearing a few screens. "You remember your passwords?"

"I wouldn't have asked if I didn't."

"Don't tell me you're one of those people that has one password for everything." People were so naïve to think they were the only one who would never get hacked.

"You don't think very much of me, do you? How do I know you don't have an app on your phone that will capture my user IDs and passwords?" she shot back.

He'd be pissed if he wasn't amused. "Check your accounts," he said. "Then we'll get out of here."

As they made their way into Fort Myers, Rick noted that Finch's squared shoulders were now relaxed. The relief of knowing that no one had accessed her bank account or credit cards must have taken some of the weight off of those shoulders. She'd also reported her phone as lost. At his suggestion, she had new cards overnighted to Steve's office. Her financials were untouched, but her keys were another matter.

He didn't know what they would find at her place. All they had was her word that the events she related actually happened. She either had a vivid imagination, was lying, or she was in trouble. She was also beat. It was his job to notice things, and it was hard to miss the dark circles forming under her eyes. The spark he'd seen flash earlier in those eyes had faded to resemble a tarnished copper penny.

She was headed for a big crash. Sheer willpower, he suspected, was holding her exhaustion at bay.

Rick stood back while Finch spoke to the manager and dealt with the details of getting her locks changed. He didn't miss the manager's eyes flick to him several times during the conversation with Finch. Not only was Rick a big man, but he was wearing his on-duty clothing—dark green polo with the department's name and logo, khakis and police issued weapon. The manager pulled her out of Rick's earshot at one point and whispered into Finch's ear. She reached out and put her hand on the small man's arm. Whatever she said, appeared to satisfy him.

Finch's apartment was in the rear of the complex and at the end of the last building. The location would give her privacy, but the isolation could make it less safe—even for a tough as nails woman like Finch.

"Second floor?" he asked, looking at the unit numbers.

"Yes." She slid from the elevated seat of his truck onto the ground.

"I'm going first," he told her. "Let me have the key."

He was growing accustomed to her snarls and angry scowls. Going on the assumption that her abduction was real, she had no business entering her apartment and possibly surprising a visitor.

Unlike multi-family units on Sanibel, her complex had a cold feel to it. Nothing personal or welcoming. It wasn't new. He noted the wear and tear on the façade and stairwell. The one aesthetic benefit was the rear of her particular building skirted farmland that had yet to be developed. The location was quieter and more peaceful than the buildings closer to the road.

"How many rooms?" he asked, his voice soft and low.

"Four," she held up four fingers. "Bedroom, bath, kitchen and living area," she answered in a low whisper.

He pressed her gently against the stucco wall next to the door. "Stay here until I tell you it's safe."

"Aren't you overdoing this?" She'd maintained the scowl, but her eyes were wide. Good. She had enough sense to be frightened. It would keep her on her guard.

He unholstered his weapon before inserting the key into the lock. Forcing his focus away from Finch, he pushed the door open wide until it hit the interior wall. The kitchen opened to the living room. Both were clear. A short hallway led to the back of the unit. It was empty as well.

The bedroom was small, with hardly enough room for a double bed, what looked like a second-hand kid's desk, and a chest of drawers. It was neat as a pin. The bathroom was a tight fit and impossible to hide in. There was no tub and the curtain on the tiny shower was pulled back. The room held the fragrance of jasmine and woman, he reflected. His last stop was the balcony off the bedroom. A single, plastic chair occupied the terrace. Not two chairs, as most people would have. It spoke volumes about her life.

"Okay if I come in?"

He was somewhat surprised she'd waited as requested. "It's clear. Nothing seems to have been disturbed," he said as she approached. "You'd better check to see if anything is missing."

She made a beeline for the bedroom and the desk that was shoved into the corner. A laptop pretty much covered the surface. First, she opened the top drawer and grabbed a set of keys from inside. Juggling them in her hand, she smiled. She then booted up the computer, entered her password then let out a sigh he imagined feeling across the room.

"I'm going to check a few sites, report my license missing and change the most important passwords," she said, glancing over her shoulder. "Would you mind waiting? I don't want to keep you but now that I know I have my car keys, I need a ride to the spa."

"Go ahead. I'm not expected back at the station today. If they need me, they know how to reach me."

"Thanks," she said, turning back toward her computer.

"Don't you want to check the place? Make certain nothing is missing?"

"Why? If there was a break-in, they'd have taken this computer. I have nothing else of value."

"What? No jewelry? No family heirlooms?" He realized the gaffe the minute the question was out of his mouth. The hooded look she gave him put a point on it.

"Family heirlooms only apply if you have a family," she said. "What little I wear is all costume jewelry."

She'd made the comment without inflection. He assumed it hurt to be reminded of being literally tossed to the curb, but she responded without emotion. She wasn't looking for sympathy. He felt it, all the same.

The woman was efficient. It didn't take her long to do what she wanted. The printer kicked in at one point. She snatched the paper from it, reached in the cubicle that passed for a closet and dug out a small crossbody bag.

"This," she said, waving the paper at him, "will make it legal for me to drive until I get my license, in the event you were ready to pull me over the minute I got behind the wheel." She tucked the paper into the bag.

"What's the plan after you get your car?" Being alone wasn't a good idea.

"There's no way I can get a new phone or anything else until my credit cards arrive. I should swing by the spa and ask for a few days off to take care of this shit, and it would be nice to know if they've heard from Tony."

He'd like to know the same thing.

"Give me a second." Opening the file drawer, she flipped through tags on the folders. "I don't want to forget to contact anyone. I think I've got it covered…" her voice trailed off.

"What is it? Something missing?"

"I don't know." She fingered through the drawer a second time.

"What do you mean you don't know?" His radar was on high alert.

"It's got to be in here." She started pulling files and papers from the desk.

"What are you looking for?"

"My history. My life." Tension crept back into her voice.

"What the hell does that mean?" In two steps, he was standing behind her chair.

"All my legal records. From the time I was assigned my first social worker until I changed my name. I don't need them except for the occasional issue with my name change. Otherwise, they sit in the file."

"When was the last time you handled them?"

"A few weeks ago. I was in an organizing mood. Documents that need saving tend to wind up in a pile until I can't ignore them anymore. I cleaned off the desk and filed what needed filing at the end of last month."

"Two, three weeks ago?"

She nodded.

"I can't imagine who would want them. They're no good to anyone but me. I must have misplaced them."

The statement was spoken in a smooth, even tone, but her body reflected a different level of concern. He literally saw the cords in her neck tighten. Her breathing was rapid. Her breaths shallow. Placing his hands on her shoulders, he gave them a gentle squeeze, reminding her she wasn't alone. The missing papers had her spooked. He didn't like it either.

"We can come back and look for them," he suggested, but his gut told him they wouldn't find them. "We need to get going if you want to stop by work before they close for the day."

Finch circled the room as if another look would miraculously produce the missing documents. "You're right. I can look tonight."

"Why don't you grab a few things. It's unlikely they'll get to the locks this late in the day and it's not safe for you to stay until they do." He closed her laptop and pocketed the charger.

"What do you think you're doing?" She snatched the computer off the desk as he was reaching for it.

He suspected this conversation would not be easy. She was stubborn and independent. Spending time in detention, she probably figured she was tough. He also doubted she'd carelessly leave important documents lying around. If the papers were missing, she'd had a visitor. Changing the locks would help, but they wouldn't stop anyone determined to get to her. She'd be safer on the island.

"Look," he started. "I'm not trying to bully you, but there's a possibility you had a visitor."

"And why is that your problem? I can take care of myself."

He tried another tact. "Swallow that pride and think about Shayne. She's your friend and worried about you. Knowing her, she'll plant her ass on your doorstep tonight if you don't return with me. Do you want that?"

Bringing Shayne into the conversation lowered the heat

in the room. He wasn't exaggerating. Shayne would show up and Troy would be with her even if that meant they spent the night in the car. Finch, apparently, knew her friend well enough to be thinking the same thing.

She stormed by him, grabbed a tote bag, and began shoving some clothes in it. "I'm going to rinse the salt off and change out of Josie's things," she said, stepping into the small bathroom. "I'll only be a couple of minutes."

She was true to her word. In less than ten minutes she popped out of the bedroom, running a comb through her wet hair. She was wearing a pair of jeans and a black t-shirt that read *Nevertheless, She Persisted.* He grinned. How fitting was that?

"Let's go get my car and see if the spa has had any contact with Tony," she said, laying Josie's clothes on top of the ones she'd packed.

He grabbed the doorknob before she reached it and stepped out onto the concrete walkway. No one else was present. He glanced at the apartments across the parking lot. There was no one milling about—no sign of movement. Motioning her outside, he didn't miss her eye roll. God, the woman was obstinate.

Arriving at the spa, Finch made a beeline for her car.

"Is this where you left it?"

There was a brief, questioning look in his direction before his inquiry struck home. "Yes. Same parking place I normally use."

"Let me have the key." He reached out his hand.

"I don't know whether to be scared or angry." Still, she tossed him the keys.

"It's all right to be scared. It keeps you on your toes, but anger can blind you. So, you might want to keep that in check."

He slid in the driver's seat and for the second time this

afternoon, sirens went off in his head. Finch was tall but not near as tall as he was, yet he slipped behind the wheel comfortably without moving the seat back.

"Did you lend your car to anyone?"

"No. Why?"

Opening the glove box, he pulled out her registration and insurance papers. Nothing else was there.

"Do you keep anything in here besides these?" he asked holding up the documents.

"No. What the hell is going on?"

"Did you adjust your seat the last time you were in the car?"

"Why would I? You think someone was in my car?" She was now planted between him and the open door.

"Seats don't move on their own." He looked over his shoulder into the back of the car. Nothing there. "And your rear seat was empty?"

"It should be," she answered, her voice wavering. Cautiously, she reached for the door handle.

"I'll get it." He checked under the floor mats and the front seats. Nothing. As he opened the trunk Finch didn't join him. He would have asked her to step away if she had. He breathed a sigh of relief as he opened the trunk. Apart from reusable grocery bags and a spare tire, the trunk was empty.

"Nothing here," he assured her. "Let's get inside and talk to your boss."

As Finch had indicated, the spa was upscale. A soothing fragrance drifted from an aromatherapy machine tucked discreetly out of sight. One wall was filled with shelving, giving the business a place to showcase the products they sold. On the far wall, someone had painted a mural of a forest which included a life-like waterfall.

A table nearby offered chilled water from ice filled

dispensers. One contained citrus fruit. The other held what looked like cucumbers. Fancy paper cups and cocktail napkins were available from a tray separating the two urns. Lounge chairs filled the remaining space.

"No Tony?" Finch asked softly as she passed the reception desk. The young woman shook her head. Rick followed Finch down a hallway lined with closed doors on both sides. He assumed they were the treatment rooms. Reaching the end of the hall, Finch made a short right and tapped on the door that said "manager".

"Come in."

A woman, somewhere in her fifties with short, brown hair and a stern look sat behind the desk. "Are you back?" she asked, straightening in her chair as Finch entered the room. Despite her posture, there was no anger in her tone.

"Not yet," Finch replied. "I need a couple of days. I hate to leave you short..."

"I'm Detective Rick Wilcowski." He'd intentionally interrupted Finch. Her apologetic tone suggested she'd be an easy mark for the formidable looking manager. He understood she want to keep her job, but he needed more information before he was comfortable leaving her on her own.

"A police officer." It was a statement, not a question. "I'm Mrs. Gonzales. I manage this place. Or try to."

"I can confirm Ms. Finch isn't in any trouble, but besides the time she needs to get organized, we can use her help."

"With what?"

Rick took a quick glance toward Finch. Her expression was neutral. Thankfully, she didn't question his tactics.

"I'm not free to discuss it," he lied. He didn't know what was going on, but he wasn't sharing that with the manager. "Give us a few days and we'll have her back to you," he added.

"We're already short a guest service attendant, but if it can't be helped, I suppose I have no choice. I need you here as soon as possible," she said to Finch. "I don't want to replace you, too."

The last comment brought a little color to Finch's face. She wasn't being fired. Just the opposite.

"What happened to Tony?" Finch asked.

"Quit by text. I hate that. Didn't even have the decency to call or come in. No notice, either."

"That happen often?" Rick prompted her. He stood with his arms crossed. Finch had initially taken a seat in front of the manager's desk but now was on her feet.

"It happens. He said he had a better offer."

"I wonder where? He never mentioned changing jobs."

"He didn't say. They didn't call for a reference, so I don't know. Not that they would have gotten one under the circumstances." Gonzales got to her feet. "I don't want a resignation by text from you, young lady. Do you hear me?"

"Yes, ma'am. Thank you."

"I need to know how to reach you. Are you staying at your place? Do you have a new phone yet?"

"If you need her, you can contact me," Rick said, before Finch could answer. "I'll get in touch with her." He handed the manager his card. "Let's go." He ushered Finch quickly out the door. Until he uncovered who was behind Finch's attempted abduction, he wasn't in the mood to confide in anyone.

8

____

unny how getting behind the wheel of her own vehicle was freeing. She always breathed a sigh of relief as she settled into its worn seats after leaving work. It was her decompression zone. Today felt different, though. She was almost giddy to be in control of something, even if it was only her old Toyota Camry.

Rick had insisted on following her to the island instead of taking the lead. It would have been easier the other way around since he knew their destination. Instead, he'd given her directions, an address, and a few landmarks that would tell her she was getting close. It sucked not to have a phone, particularly when you used Google maps to find everything. Her sense of direction wasn't the best.

As she drove through one of the toll booths onto the Causeway Bridge, a black SUV was coming through the booth to her left. She let off the gas, offering the driver an invitation to go ahead of her before the road became a single lane bridge. Instead, the vehicle slowed, then forced its way in behind her, cutting off Rick. Horn blaring,

Rick's truck disappeared behind the large vehicle. Fuckin' asshole.

Stepping on the gas as she crossed the bridge, she was able to put a little daylight between her and the large SUV. She'd pull over when she reached one of the small causeway beaches on the other side of the bridge. That would allow her to pick up her escort again. She imagined he was cussing out the driver behind her. Rick appeared to take his protection duties seriously.

Abruptly, everything vanished from her rearview mirror but the grill of the vehicle behind her. What the hell was his problem? She was already speeding, which wasn't wise on this stretch of road. The beaches on the causeway drew families and fishermen, many crossing the two-lane thoroughfare to use restrooms at different points on either side. She increased her speed as she crested the span. She could see the water and beaches below. They were packed. The bump against her rear fender, thrust her heart into her throat. Her grip tightened on the wheel. She was quickly gaining on the traffic in front of her. She'd rear-end them if she gave her Toyota any more gas. The crowded beaches and cars parked along the side, left her nowhere to go. Even if she found an escape route, at this speed it would be hard to control the vehicle on soft sand.

Bam. This time, the hit was harder. Her palms were slick with sweat, making it difficult for her to hang onto the wheel. Her chest pounded. The Toyota rattled. There was too much traffic coming off the island for her to pass the cars in front of her. For a split second, Rick's truck appeared in the side-view mirror before she was jolted again. Standing on the brake, she tried to give the vehicles in front of her time to escape the mayhem. The massive SUV retreated, but the reprieve was brief. Metal crunched and her head snapped back, sending her sunglasses flying over her head and onto the rear seat.

Her Toyota propelled forward despite her efforts to stop it. The smell of burning rubber filled her nostrils. A horn blared. Rick, she assumed. Oncoming traffic on one side and a sandy beach crammed with families on the other—locked them firmly in this lane. There was no way for Rick to get past the monster vehicle. What could he do if he managed the feat?

The SUV let off the gas again. While she hadn't been able to stop her vehicle, she had attained a bit of breathing room between her and the cars in front of her. Stepping on the gas, she cleared a shorter bridge span, managing to distance herself further from her pursuer. The attempt was short-lived. The driver used his vehicle to force her to the right. Pulling the wheel hard to the left, she fought to avoid the beachgoers. Her tactic worked, allowing her to straighten her car. Flooring it, she pulled away from the populated area.

With the traffic headed to Sanibel now in the distance, she flew across the last bridge that led to the island, but she wasn't fast enough. The SUV slammed into her again. And again, it was to the driver's side bumper. She wasn't able to hold it this time. Tires slid across a patch of grass before skidding across a sidewalk which was, thankfully, empty. The madman struck her one last time, sending her into a spin. She'd have completed a full three-sixty if the driver's side door hadn't hit a palm tree.

Tensing for a final blow, she was stunned when gravel and sand peppered her car as the SUV peeled off toward the interior of the island. She dropped her forehead against the steering wheel. Heart pumping, hands shaking —her breath came in gasps. What the hell had happened?

She squealed as the passenger door was yanked open.

"Are you hurt?" It was Rick. His striking blue eyes intense. Worry? Anger? Or both?

"I think so." Then it clicked. "Why didn't you go after the asshole?"

"And leave you? I already contacted the department. He won't get far."

Her mind cleared as her heart settled. She nodded. She wouldn't have left the scene either if she'd witnessed the road rage incident. A few cars besides Rick's had pulled to the shoulder of the road and were heading their way. Good Samaritans or witnesses, she supposed.

"I'm sorry I wasn't able to get to you." He reached over to undo her seat belt.

"You couldn't get to me any more than I could get out of his way." She started to haul herself over the center console since the palm tree blocked the driver's door. "Did you get his license plate number?"

"Stay put," he snapped. "Wait until the paramedics get here to check you out."

"I don't want to be checked out. I'm fine."

"We're not going through this again. You don't have a say this time." Rick parked his ass on the seat next to her. "You've taken a beating these last few days. You're going to wait right here until they say you can leave."

"Anyone ever tell you that you were a jerk?"

"Being a cop and a soldier, I've been called all sorts of names. Jerk would be one of the nicer ones." He tucked her hair behind her ear.

"Did you at least get his tag number?" she repeated.

His eyes met hers. "Yeah. Called it in as soon as he cut me off."

"Why the face?" He knew something.

"While you were being slammed into the tree, I received a report that the vehicle was stolen."

Her teeth dug into her bottom lip as she digested that information. "This wasn't a simple road rage incident, was it?"

"There probably was some rage there, but he deliberately targeted you. He forced his way in front of me to get behind you. He wanted you."

"I don't understand any of this," she said, resting her head on hands now gripping the steering wheel. "I can't think of anything I've done to warrant this kind of attention."

Rick tenderly grasped her chin, turning her head so she was facing him. Aware her lips were trembling, she willed back the tears. She'd be damned if she let anyone see her cry, especially this man. Why was that so damn important?

"We need time, but we'll figure it out."

The police and medics arrived. Rick slid out of the car and headed toward the uniform cops, stopping briefly to speak to the paramedics as they passed each other.

She recognized the two paramedics from the beach. The big woman now occupied the seat Rick had vacated. Her kit remained on the ground next to the vehicle. Her partner approached the driver's door.

"There's no way we're getting her out of this side unless we move the car. Can you lower the window?" he asked Finch.

She turned the key and was half surprised when the engine caught, and she was able to lower the window. She'd assumed her car was a total goner.

"I'm Mike and that's Leslie." The medic tipped his head in the woman's direction.

"I'm Finch and I'm okay. I just need to get out of here." She was feeling claustrophobic with the two medics crowding her.

"Let's take a quick look at you first," Leslie said.

"You can do that when I'm not trapped in here. Move, please."

She crawled over the center console, forcing the woman to get out of her way, then planted her butt sideways on the passenger seat. The paramedics then did what paramedics do. Other than a few minor cuts and bruises, she passed their tests. Leslie helped her to her feet. Finch let out a slight groan as she straightened to her full height. No one had to tell her she'd be sore as hell tomorrow. First, a night swimming across the bay and now this.

"What's the verdict?" Rick asked, returning to the car. He put his hands on her shoulders as if to steady her.

"She says she didn't hit her head," Mike told him.

"She's going to ache like hell. A hot bath or shower will help, then ice down the bruises that are going to appear," his partner added.

"Thank you," Finch said as they stowed their gear.

She took a close look at her Toyota. If the insurance company didn't total it, she'd be shocked. Was this shit ever going to stop? Glancing up at the clear Florida sky, she half-expected to find a metaphorical black cloud hanging over her head.

"What are you looking for?" Rick asked, following her line of sight.

"Nothing." He already doubted her veracity. No point in adding crazy to his list of grievances against her. She studied the car's trunk. It was going to take a crowbar to pry open the crumpled metal. "Good thing I put my stuff in the back seat."

She found her laptop under the front seat. Her bag of clothes had upended. She grabbed the items from the floor and crammed them inside. With his arm over her shoulder, he led her toward his vehicle.

"I gave them my statement." Rick indicated the two officers leaning against a black and white unit. "They need your perspective on what happened. Did you see the driver? Did you recognize him?"

"I can't tell you if it was a man behind the wheel. All I saw was a lot of chrome. Did you get a look at him?" she asked as they approached the cops. More cops. She hadn't seen this many law enforcement officers since her stint in juvey.

"I caught a couple of quick glimpses in his side mirror. White male with dark hair."

"Big guy?" she asked.

"You're thinking about the men on the boat?"

"It's a possibility."

"If we find the SUV, it may give us additional information." He opened the rear door to the cruiser and directed her to sit. She stared inside. The last time she was in the back of a police unit, it was not under her own volition— and she'd been cuffed.

"You need to sit before you fall," Rick said, coaxing her onto the seat.

She swallowed hard before dropping onto the bench seat, reminding herself she wasn't under arrest. And to be honest, her legs weren't going to hold her much longer.

Rick uncapped a bottle of water and handed it to her. "Tell them exactly what happened."

Finch took a long drink, swallowed hard and then began.

9

———

The questioning trailed off as radios cackled to life. The cop who'd been interviewing her stepped away to join the others. Finch was glad for the break. She sat, twisting the cap on and off the bottle. Thoughts raced through her head, but she didn't have the energy to keep up with them. No longer intimidated by the official vehicle, she slumped against the seatback and rolled her neck, trying to loosen her muscles. She was aching, tired, and scared.

Rick had joined the officers. Finch could hear them talking but wasn't able to make out what they were saying, which was fine with her. She wanted a few minutes of peace. Tuning them out, she closed her eyes. The respite didn't last long.

"Finch?"

Turning her head toward his voice, she studied the chiseled features of the man she couldn't decide whether she liked or distrusted.

"Present," she raised her hand. "Physically, anyway.

What's going on?" she asked, sitting up straight. It took more effort than she'd anticipated.

"They found the SUV. It was abandoned."

Of course, it was. "I'm not a rocket scientist, but he's either on foot, which I doubt, or he had a car waiting."

"Probably the latter," he said, his face expressionless.

"Which means the whole shitshow was planned. How did he know where I was? No one but you knew we were headed to the island."

"It wasn't me, if that's what you're insinuating," he snapped. "We'll look at your car. Let me have your computer, too. We'll check them both for tracking devices."

"You're not serious." Still, she handed the laptop over to him.

"As you said, only the two of us were aware of where we were going. You did, however, pick up your car and your computer."

She was staring at him as if he had two heads. Who the hell would go to that much trouble to hurt her?

"My friends," Rick continued, "have the equipment to check your computer, but if there is any sort of locator on it, I don't want to lead anyone to our location. The guys at the station will check it." He handed the computer to a uniformed officer who was standing behind him. "We'll return it as soon as its cleared."

"And my car?" They looked at the beat-up piece of metal.

"We'll get it towed and check it as well. C'mon. You look like shit," he said, clasping her elbow.

She wished she was able say the same about him. He'd gone from good-looking cop to a hot commander as he'd taken charge of the scene. If she wasn't so tired, she'd kick herself in the ass for even thinking it.

Reaching into the rear of the cruiser for her sack of

clothing and crossbody bag she stopped. "Please tell me I can bring these with me." Being stripped of everything would be a bridge too far. She felt isolated and alone, even surrounded by all these people. She needed something—anything—that belonged to her. Silly. She wasn't a child clinging to a stuffed animal any longer.

Finch noted his moment of hesitation, then the quick study of her face. He was tempted to say no, but took the bags from her, then steered her toward his truck.

It took less than ten minutes to reach what had been their original destination. Rick pulled into the parking area of a building, which she assumed from its façade, had once been a home. The split sign out front announced the two businesses now housed inside, *Sanctuary Gardens* and *Island Securities & Investigations*.

Before Finch was firmly on the ground, Shayne was bursting out the door. "Are you okay? Rick called and told us what happened."

Finch didn't have time to answer the question before a petite woman with sable brown hair flew past Shayne.

"Hi. I'm Cat James," she said, pulling Finch in for a quick hug. "Shayne's told us so much about you. Come meet the rest of the gang."

Shayne and Cat were tugging her forward, but Finch's feet wouldn't move. Neither would her mouth. She couldn't seem to get her brain to engage. She blinked several times, trying to clear her head. The only thing that registered was the fact that her knees could buckle at any second.

"Finch? What's wrong?"

She recognized the worry in Shayne's voice but couldn't form any words. It wasn't possible to reassure her friend. It was taking all her concentration to remain standing. A band tightened around her chest. She wasn't getting any air. What the hell was wrong with her?

"Let's get her inside and have Kevin look at her." A voice rumbled in her ear as her feet left the ground. She recognized it but didn't have the energy to look up to confirm its owner. She simply closed her eyes.

10

———————

$\mathcal{R}$ick cocked his head to scan the business next door as he helped Troy haul a picnic table away from the rear wall of the photography studio. Colton James, the team's former commander, along with his business partner, Gibson McKay, owned the studio and the two condos perched above. Kevin and their former lieutenant, Steve Brody, were following suit with a second table. The group had been growing over the past few years with the addition of their spouses and now a child. They could all squeeze into one of the two condos, but it would be a tight fit. On nice evenings, they opted to eat outdoors, which provided them with a generous amount of elbow room.

"She's fine," Troy said. Rick continued to stare across the driveway. "Shayne's with her. If Finch needs anything, she'll let us know."

The men placed the tables end to end to make one long eating surface. "She's exhausted," Kevin told him as they angled the wooden tables into a straight line. "I doubt she got any sleep last night and after that long swim her body hasn't had the chance to catch up."

"She looked like crap," Rick said.

"I wouldn't repeat that to her face," Kevin chuckled.

"Trust me, he's right." Steve walked past them, heading toward the building. Gib and Colt were making their way down the stairs. Colt was loaded with tablecloths, cutlery, and other items needed for the upcoming meal. Gib had Steve's daughter on his hip. She was clutching a stuffed unicorn. Steve reached out and took Cece from his friend. "Where did this come from?" He held out the colorful fluffy animal.

"You'd better watch him," Rick commented, grabbing a beer from the cooler. "He'll be buying her a pony next."

"You're right. She needs a pony." Gib's eyes brightened.

"No. No pony." Steve glared at his friend. "You need to stop spoiling her."

"I enjoy spoiling her. A princess deserves to be spoiled."

Rick rolled his eyes. The notorious womanizer was thoroughly enchanted by his goddaughter. It was fun to watch him being wrapped around a woman's finger, regardless of her age. He suspected Gib would get that pony now that the idea had settled in his head.

Steve tickled his daughter's tummy. "Mommy will be back soon."

Cece's giggles lifted Rick's darkening mood.

The women were absent, having assigned themselves different chores. Steve and Kevin's spouses, Josie and River, had gone shopping. While Finch had brought clothing with her, the women decided more was better. Who knew how long she'd be gone from her home? Cat was making the food run while Shayne had stayed with Finch. The women of this group were a force unto themselves. Hardly a word was said before they'd split up, each knowing what needed to be done without discussion. They constantly amazed Rick.

Twisting the top off his beer, Rick dropped to the wooden seat. "Which one of you are going to traipse over to Fort Myers Beach tomorrow?" he asked.

"That would be me." Troy wiped his mouth with the back of his hand after taking a swig of his own beer. "I'm hoping we can get a bit more information out of Finch so I can narrow the search for the boat."

"She's going with you assuming she feels better. She thinks she can find the place again," Rick explained.

"Be sure you talk to other boat owners and local businesses nearby," Colt added.

"Damn. I hadn't thought of that." Troy thumped the heel of his hand against his temple.

Rick grinned. Colt would occasionally slip back into his leadership mode. None of the guys minded. As their commander during multiple tours, his instincts and skills had saved their asses several times.

"Sorry." Colt grinned. "I've got a magazine deadline to meet which will keep me tied up most of tomorrow. I know you guys can handle anything that comes up, but don't hesitate to holler if you need me."

Their former captain had become a renowned nature photographer. His pictures not only sold as works of art but appeared in various publications and books.

"I'll be on duty all day tomorrow," Rick said. "Don't let her overdo it. I'll do a deeper dive into her background," Rick told them. "I only got a cursory look today.

"We need to talk to her case workers from her time in the system," Rick added, taking a final swig of his beer. "It would help to know why those documents are missing."

"You don't think they've been misplaced," Kevin stated.

"Do you know the location of your discharge papers? Your marriage license? Birth certificate?" Rick shook his head. "No. I don't believe she misplaced them for a minute. Besides, she hadn't needed them recently. It doesn't make sense."

"Who would want them?" Gib asked, planting his ass on the table.

"An excellent question."

"Josie plans to get busy," Steve added. "She did a story a year or so ago on foster homes and adoptions. She still has contacts in the Department of Children and Family Services. DCF can be a hard nut to crack. They're protective of the kids, as they should be, but the media sheds a negative light on them. Josie made a few friends who can check for those red flags."

Steve's wife was a freelance investigative reporter. Rick was amazed at her contacts in and out of journalism circles. Those contacts and her research had been invaluable in leading to the arrest of a crooked state attorney.

"I'll check with her," Rick said, reaching for another beer from the cooler.

"We haven't addressed the elephant in the room." Colt waited a beat. "How was she tracked to the island?"

"I had her vehicle and computer taken to the station." Rick glanced at the garden next door, then again at Steve. "I'd appreciate if either you or Troy would look at her computer after my tech guy is done with it."

"And the stuff she brought with her?" Troy asked. "I'm surprised you didn't drop that off at the station, too."

He remembered the look of near desperation when she thought he was going to take them from her after the accident. "It's doubtful anyone would know what personal items she'd take, assuming they even guessed she would leave, but it wouldn't hurt to clear them. Can we do it without her knowledge? She's pretty defensive."

"I'll slip in there. We have the equipment on premises. It should only take a minute and she won't know I touched a thing—unless I find something."

"We haven't discussed what to do with Finch while this plays out. We can't keep her a prisoner, but she isn't safe on her own." Steve planted his foot on the end of the bench.

"Do you think she'll agree to stay out of pocket?" Colt asked Rick.

"I used the guilt card to get her over here. I told her Shayne would plant her ass on her doorstep. Do you think your wife would be willing to play that part and help keep her on the island?" he asked Troy.

"You read Shayne right. She'd be beating on Finch's door. We can push that angle. Shayne won't hesitate to use it."

"Finch's mind may have changed since the attack on the bridge," Kevin suggested. "It may not take much to convince her."

"I don't see these guys stopping. They want her for a reason." Frustrated, Rick ran his hand through his short hair.

"Then why was that guy trying to run her off the road?" Troy asked. "How does that fit in? They could have killed her."

"If they wanted to kill her, they could have done it on the boat. Instead, they knocked her out and locked her in a cabin." Gib stood and stretched his arms over his head. "The boat incident feels more like a kidnapping, but she's not a person of means and doesn't have any family to pay a ransom."

"That we know of," Rick mused. "Was it a kidnapping or an attempted murder? Finch didn't spend any time listening to the men arguing on the bridge. She was frantic to get off the boat."

"Are we confident the two incidents aren't connected?" Steve asked.

"Oh, shit. Don't go there," Rick warned. "One mystery at a time."

Cat's roadster pulled into a parking space between the building and the makeshift picnic area. "Could use a little help here," she shouted as she popped the trunk. Steve took the toddler from Troy who was having his turn at spoiling her. The rest of the men headed toward the car.

As they finished unloading the food, Rick heard a vehicle pull into the parking lot in front of the business next door. Josie and River were filling their arms with shopping bags when he reached them.

"I thought you were only getting her things for a couple of days." Rick smiled as he glanced at both women.

"Who says this is all for her?" River volleyed back.

"Touché," he answered. "If Finch is up to it," Rick said, changing the subject, "we need to get moving. Cat's here with the food and Colt has the grill going. After we eat, we need her to answer a few questions."

The pair nodded their understanding and headed inside. As Rick made his way to the picnic area. He smelled the grilled meats as he rounded the corner. Did Finch even eat meat? They'd know soon enough.

Close to half an hour later, Josie, River, Shayne, and Finch came through the garden gate. Rick had to admit that Finch looked a damn site better than she had when he'd left her on the break room sofa. In fact, she was stunning. Wearing a magenta tank top that almost matched the streak in her hair and a pair of snug jeans, she crossed the driveway. As his dad would have said, she cleaned up nice. Her hair fell like silk on her shoulders. Her skin was vibrant, despite the bruise on her jaw. Instead of wobbly knees, she strode sure-footed in their direction. The look in her eyes was determined. Kevin's diagnosis appeared to be true. A little rest and she was a different person. There was strength there.

The other women parted, each heading toward their respective mates. To his unexpected annoyance, Gib made a beeline for Finch. Rick stepped in, blocking his way. "I need to talk to her," he said softly so Finch wouldn't hear.

"Uh huh." Gib smiled. "Business or pleasure? Because she's definitely a pleasure to look at."

"Knock it off, Gib."

"Do I sense some territorial posturing?"

"It's police business," Rick snapped. But seeing Finch so vulnerable and now so vibrant, stirred something within him. He didn't like Gib setting his sights on her.

Gib's grin widened as he met Rick's stare. "If that's all it is then you won't mind if Finch spends the night at my place."

"What?"

"What's going on?" Finch asked as she reached the two men.

Rick's eyes narrowed at Gib before greeting her. "How are you doing? You look a lot better," Rick sidestepped the question.

"I feel better. What were you two talking about? I heard my name." She eyed both of them, waiting. She wasn't dropping the subject.

"I'm Gib. Sorry to meet you under these circumstances." He lifted her hand to his lips and brushed a kiss across her knuckles. "I was offering my spare room for your use tonight," Gib explained. "You need a place to sleep and I have an extra bedroom."

It surprised Rick that he had to restrain himself from

breaking the connection. She was a case, he mentally chastised himself—and had a history.

"Thank you, but the couch I passed out on will do well enough, if no one minds."

"You shouldn't be alone," Gib coaxed.

"She won't be," Rick's mouth engaged before his brain did. "She'll stay in my guest room. It's not likely anyone will look for her there."

He noted the instant the statement registered with Finch. "You think someone is still looking for me. I can take care of myself and I'm more aware of things now. Plus, I noticed they have a security system next door."

"You're coming with me," Rick argued. "We don't want you disappearing in the middle of the night."

"What the hell is that supposed to mean?" Finch's jaw clenched. "I don't run from my battles."

"That's not what I meant. You've been attacked twice. Being alone, regardless of the security, isn't a good idea. The rest of these men have wives and family we wouldn't want to endanger." Good argument. He gave himself a mental pat on the back, despite the grin he witnessed on Gib's face.

"And what about Gib?" she asked, cocking her head. "Shayne said he wasn't married."

"Because he's too busy entertaining members of the opposite sex. You'd be in his way."

Rick ignored his friend's laughter as he led Finch to the table where the rest of the group waited.

11

———

$\mathcal{N}$o one bombarded her with questions as they introduced her to the individuals she hadn't met. Either they weren't the curious type—unlikely—or they were waiting until after the meal. Finch was, admittedly, a loner, but she'd learned how to be personable. She had to work at it, but if she wanted to make a living in a service industry, the skill was required. With this group, however, she fell into it easily. They were friendly, funny, and talkative.

While the women had paired off with their husbands, they kept Finch included in all conversations. They were lively, but she suspected they would be a force to be reckoned with if the situation called for it. The men surprised her. Watching these former soldiers tenderly touching their wives, playing peek-a-boo with a baby, and bantering with each other, she realized she'd been half expecting a wall of men who could pass for a defensive line of a football team ready to tackle the opposing quarterback—her.

During the meal, whenever the opportunity presented itself, she'd sneak a peek at Rick. The detective was an attractive man. He cut his silver-blond hair military short. His blue eyes stood out against his light hair and tanned skin. A shoulder holster accentuated his broad chest. The badge on his hip drew her attention to his solid thighs.

Jeez. What was wrong with her. She had more important things to fret over than the sexy man sitting to her right.

During the early part of the evening, the conversations had been light. It was obvious the friendships were close. Sitting between Gib and Rick was an interesting experience. She felt like a tennis ball at Wimbledon. The banter between the two was relentless. She found herself laughing at their antics. She hadn't figured out why, but each time Gib paid her a compliment or did his best to charm her—which came easily to him, it would seem—Rick would snarl and lob another warning to back off. In return, Gib would be hit with a fit of laughter.

By the time they finished the meal, Finch felt… normal. Had she ever felt normal before? It was a peculiar feeling.

After the tables were cleared, they began to pepper her with questions surrounding the boat ride and her co-workers. Josie was particularly interested in her personal history. The woman asked thoughtful, detailed questions regarding the case workers that supervised her foster homes, her various foster parents, and even asked what she knew about her birth parents.

Finch wasn't going to be of any help with regard to her parents. She'd never looked for them. Why should she? Their sole act of charity toward her had been to leave her at a fire station instead of in a trash can. Why was Josie so interested in her past? Finch couldn't imagine any of her current catastrophes being connected to her abandonment but because these people wanted to help, she told them what she knew.

"You understand it's not safe for you to stay in your apartment, right?" Rick asked as the questioning tapered off.

Finch pressed her fingers against her eyes, then pinched the bridge of her nose. It appeared she had little choice but to rely on Shayne and her friends in the short term. God, she hated being a burden. Memories of time spent in the foster care system came rushing in like a storm surge. She'd done her best to put those days behind her but, once again, she needed help to survive.

"I'm not stupid," she answered a bit too harshly. "Sorry. My nerves are still a bit frayed. Too many fast balls coming at me," she added.

"Then you're staying with me until we get to the bottom of this. I think it's safer for everyone," Rick reiterated.

"Why can't I stay with Gib? He's certainly pressed the option," she pointed out as Rick followed her to the cooler. Spending the night under the watchful eye of an officer of the law was a bit too reminiscent of her youth.

"He'd spend the night trying to charm you into his bed."

"And you won't?" Finch asked. Her mouth had engaged before her brain had. Wishful thinking?

"Only if you want it," he answered.

12

———

hat the hell had possessed him to make that remark? He had no business getting involved with Finch. She was a friend of Shayne's—which almost made her family. She'd been targeted by only God knew who. And to top it off, she had a record. He didn't hold people's pasts against them, but he didn't imagine it would be a good look for an officer of the law to get involved with a person who'd been accused of breaking it.

Rick opted to stand after they returned to the table. It served two purposes. He wasn't thigh to thigh with Finch and neither was Gib.

"Do you think you'd recognize the boat again?" Steve asked. "Or the man that dragged you onto it?"

"The boat was unusual looking to me, but I don't see a lot of boats so it may be more common than I'm assuming."

"How was it different?" Colt leaned forward, resting his elbows on his thighs.

"The enclosed space was larger than the outside deck, at least on the level I was relegated to."

"A houseboat?" Troy asked.

"It wasn't big enough to qualify, unless their making compact versions."

"And the man that hit you? Would you be able to identify him if you saw him again?" Steve continued to question her.

"I think so. Things happened quickly once I balked, but I got a good look at him before that."

"I'll do my best to sketch what you remember." River, who'd been sitting on her husband's lap, slipped off and headed toward a vehicle parked in the lot behind the building.

"Wait a minute," Rick said, stopping River's progress. She always had a sketch pad nearby in case a creative idea for one of her masquerade masks hit. "Why don't I drop Finch off at your place in the morning if that's okay. Give Troy a call when you're finished with the sketches. He can swing by and take her to the marina."

"Sounds like a plan," Troy agreed. "If we have drawings resembling people or a boat, all the better."

"Who's going to be with River and Finch in the morning?" Kevin asked. "I've got a twelve-hour shift at the hospital tomorrow that starts at 7:00 a.m. I don't want them by themselves."

"Can you spare me for a bit in the morning, Colt?" Gib asked. "I'll keep the ladies company while they work on the sketches."

"I'm good. There are no shoots on the calendar for the next few days. Besides, I'm stuck on this layout for the magazine spread. I should be done by the time Troy and Finch return from the marina so I can relieve him."

"Relieve him of what?" Finch asked.

"Keeping an eye on you," Rick explained.

"I don't need a babysitter and I don't need anyone to watch over me."

"Besides, after the last two days, I beg to differ with you about needing a watchdog. You can't be oblivious to the fact that you're a target."

"Excuse me?" She twisted in her seat to face off with him. "Is that a roundabout way of calling me an idiot?"

"You need to get rid of that chip on your shoulder. We're trying to help."

"Finch," Shayne said, gaining her attention. "No one wants to see you get hurt—or worse. You jumped from a boat to save yourself and were almost run off the road and into the bay. This isn't our first rodeo, as they say. Come on," Shayne added. "Let's take a walk,".

"Stay where we can see you," Troy said, rising to his feet.

"Yes, dear." She grinned, standing on her toes to kiss his cheek.

Rick watched the women as they entered the garden next door. With trouble brewing, Shayne would know better than to disappear into the tropical landscape. The two stood just far enough away so no one could overhear their conversation.

Shaking his head, he turned to face the group. Troy kept a watchful eye on his wife, the others were staring at him.

"What?"

"Why does she get under your skin?" Colt asked.

"What makes you say that?" Was it that obvious? To Colt, it would be—and based on the looks the others were giving him, no one had missed his reaction to the bundle of trouble with the copper-colored eyes.

"Really, Rick?" This time it was Kevin. "You've been an ass half the time. What's going on between you two?"

"He's attracted to her," Gib laughed. "He doesn't want to be, but he is."

"Why is that a problem?" Josie asked bouncing Cece on her hip.

No point in arguing. "First, she's Shayne's friend. I shouldn't have to spell out the complications that could create."

"And second," Steve interrupted, "she's not a saint. She's got a record and that bothers you."

"That would be petty," he snapped, but hadn't that been one reason he'd silently listed for keeping his distance?

"I'm surprised at you," River chimed in. "Since when did any of us hold a person's history against them? If we did, half of us wouldn't be here now."

"We all make mistakes," Cat said. "It's how we learn from them that counts." She snuggled closer to Colt.

"I never said that I wanted to do anything more than protect her," he argued. "You're listening to this trouble-maker here." He pointed to Gib.

"Then why can't she stay with me?" Gib asked.

"Because we don't know if she was tracked here."

"Bullshit." Troy took his eye off his wife long enough to give Rick a scathing assessment. "I told you I checked her belongings. There are no tracking devices in her computer or personal items."

"Still, she'd be too close to Cat if she stayed with Gib," he argued.

"Give it up, man," Gib said. "You know damn well no one is getting close to Cat. Colt would tear them limb from limb. Plus, our security systems here and next door are top-notch. Stop trying to convince yourself you don't want her."

"Knock it off." Troy tilted his head toward the returning women.

"Sorry I was being so contrary," Finch said, approaching the group. "I didn't mean to insult anyone by my refusal. I'm accustomed to looking out for myself."

"I can sympathize," River told her. "But you can trust us. I learned it's better to have a good team at your back than go it alone." She smiled at her husband, who laid a kiss on her temple.

"And you're definitely not alone." Gib smirked.

"What did we miss?" Shayne asked.

Gib burst out laughing.

13

"Did you get any rest last night?" Troy asked as they drove across the causeway toward Fort Myers.

"A little. I had a hard nap yesterday afternoon."

"Nap?" Troy chuckled. "You passed out cold from exhaustion."

"I guess I did." No point in arguing it.

"You've got more color this morning. Shayne will be glad to hear that."

She fidgeted in her seat. She wasn't comfortable having others worry about her. If only she could return to her apartment and work. But if she was a target—and these guys were certain that she was—then she'd be putting additional people in danger. She was reckless if she didn't accept the help, but selfish if she did.

"Can I ask you a question?" She wiggled in her seat so she was facing him. His left eye was covered with a patch. His right eye compensated, constantly moving across the horizon. She couldn't say for certain, but it appeared the

74

side-view mirrors were a little larger than standard. If so, was it to compensate for the loss of his eye?

"Shoot."

"Would it be wiser for me to get out of town?"

"Like what? Go off the grid?" he asked. "Extremely hard to do. Ask Josie. She only managed for a few days before being tracked here."

"Why did she need to do that?" Damn. These people had intriguing histories.

"Ask her, but the bottom line is she was smart enough to know it wouldn't last and needed help. We don't know why you're being targeted. Until we do, it's best if you stay put while we sort things out."

Escaping would be the easiest solution to leaving this mess behind. "It's a chickenshit way out, anyway," she admitted. "I'd like to be able to pay you. I'm sure you don't normally supply security for free."

"You're a friend of Shayne's and, therefore, family. Consider it the *friends and family discount*."

"I'll make it up to all of you. I promise." They'd be getting free massages for life. Her mind flashed to having her hands on Rick. Her thighs tightened. She hoped she didn't have to spend another night at his place. Images of him in the room next to hers kept her awake a good portion of the night. Did he sleep commando style? Boxer shorts? How big was his bed? She was an idiot.

"Can we work out a way for me to stay at my apartment or, at the very least, sleep on the couch in the garden center's break room?"

"Why?" He shot her a quick, hard look. His eye narrowed and his features hardened. "Rick is a good guy. Did he give you a reason to feel uncomfortable?"

It was obvious she'd offended his friend. Despite that,

he still showed concern for her. "No. Being alone is my comfort zone. I know I'd sleep better in my own bed."

"I imagine we'd be able to work out a schedule to watch your place if you insist. But it would be less of an inconvenience for us and less worrisome for Shayne if you stayed on the island."

As they made the turn onto San Carlos Boulevard, she didn't note any anger in his tone or reactions. They were giving up their time, and certainly some business, to help her, and she was whining. "No. It's fine. Really. I'll adjust. You'd think I'd be used to strange places as often as I moved when I was a kid. It's probably why I like sleeping in my own bed."

"Relax. Rick's one of the best people I know. But if he makes you feel uncomfortable, I'll talk to him."

"No. No," she repeated, her tone softer this time. "He's fine. I still feel you're all overreacting," she added.

"Or do you just hope that we are? Let's err on the side of caution. Give us time to work on this."

She certainly hoped so. Being in the same place with Rick was like telling a child there was candy in the house, but she wasn't allowed to have any. He didn't even like her, she reminded herself.

For whatever reason, Troy was grinning as they made the last turn onto Estero Boulevard. Fort Myers Beach's main road. Finch suspected he could read her mind. Note to self… don't talk about Rick.

"Does this area look familiar?"

"Make a left at the next street. I didn't know until the other night there were marinas tucked behind these businesses."

"How'd the sketches come out?" he asked, zipping in between oncoming traffic.

"Good. I remember the boat better than the guy's face."

"All the better. People are more apt to remember a boat, especially if it's distinctive, before they remember a person." He slowed down. "Is that the place?"

"Yes." She sat on the edge of her seat and stared out the windshield as they entered Paradise Marina. "I don't see the boat."

"It's a big marina. If it's not here, we'll ask around. I want to talk to the dockmaster first. See if he has any record of it."

Troy took the drawings from her as they walked toward a small building at the first dock.

A man with sun-weathered skin, gray at the temples and a less than welcoming smile, glanced up from a logbook. "What can I do for you two? We don't rent boats here."

"We don't need a boat. We're looking for one that was docked here a few days ago." Troy held out the sketch.

"Why do you want to know?"

"I'm a private investigator," Troy explained, pulling out his business card. "We're investigating an incident that happened on a boat that looks similar to this one."

"What happened?" The man eyed them both suspiciously. "Does she work with you?" He nodded his head in Finch's direction.

"We don't intend to cause you or your customers any trouble. We only want to look for this vessel."

"Haven't seen it or one like it."

"That can't be," Finch raised her voice. "I was on it the other night."

He shrugged. "Could be it tied up after hours. You sure it was this marina?"

She caught the turn of Troy's head. He was waiting for

confirmation. "Yes. The sun hadn't set yet, but it was close to seven o'clock."

"I'm gone by five, at the latest. It wouldn't be the first time a boat slipped in here and moored for a while. It's either that or you've got the wrong place."

"You weren't at capacity, I assume," Troy asked.

"Not this time of year. Plenty of berths open." The dockmaster examined the drawing again. "My guess is that's a Mainship Trawler. Good size pleasure boat. Don't see many of them, at least not around here. If it stole a berth for the night, it would have been one of those close to the open water. Easier in and out for a boat that size."

"Do you mind if we check out the docks and ask a few questions?"

"Don't see any harm, as long as you don't annoy any of the guests," the man's voice had softened. "Did something happen to this young lady here?"

"They tried. She didn't give them a chance."

"Why aren't the police involved?" the man asked, grabbing his keys and locking the office behind him. "I'm Bob," he said, reaching out his hand to shake theirs.

Troy kept Finch next to his side as they followed Bob toward the docks. "The police don't have enough to go on. We're trying to change that."

"We don't get many troublemakers here," Bob told them. "Most of the owners of these boats have had a berth here for years."

"We're not accusing anyone," Finch felt compelled to say. "I'm simply trying to refresh my memory."

"We're looking for info to turn over to the authorities," Troy added. "We won't cause any problems."

Finch cocked her head in his direction. Was that the plan or was he trying to make the dockmaster more at ease?

"This is it." Finch stopped at the end of a dock. "I remember this boat."

"That's not a Mainship Trawler," Bob was quick to point out.

"No. But I remember this boat. We turned left at this dock. You're right," she said looking at the dockmaster. "It was at the end."

"Then let's go have a look." Troy took her elbow.

The slip was empty. She hadn't expected otherwise. Still, there was a twinge of disappointment. Bob and Troy inspected the dock and the surrounding area. She didn't know what they were looking for, but Troy was the expert. When the inspection didn't reveal any clues, the dockmaster didn't object when Troy told him they were going to check with a few of the other boat owners.

"It'll be faster if we divide and conquer," Finch suggested to Troy. She was met with a scowl. "I'll be careful and stay close by." Being here gave her the creeps, but she wanted to prove that this part of her story was true. She was the only one who had seen the boat. Surely, someone else could attest to its existence. Then maybe Rick would believe her. She wasn't convinced he did.

"Stay where I can see you and shout out if you need help or find anyone who may have heard or saw something."

Which had been her plan. The two made their way up the dock. Most of the boats moored there were vacant. Weekend boaters, she assumed. Since her boat ride hadn't taken place on the weekend, they wouldn't be of much help if they had been here today.

Troy never veered far from her. Every time she glanced his way he was watching her, even when he was speaking with someone. Apparently, he could multi-task. She reached the next boat on her side of the dock and shouted a greeting. She was ready to move on when a woman appeared from below deck.

"Can I help you?"

Finch guessed the woman was in her forties. Deeply tanned, dressed in tight shorts and halter top, her expression was curious but not fearful.

"Hi. We're looking for our friends who said they'd be docking at this marina. They were supposed to meet us for dinner last night but didn't show."

"Maybe be they didn't have time to see you," the woman suggested, politely.

"True, but we felt better if we'd checked on them. Their boat isn't here. Did you see a boat similar to this one?" Finch held out one of the two drawings she'd brought with them. River had made copies in the event the original got lost.

"Yeah," the woman responded. "It was here the other night, but it mustn't have tied up long. I didn't see it when I went below deck to start dinner. We live on our boat, but my husband works in town. We were clearing the dinner dishes and we heard shouting. We came up on deck to see what the fuss was about. The boat was pulling away from the dock."

"Did you see anyone?"

"No. Just heard voices that sounded angry. I was glad they left. This is a peaceful place."

"Troy," Finch hollered. He wasted no time getting to her side. "This woman… I'm sorry, I didn't get your name."

"Amanda."

"Amanda saw our friends' boat the night before last. Right?"

"Yes."

"Did you get the name of the boat? See anyone?" Troy asked.

"You don't know the name of their boat?" Amanda's eyes narrowed, taking a step back. "I told you what I know. I hope you find your friends," she said then disappeared below deck.

"Sorry," Finch apologized to Troy. "The friends angle was the first thing that popped into my head."

"At least we have a time frame to work with," he told her. "Let's head a dock over and see if we can dig up any more eyewitnesses. She's probably watching us, wondering if she should call the police."

She and Troy canvassed each dock, seeking anyone else who might have seen a boat that fit her description. No one had.

After they returned to the garden center, Troy deposited Finch in the garden's gazebo. He assured her he would return to the marina tomorrow to ask more questions.

Finch settled into the deck chair and took in the lush garden that surrounded her. There hadn't been time to admire its beauty while being whisked through it the night before. Shayne had invited her over several times to meet her friends. Finch always had an excuse. Now, she wasn't only meeting them, but they were bailing her out. Closing her eyes, she fought against the darkness seeping into her soul.

It had been a long time since she allowed those feelings of despair to inch their way under her skin. She'd put them firmly behind her, or so she'd thought. Burying her face with her hands, she let the ache, the hurt, and pain swallow her. It had been years since she'd let her history rule her. She'd battled so hard to forget it—to get past it, but she'd been holding in her fears, and her tears, since long before the events of the other night. Her counselor had once told her after she'd fallen apart, that a good cry could be cathartic. Still, she didn't see it as a positive. How many times had she been backhanded when she'd let tears slip? Too many to count.

Fisting away the moisture, she sucked in an enforcing breath and squared her shoulders. None of this was her fault. She had to remember that. Her own stupidity had earned her stay in detention but accepting an invitation from a co-worker, she'd had no reason to distrust, wasn't deserving of self-flagellation.

She needed to stop acting like a child. It wouldn't get her out of this situation.

14

---

*T*roy was on the phone when Rick arrived. He was eager to know the details of the trip to the marina. His friend had called earlier to confirm the boat Finch had described had docked at the marina for a short while. Troy didn't disconnect from his call, instead pointing toward the rear of the building. Rick dropped Finch's laptop on Troy's desk. The department had cleared the computer of any tracking device, but Troy would double check their work.

Rick passed through the empty break room and out the rear door. Shayne was at the potting bench, an earbud in one ear, her foot tapping to whatever tune she was listening to.

"She's in the gazebo." Shayne directed him to the center of the garden with a nod of her head.

"Alone?"

"Seriously, Rick? Nobody's ever alone here. Troy's watching us all on the security camera right now." She chuckled. "I could throw myself into your arms and test how fast he gets out here."

"No thanks. I hope to live a little longer," he laughed. "Although it might be fun to see how fast he can move."

The team tended to draw attention, and often that attention came with trouble. The result was the best security system on the island for this place, as well as the home and business next door.

As he stepped onto the garden path that led to the gazebo, Rick recognized the sound of sniffling and paused. He wasn't good around tears, and he didn't think Finch would want a witness to them. She'd appeared tough, bordering on arrogant. It would take a thick skin to make it through multiple foster homes and a stint in juvenile detention. He'd assumed that her cocky attitude was her normal persona. Now he speculated if it was a front. Crying in juvey would have made her look weak and, therefore, an easy target. The same could be said for many foster homes.

His phone beeped. A text message from Troy. "Afraid of tears? Get a move on. And be nice." Proving the point that Troy did, indeed, have eyes on everything. It was tempting to tell Troy to get his ass out here and deal with it, but he'd be proving Troy's point.

"What's that supposed to mean?" he texted. "I'm always nice."

"Then why does she act as if she's afraid of you?"

That gave Rick pause. Finch was afraid of him? In what way? Did she pick up on his attraction to her or his struggle against it? Perhaps he should let her stay with Gib, but the idea immediately soured in his stomach.

Rick continued his trek toward the folly Cat had added to the garden. Fortunately, the sounds of distress faded before he reached it. The small jungle was quiet except for the sound of birds and insects. As he rounded the last obstacle—a stand of tall plants—he spotted Finch sitting on the hard plank flooring, her legs crossed, and her eyes closed. Her wrists rested on her knees. He recognized the meditation pose and debated withdrawing away quietly when Finch opened her eyes and looked straight at him. Those copper discs sucked him in.

"Sorry. I didn't mean to disturb you," he said, feeling a bit like a voyeur for lingering.

"You're fine. I needed a minute to regroup." Finch dragged her sleeve across her face, erasing any remnants of the tears she'd shed, then stood.

"I can come back," he said, retreating. "I wanted to check on how things went today. Troy was busy, but I can wait for him to finish." Damn him for interrupting what little peace she'd had these last few days.

"Stay. I've had enough time to myself. I didn't want to follow Shayne around the garden while she worked." She took a sip from a diluted glass of tea. Her friend had brought a pitcher of iced tea along with several glasses before she went back to work in the garden. Had Shayne been expecting visitors?

"This place is amazing," she said, changing the subject and gesturing toward their surroundings.

"A garden already existed before Cat purchased the property. The former owners had a green thumb. After she closed on it, Cat worked her magic and created this place. It makes a great sales tool, I'm told."

"Visuals. I imagine it helps a lot when selling plants and landscape designs."

"I guess it does. She and Shayne stay busy."

"Do you like being a cop?" Finch asked, cocking her head.

"I don't imagine you have many fond memories of the police," he said, instead of answering her question.

"For the most part, when the cops arrived at one of the foster homes, they wanted to help. A lot of the officers at the detention center were good people, too, but there are a number I'd rather never see again."

"Most of us become officers of the law because we want to help people. Like every profession, you'll find good and bad. I'm sorry not all your interactions were positive." Was it his career choice that made her skittish of him? He hadn't been particularly friendly. If he was being honest, he didn't want to get close to her. He was drawn to her and that was terrifying as hell.

"It didn't help matters that I wasn't a model foster kid."

"Did you ever hear from your birth parents?" Business. Keep things on a business level.

She exhaled deeply before answering. He could feel her pain from where he stood.

"No. As far as I know no one ever came looking for me."

"You also said you'd never looked for them."

"Why should I? Besides, the Division of Family Services didn't know how to find them. How was I supposed to if I had the desire to?" Her fists had tightened as she spoke. The knowledge that they dumped her within days of being born would cut anyone deep.

"Have you ever considered one of those genealogy sites? Could be they're looking for you. Times change. People change."

"Not interested."

Knowing her history could be a key to solving the attacks on her, but he didn't press. He didn't want her shutting down, so he temporarily tabled the subject. With any luck, Josie had discovered additional information from her contacts.

"What happened to Mary Pierce?"

"Mary Pierce disappeared as soon as I was old enough to legally change my name. And, in case it wasn't in the records you found, that name was assigned to me by my first social worker. They left me in an alley behind a fire station. No note. No name. The fire station was on Pierce Street. I guess she preferred the name Mary over Jane."

"Still, why change it?"

"It was a constant reminder that I wasn't wanted. I picked a new name for a new beginning when I got out of detention, and it finally sunk in no one was going to better my life for me. I had to do it myself. A new name and a new future, I'd hoped." She shrugged, breaking the connection to gaze at her hands in her lap. He immediately missed the warmth in her eyes. He was nuts.

"Savannah Finch. Why that name?" Stay on point.

Her eyes rolled as she lifted her head. "No big mystery. I liked the sound of it. I didn't expect people to call me Finch when I picked it." She shrugged again. "But either name is fine with me."

"Tell me what happened today."

"Good news is we found the marina. The bad news is there was no boat or a trace of it. The dock manager, or master, or whatever he's called, doesn't have a record of a boat fitting my description mooring there recently. He admitted it wouldn't be the first time one slipped in and out of the marina while the office was closed."

"What about the other boat owners? I know Troy didn't stop with the dockmaster." Rick pulled up a chair. The angle allowed him a direct look into her glimmering eyes. It was hard not to stare.

"We had a little luck there. Very little. One woman reported seeing the boat leaving the dock. No one else claimed to see anything, or if they did, they wouldn't discuss it. Troy said he was going to take another swing by there tomorrow."

"Good. To be safe, I think you should stay at my place

again tonight. You can't go home even if they've changed the locks—not after today."

"I'm used to being on my own." Exasperated, her head dropped back against her shoulders, taking the gleam of polished metal with it.

"It's not smart to go it alone—not if you really are a target," he reminded her.

"Excuse me? Do you think I jumped into the bay for fun? Why do you continue to insinuate that I'm stupid?" Her eyes locked onto his. This time, they were a fiery bronze.

"I'm not, damn it. Stop putting words into my mouth. It's clear something is going on…"

"Ya think?"

"Can you be quiet for a minute?" He stopped. He was digging a hole that would be hell to climb out of. "Sorry. What I'm trying to say is that I'm trained to investigate not leap to conclusions. What is obvious is that you are in danger and Shayne would never forgive me if I let anything happen to you."

"I understand that, but I don't need or want charity. I'll sleep on the break room couch," she said. "And don't try laying a guilt trip on me about Shayne fretting over me. She won't like it, but she won't stop me."

"Shayne is family. I don't care if you think I'm trying to manipulate you. You need to stop being so damn selfish and stubborn and take the help that's offered to you."

He was finally getting a handle on how to read her. The secret was in her eyes. He'd been distracted and fascinated by their beauty. While the rest of her face remained placid—a skill he suspected she'd honed while growing up —her pupils were telling him he'd hit the mark he'd intended.

"Why does it have to be your place?" she argued. "You

don't like me. You don't trust me. Why can't I stay here? You said it was secure."

"You're not reading me very well," which was probably a good thing, "but that topic can wait for another time. As for your other question, you'd still be alone in that building. Even with the security system in place, it would take time to get to you if you needed help."

She rubbed her eyes and sighed. "Fine."

He didn't think she was any less frightened of him, but he was certain she was furious as hell. *Fine.* There wasn't a man alive that hadn't heard that word in that tone.

"Tell me what was in the papers you didn't find in your desk." Perhaps a change it subject would lower the room temperature.

"I must have misplaced them."

"Do you actually believe that?" He rested his forearms on the tabletop.

"You must think I'm a compulsive liar. You seem to doubt every word that comes out of my mouth."

Those heat-seeking missiles locked on him again, and his groin tightened. Shit.

"You need to work on that chip on your shoulder. It's pretty damn sharp. You might cut yourself."

"Funny." She wasn't smiling.

"Anything else you can tell me about those missing papers? By the way, Troy has your computer. The department cleared it for bugs and tracking devices. Troy's double checking their work. At least you'll be able access the copies you scanned and saved."

"Don't you trust anyone? Your own department isn't good enough?"

It was Rick's turn to sigh. "Check. Check. And double check. Fewer surprises that way. The last thing you want in the military or in law enforcement is surprises."

She appeared to accept that with a simple nod. Progress?

"And my car?"

"They'd found a locater device under the dash, which explains why the seat was moved. Whoever planted it was sloppy and forgot to return the seat to its normal position." An amateur's mistake. If they were talking organized crime, which was still way out there in his opinion, they wouldn't have made that error.

"I don't get any of this."

Neither did he—yet.

"What's in the missing documents?" The fine hairs on the back of his neck tickled every time the subject came up. He was convinced they'd been taken. The question was why?

"Reports by caseworkers. Notes I'd taken about foster homes where I'd been placed. Stuff regarding my stay at Hillsborough Detention Center. Then, of course, there are the legal documents regarding my name change."

"Do you need to access any of the papers on a regular basis?"

"I occasionally have to submit a copy of the court document changing my name. There's really no good reason to hang onto the rest of the papers, but I've always had a fear if I got rid of them, I'd need them."

"When was the last time you had your hands on them?"

"When I applied for the job at the spa. Occasionally, an employer will come upon the name change when doing a background check." Finch was drawing circles in the condensation that had formed on the tabletop near her glass. "I always keep them in the same place, but I can't swear I put them in the drawer. I wouldn't have given it any thought—like locking a door. You do it without thinking."

"We'll double check the apartment," Rick told her.

"And if they aren't there, why the hell would anyone take them?"

15

———

etween arranging for new credit cards, identification, and such, Finch had put the file out of her mind. It was front and center now. A pit formed in her stomach. Why would someone want those papers? What good would they do them?

"I need to get home and look for the file." She pushed back her chair.

"You didn't mention if they had changed your lock."

"I called this morning. They're finished. I have to stop by and get the keys—and pay them." She'd lost her keys, therefore, she was financially responsible for the new lock. Crap. She'd need money before they'd release them. She started to look at her watch and stopped. Besides her bag and phone, she'd lost her watch in the ruckus on the boat. Where the hell was the delivery driver with her credit cards? One card is all she needed to get things moving.

"I need a phone. A watch. Preferably both. Otherwise, I'm going to have to learn to tell time by the position of the sun."

"We can get you a burner phone until you can get situated," he suggested.

"A burner phone?"

"A temporary phone. We use them when we don't want a number traced or tracked."

"Another debt I'll owe." Another weight added to her shoulders.

"I wish you'd stop looking at it like that," Rick argued. "No one here is expecting compensation."

"I don't get it. You guys don't know me."

"No, we don't," Rick admitted. "But you need help and helping is part of our DNA, Besides, Shayne knows you and trusts you. Don't let her down or you'll have to answer to me."

She stared at her glass, which was now mostly melted ice. At least she knew where she stood with him. Knowing made her feel better. He was helping her because of the bond with his friends. Loyalty was one characteristic she rated highly. Few people had faith in her when she was a child. None were loyal. Seeing it in others was refreshing and comforting.

She'd find a way to thank them. Another item she needed to add to her list.

"Do you think I could get a pen and some paper?" She needed to start a written list. Too much was going on to remember everything she needed to do. Besides her personal stuff, she wanted to have something to write on in case a memory suddenly popped into her head. She'd always been a list maker. Starting one might help relieve some of the pressure building inside her.

"Not a problem." His long, broad form cast a shadow as he rose from his chair. "You okay coming home with me tonight?"

She nodded while her cheeks heated. The statement

sounded more like a date than a security detail. She was grateful when he disappeared behind the outcropping of plants. It gave her a minute to clear her head, but he wasn't gone long. He returned with the items she'd requested accompanied by Shayne who was bearing a fresh pitcher of iced tea and extra glasses.

"We're closed now," Shayne said, pouring herself a glass. "Mind if I hang out until Troy finishes?"

"Sure. Is he going to be much longer?" Finch asked.

Her question was answered a minute later when Shayne's husband appeared. He leaned over and gave his wife a kiss so intimate that it had Finch looking away rather than intrude on the moment.

"Your computer is good to go," he said, handing her the laptop. "I encrypted it so it can't be tracked through its IP address. Cleared out your history and a few other things. No one should be able to track you using this."

"Check your emails. It wouldn't be the first time a stalker reached out that way. Your pursuer may try to bait you out into the open."

Finch quickly logged into her server. Her password still worked. A good sign, she suspected. Or was it? She'd best change it, but she wanted to check those emails first. And, damn, there were a lot of them. Mostly junk and a few bills. There were a couple from the credit card companies and her bank notifying her of the changes she'd made. She deleted the junk from the first page allowing older messages to scroll onto it. Clicking boxes to delete more crap, she stopped when she spotted a notification from her provider that a sender was requesting to be added to her contact list. She hovered the cursor over the email address, her stomach doing flips as she did. Tony G.

"Ah, guys?" She waited a beat. "This may be a message from Tony."

"You don't know?" Rick asked.

"We've never exchanged emails, so he's not in my contacts. It went to my suspect folder. How'd he get my email address?" She was certain she never gave it to him.

"Probably from work," Shayne suggested. "Maybe he got a hold of your file."

"Do I open it?"

"Yes." The answer came in stereo as Troy and Rick responded at the same time.

She transferred the message to her inbox, then opened it. Rick was lurking over her shoulder. "Odd," she said.

"What does it say?" Troy got up from his chair and joined Rick.

There was nothing in the subject line.

"*Watch your back*," she read. "Is that a warning or a threat?"

"The email is dated yesterday," Rick said, hovering over Finch's shoulder. "That's after he was last heard from —at least as far as we know."

"Is the spa still open?" Troy asked. "See if they'll give you his phone number."

"Gonzales should be there."

"She's not going to give out that kind of information to another employee," Shayne corrected her husband. "Rick would stand a better chance of getting it."

"Not without a warrant," Rick explained. "As soon as the authorities get involved, those are the first words we hear—unless they're idiots," he said to Finch.

"What makes you think she'll give it to me?"

"How well can you act?" he asked. "Tell her you're worried about Tony, but you've lost his number since you lost your phone."

"I'll need a phone to place the call," she pointed out.

Shayne pulled hers from the pocket of her shorts and held it out to Finch. Rick put his hand over hers.

"Troy? Can you get one of the burner phones from your office? It's best if no one can trace a call to any of us."

Troy didn't take the time to acknowledge the request. He took off for the building and was back in less than five minutes, handing a fully charged cell phone to Finch.

The call took longer than she'd expected. Finch had never spent more time than necessary when talking to Mrs. Gonzales. She was surprised her boss was such a chatterbox. She did, eventually, get the number.

She disconnected and called Tony. There was no answer, and his voice mailbox was full.

"That got us nowhere," she said, sliding the phone across the table to Troy. He slid it back.

"Keep it," he said, echoing what Rick had said to her earlier.

"Any news on Tony?"

"No. She wanted to know what I knew. As you probably picked up from my end of the conversation, I was as vague as I could be. She appeared concerned about him today—which is weird since she was seriously annoyed at him yesterday."

"Did she say what was bothering her?" Rick rested his forearms on the table.

"No. Other than giving me his phone number, neither of us got much from the conversation. We were dancing around one another."

"I have to wonder why his voicemail was full," Troy commented, leaning against one of the posts of the gazebo. "Maybe something is wrong with his phone or provider, or he has a hell of a lot of messages he hasn't answered."

"I've never known anyone's voice mail to fill up. That

would take a lot of calls, wouldn't it?" Finch glanced at the men, trying to judge the seriousness of this development.

"It might depend on his provider," Rick answered. "There could be any number of reasons. This only adds another layer of mystery to this puzzle." He took a gulp from his glass of tea. "Gambino could be on the run from the same people who are after Finch."

"Then why lead her to the boat? You'd think he'd have explained in his email," Shayne asked. "Telling her to watch her back isn't very helpful. It's scary."

"Which may be the point." Rick eyed Finch. "Perhaps he doesn't want you trusting anyone."

"There's no way to track his phone?" Finch asked.

"Only his service provider can do that," Rick explained. "And an official request is a long, messy journey."

"Can you tell me anything more about today?" Rick asked Troy, redirecting the conversation.

"I'm sure Finch filled you in on our trip to the marina. I'll take another stab at it tomorrow." Troy gave Finch his full attention. "Good job remembering the details of your trip to the beach and the guy's description."

"It didn't help much." She was good with details. It came naturally to her after her time behind bars. Juvenile detention wasn't a picnic, and while they separated the girls from the boys, that didn't mean she'd been able to let her guard down. She learned who to trust and whom to avoid. She'd studied every idiosyncrasy of her jailers and fellow detainees.

"On the contrary. We may not have found it without your keen eye."

"What else have you been working on?" Rick asked.

"We're digging into Tony Gambino," Troy answered. "His last name raised flags, of course. The Gambinos are still an active organized crime family with tentacles here in Florida. If Tony is connected to them, I haven't found a link."

"Why would an organized crime group be interested in me?" Finch stared at Troy. What she knew about organized crime, she'd learned in the movies and on television. It surprised her the actual *families* were still active.

"They have their hands in a lot of illegal activities. You may have inadvertently bumped into one. But just because his name is Gambino doesn't mean he's part of that family or, if he is, whether he is active in it. Not everyone related to a member of an organized crime family is a bad guy. Steve and I are still digging." Troy took another swallow of his drink.

"Anything unusual so far?" Rick pushed.

"Other than a few speeding tickets, he appears clean. We haven't entertained the idea that he might have been tricked into getting Finch to that boat. It's a possibility."

"Which could explain the email and his argument with the two men on the boat." Finch massaged her temples. Her head hurt from thinking. Another string to untangle. Snatching the writing pad off the table, she started sorting through her thoughts. Putting them on paper always helped. She'd kept a diary of sorts over the years, but she'd rarely written in it since she left detention. Her life had finally settled—or at least she'd believed it had.

"We have connections that can check out any links to a crime syndicate—or are you forgetting our friends at the FBI in Tampa?" Shayne asked.

"Hernandez and Morgan," Rick confirmed. "I can call them and let them know we have a Gambino in the area."

"Let me call them." Shayne grinned. There was a flicker of mischief in her eyes. "They still owe me after the mess they created when they sent me here without telling you guys why."

"Regardless of why, I'm glad they did," Troy said, touching his lips to the crown of Shayne's head.

"It still doesn't let them off the hook." This time, Shayne spit out the words. There was anger in her tone.

Finch knew a bit of the backstory on Shayne's relocation from Tampa, but there were a lot of details she hadn't shared. Knowing Shayne could simply pick up the phone and call an FBI agent was intriguing and pretty damn cool.

The moment was interrupted as they heard the slow roll of tires on the drive between the two businesses. The lush greenery prevented anyone from seeing the vehicle. Finch locked onto Rick. His head was cocked in the direction of the sound and his hand was on his weapon. She held her breath.

16

Troy pulled his phone from his pocket and swiped the screen with his thumb. "Relax," Troy told them. "Colt here. Pizza tonight upstairs. We'd better get our asses over there before Kevin gets here. He inhales food after a full day at the hospital."

"What the hell is Colt doing creeping in like that?" Rick snarled.

Troy shrugged. "Maybe he didn't want to alarm anyone."

"He managed the opposite."

"You can debate his stealth tactics with him later," Troy countered.

Additional vehicles were arriving, filling both the front of the businesses and the lot behind the photography studio. Shayne grabbed the pitcher of tea and Troy gathered the glasses. "We'll rinse these out and join you upstairs in a minute," Shayne told them.

Rick ushered Finch through the garden gate, then up the stairs to the unit on the right. Boxes of pizza lined the kitchen counter. Someone had put a salad together to round the meal out. He waited by the fridge while Finch filled her plate with greens and a slice of pizza. After filling his own plate, he grabbed a couple of beers and joined the others in the living and dining area.

Finch only made it a few feet inside the doorway before she came to a halt. Her eyes widened as she scanned the area. It took a second before Rick noted she wasn't staring at the people in the room, but the room itself. He and his friends were accustomed to its decor. They practically lived here, but this was Finch's first visit.

The area was decorated with an artist's eye—Colts. The colors and furniture were tropical in nature. Cat had added a few touches of her own, but she'd pretty much left it as it was when she moved in. The two condos on the second floor of the business were mirror images of each other. A long hallway ran from the kitchen to the front door—shotgun style. Every room was nestled against the outside wall. The layout gave each space copious amounts of sunlight.

The natural light set off the stunning photos. Rick still appreciated the art but had seen it so often he shamefully began to take them for granted.

"My God," Finch murmured.

"We're the same group we were last night. The guys are more intimidating, bunched together," Cat said, approaching her.

"It's not you," Finch explained. "It's the pictures. You've got an art gallery in here."

Cat beamed. "Colt took most of them. We threw a few of Gib's in so his feelings wouldn't be hurt." Cat laughed outright when Gib stood and playfully grabbed her around the waist.

"You love them as much as you love me. Admit it," he said, and gave her a quick squeeze.

There was a special relationship between the two. Gib had taken a bullet for Cat shortly after they'd met. Rick considered them closer than most brothers and sisters.

"Let's eat," Colt said, gesturing to his wife to rejoin him on the couch. "We have a few things to cover when we're done."

Troy and Shayne weren't far behind Rick and Finch. Everyone settled with their food and, as they'd done the previous night, made small talk while they ate their meal. Finch relaxed, asking most of the questions. She was bursting with them, inquiring how each couple met, wanting to know more with each answer. How much of the questioning was to get her mind off her problems and how much was genuine interest? Hard to tell. He had to admit, the tales were legendary.

With the meal done, glasses and beers refreshed, Finch slowly withdrew into herself. She was fully aware that the inquiry was going to turn on her.

"I spent a good part of the day researching and talking to social workers," Josie said, retrieving a notebook from her large handbag. "If no one minds, I'd like to start with a few questions."

Rick felt Finch's deep intake of breath, but she let the breath out slowly and didn't retreat. He didn't think she retreated much—or often. He should get extra points for convincing her to stay with him tonight. Points toward what, though?

"Finch," Josie started, "first off, I want you to know I took no pleasure in digging into your past. Unfortunately, everyone here has learned that the past sometimes holds secrets that can come back and bite us in the ass."

"No one here would do anything to hurt you, physically or emotionally," Shayne assured her.

"Go ahead," Finch urged Josie. "There's a lot of bad stuff—much of it I brought down on myself."

"You were a child." River reached across the coffee table and took her hand. "There are times in our lives we all want a do-over." Kevin tucked his wife closer. River had experienced one of the ugliest, most heart-wrenching childhoods anyone could imagine—and Rick could imagine a hell of a lot.

"I won't go over each of your foster care placements, but there are a few that stand out."

"Why is that, Josie?" Rick asked.

"Because of the number of calls to the authorities while I was in those homes. Right?" Finch answered softly.

Josie nodded. Rick had been watching Finch. For a split second, she morphed into a vulnerable child. He'd seen the look far too many times while deployed and during his stint with the Chicago PD to miss it. The urge to pull her into his arms was almost overwhelming. It wouldn't have been a bright move for either of them. She didn't like to show weakness, and he didn't want to advertise his attraction to her.

"Until I reached my teens, foster care wasn't fun, but it wasn't bad either. The last pleasant home I was in, however, hadn't signed up to house kids over the age of twelve. When I turned thirteen, they moved me to make room for a younger child."

"And landed at the Simpsons," Josie stated. It wasn't a question.

"Definitely not the quirky animated TV characters, I'm afraid. I wasn't there long before I was beaten the first time. My first instinct was to reach out to my caseworker. While some foster care homes were less welcoming than others, I hadn't been abused, so I'd never been down that road before. But the other kids in the house—there were three—warned me against it. They told me it would only make matters worse, and they'd all suffer if I didn't keep my mouth shut. Initially, I kept quiet and did my best to stay out of Mr. Simpson's way."

"I gather that didn't last," Rick prompted her.

"There were three foster kids, two boys and a girl, in the home when I arrived. Of course, I bunked with Wendy. She was two years older than me. One night, Mr. Simpson slipped into our room. I'd hoped he was just checking on us. I pretended to be asleep." Finch pressed the pads of her index finger and thumb against her eyelids. Rick imagined she was trying to erase a vision stuck in her head.

"He didn't stop at the door. He crept in and stood beside Wendy's bed—watching her. I don't know if she was asleep or, like me, was pretending to be. Then, as quick as a lightning strike, Simpson threw back her comforter and covered her mouth as he mounted the bed.

"I'd wanted to turn my head away. To hide under the pillow. If I didn't see it, it wasn't happening. I was also terrified I'd be next. Then I heard Wendy's muffled cry as he stripped her underwear off. I guess it tripped a switch in me."

"What did you do?" Colt had a grip on his wife's hand. Cat had turned pale.

"Put my ass in a sling, is what I did," Finch mumbled under her breath. "I yelled at him to stop. He turned on me. I hit him in the head with the bedside lamp."

"Good for you." Gib raised his bottle of beer in salute.

"Not so good for me. It stopped him from raping Wendy, but he turned on me. I must have screamed loud enough for a neighbor to call the police. I'd assumed Simpson was dumb as a rock, but he proved me wrong. He told me I was to agree with everything he told the cops, or he'd have me arrested for assault, then he'd take what he'd originally intended to from Wendy and do it in a way she'd never forget. He told me I'd be to blame."

"A thirteen-year-old assaulting a grown man?" Gib's color changed from tan to a dark shade of red.

"I was new to the home. I expected the other kids would speak up, but they remained silent as Simpson told the story of how he'd come to check on us and I got scared and attacked him. The police had separated us, but I could still see the other kids. I didn't understand why at the time, but they all shook their heads, indicating I should stay silent. There was anger on the faces of the boys—I think they were fourteen or fifteen years of age. Wendy was frightened. Still, the look she gave me was clear. I was to keep quiet."

"What did he tell the police that they did nothing with you or him? Is the bastard still around?" Gib's white knight instincts were showing as his hands fisted.

"It was simple. He told them I'd mistaken him for an intruder and attacked him. It explained his injuries—at least as far as the officers were concerned."

"They seriously fell for that?" River asked.

Finch gave her a simple smile. "I don't think those cops wanted a protracted investigation. None of the others would have sided with me."

"And your injuries?" Cat asked.

"From the fall I took when he was defending himself. Apparently, I fell a lot—at least according to Simpson. The other kids didn't contradict him."

"You should have been taken to the hospital."

Finch huffed. "We couldn't have that now, could we?" she said sarcastically. "The cops asked if I needed to be seen, but by that time I was terrified of Simpson—and the look he was giving me told me I'd actually need a hospital if I agreed. The bruises hadn't started showing yet. I told them I was fine."

"I can't believe the police let that go," Rick swore.

"Simpson was smooth. Looking back, I think he knew one of the cops personally. He hid his vicious, ugly side in public, so it wasn't hard to convince them."

"What happened after the police left?" Josie asked.

"They locked me in the room. Mrs. Simpson moved Wendy in with the boys. I think she did that to protect her. I don't think Simpson would have tried anything while they were together. The boys were both hulks. I think between the two of them they would have been able to take him, but there would have been a high price to pay if they did —juvenile detention or worse, adult court. Their age was borderline.

"A couple of days after they confined me to the bedroom, Wendy brought me food."

"They hadn't fed you?" Josie was appalled.

"I had to pay for my actions. It wasn't so bad. Being alone was actually a respite. Going hungry was my punishment. Anyway, Wendy told me they'd all be on the street or in jail if I said or did anything like that again. I wouldn't have been able to live with that, so I stayed quiet."

"For a while," Josie added.

"A long while. Wendy and the boys all aged out of the system. I don't know what happened to them. I hope they didn't end up on the street. I think about them often. I always wondered if my keeping silent was best for them."

"And you?" Kevin asked. "What happened to you?"

The sigh that escaped just about killed Rick. It was filled with resignation and pain.

"I don't know if the DCF suspected Simpson had a thing for young girls, but no other girls were placed in the home while I was there. He constantly harangued his wife as to why. He'd stayed away from me. I guess he feared I'd be more trouble than I was worth, but eventually, that fear wore off. He came to my room one night. I always locked the door and shoved a chair under it since the incident with Wendy, but he'd been drinking. It didn't stop him."

"Bastard," Cat spat out.

"It worked out okay," Finch continued. "He might have forgotten my temper, but I hadn't forgotten his penchant for young girls. There was no way to sneak a weapon into my room, but I kept a can of hairspray under my pillow. He got a face full of it. He stumbled and hit his head. His wife had to take him to the hospital for stitches. They moved me to another foster family the next day."

"I assume you reported him?" Without waiting for an answer, Rick pinned Josie with a look. "You have his name and info, don't you?" The piece of shit was getting a visit as soon as they were done with their current issue.

"I told my social worker, but it would have been my word against his, she warned me. Besides, other than entering my room, I didn't give him the chance to touch me. There was already one note in my file stating I'd attacked him. It was likely to do me more harm than good if I pressed the issue. I was out of there. I asked her to keep close tabs on any kids put in that home. I didn't know what else to do."

And she didn't think she'd done enough. Sadness and guilt along with a light sheen of tears were reflected in her eyes.

"And then you were moved from one place to another," Josie said.

"After the Simpson incident, they considered me a troublemaker. I landed in a series of places that didn't exactly house future Nobel Peace Prize winners. It was go along with the other foster kids or live with the consequences. It was petty stuff. Not enough to get me arrested, but I got moved from one home to another until I made the mistake of thinking one of the foster boys had a crush on me. I certainly had one on him. One night we were out with several of his friends from school, I waited in the car while the others went into a house. One boy said he was going to hit up his grandmother for some cash. My instincts should have told me they were up to something. The house was dark. They stole everything they could carry—cash, jewelry, electronics. The minute they all came running to the car with their arms full, I made a break for it. I didn't need or want that shit.

"The police picked everyone up, including me, that evening. No one believed my story. My reputation was tainted—by history and the company I kept. The only reason I got a lighter sentence than the rest is because of a doorbell camera and a decent public defender who pointed out I wasn't in the driver's seat, so it proved I hadn't been the 'get-away' driver. He argued unsuccessfully I was an innocent bystander and was only guilty of poor judgment. That poor judgment got me two years in detention."

She picked at her cuticles as she continued. "On the good side, they did not try me as an adult, and I didn't have to worry what my next home would be like—whether I'd luck out and have good foster parents or be thrown into another bad situation. Funny as that may seem, being in juvey gave me a sense of security and, for the first time, I had access to counselors."

"I'm so sorry you had to go through that," Cat said. "Our justice system is often rather perverse. I know. I worked in it."

"Did anyone of your foster parents ask questions about where you'd come from or what had happened to your parents?" Steve asked.

"No. I suppose they were given my history before they took me in. Occasionally, one of the other foster kids would ask. Everyone had a story. Most believed they'd go home to their families one day. That was never going to happen to me. I did my best to avoid the subject." She paused. "Why? Is that important?"

"My contact at the Division of Children and Family Services said your files were accessed a year ago," Josie said. "Do you have any idea why someone would do that?"

"Do they know who?" Rick asked, totally focused on Josie now. The woman knew how to ferret out information.

"No. The records she accessed only showed the date the file was last opened."

"That was months before I applied for the job in Bonita." Finch frowned. "So, it wouldn't have been Spa Terra."

"It wouldn't have been the spa, regardless," Troy pointed out. "There should be no reason for an employer to check with DCF. If they wanted to affirm Finch's name change, a check of the public records would have sufficed. Unless you mentioned your stint with the State. Even if you did, their HR department would know better than to look for that history. Juvenile files are sealed."

"You don't mention you were in detention when you apply for a job, do you?" Rick asked. "You don't have to reference it on an application or tell anyone during an interview."

"I don't. Mary Pierce is dead. Shayne's the only one I've told about my past since I started my new life with my new name—until now."

"Who the hell can access those files?" Colt asked.

"Anyone can log in, unfortunately," Josie explained. "My contact is going to do a little snooping, but the name and email address go nowhere. My guess is they were set up specifically to look into those records, then disappear."

"It would be helpful if we knew who and why," Kevin stated. "It would give us a place to start."

"We already have a few places to start." Steve reached for his phone. "The boat, for one. We know from the dockmaster what type of boat it is, even if we don't know the name of the vessel. It has to get gas and water. Which means dealing with a dockmaster somewhere. I'll start making calls tomorrow."

"I can make those calls," River told him. "That will leave you free to work on other things. If I run into any hardheads, I'll let you take them."

"Thanks. I need to spend time looking at the names Josie uncovered today, and Troy will visit the docks again."

"The Sanibel PD and Lee County Sheriff's Office are investigating the bridge incident. I'm checking on the vehicle owner. Right now, he doesn't appear to be involved."

"No fingerprints but those belonging to the owner, I assume." Colt stood and headed for the kitchen.

"None," Rick answered when his friend quickly returned, handing him one of the three beers that dangled from his fingers. "Interestingly enough, all fingerprints are missing from surfaces like the steering wheel, ignition switch, and gear shift."

"They were wiped clean," Troy stated the obvious, taking a slug from his cold beer.

"It would seem so."

"Where is this going? How does any of this help me?" Finch flopped back against the cushion.

"Give it time," Shayne told her. "We're not going to figure this out overnight."

"I can't afford to sit around until we do. I need to go home and back to work."

"Think again," Rick snarled.

17

Finch winced. No one had taken that tone with her since leaving detention. The memory was vivid but brief. She shot Rick a glare, then stormed from the room.

"Where are you going?" Shayne caught up with her in the kitchen.

"Honestly? I don't know. When I get angry, I have to move. I can't sit still." She paced the width of the kitchen. "Where the hell does he get off talking to me like that? What makes him think he can order me around?"

"You're not witnessing him at his best. I suspect I know why, but it's not my place to say."

"Why not? What's going on with him?"

"He's worried about you."

Finch's eyebrows rose. Her friend was wearing a cat-that-ate-the-canary smile as she leaned against the frame of the back door.

"He doesn't like me," Finch stated firmly. "I get it. I can live with that, but I won't take any shit off of him."

"I know you're skilled at reading people. You wouldn't

be good at the job you do, if you weren't. Why is it so hard for you to get a handle on him?"

"What are you trying to tell me?"

"Let's forget Rick for a minute…"

"My pleasure." The guy was an asshole.

"You're smart enough to know you shouldn't be on your own." Shayne raised her hands defensively, holding off any comment from Finch. "Use your head. You were kidnapped, your apartment was broken into, and you were damn near run off the road into San Carlos Bay."

Finch's pacing slowed as she listened. Damn, she hated it when logic interfered with a good snit.

"We've barely begun to pull on all the different threads that lead to you. Everyone out there is doing their best to help. It's insulting to walk away from them. Use the sense God gave you. You turned your life around. You gave yourself a second chance. Don't shorten it by being stubborn."

That brought Finch to a halt. Her friend rarely lectured her and when she did, name calling had never been part of it. The spurt of resentment abated as the tongue lashing hit dead center. Temper had been her default before counseling. She thought she'd mastered it. Tamed it. Apparently not. It was rearing its ugly head too often these last few days.

"It's hard for me to lean on others," Finch admitted to her friend. "I don't know how to accept help gracefully. What should I do?" She was adrift in this sea of new friendships. Few people had defended her in her past. If her actions were hurting these people, she needed to reverse course.

"Let us help. It's as simple as that. No one is asking you to take orders unless it is for your own safety."

"I'll apologize." She took her friend's hands in hers.

"But I can't stay here forever. It may not be much, but I have a life and I don't want to spend the rest of it hiding."

"I'm asking you to give us time. Those men and women out there saved my ass. Give them a chance to save yours so you can return to your life, assuming you still want the one you've been living."

"Is there a problem with my life?" She dropped her hands and straightened her spine. Temper flared again, but this time she was able to tamp it down.

"No. But wants and desires change. This whole shitshow may very well change your perspective. That's all I meant."

With a nod, Finch headed toward the living area.

"Hold up."

"What now?"

"Let's get back to Rick."

"Why?" But she knew why. He was Finch's host while on the island and Shayne's friend. She shifted from one foot to the other, waiting.

"I'm asking you to give him a break. He's not the overbearing jerk he's making himself out to be. He cares. And, in your case, I think he cares a bit more than he'd like to."

"Will you shut up?" Rick snarled at Gib. His friend was laughing his ass off. "What the hell is so funny?"

"You." Gib covered his mouth, smothering the laughter a bit, but those grey eyes sparkled as much as the ruby stud in his ear. "Is there anything you want to tell us?"

"You know if she leaves our protection, she'll be putting herself be in danger." His friends grinned in response. What the hell was their problem?

"As much as we'd like to stay for the entertainment

portion of this show, Josie and I need to get home to Cece," Steve announced. "We told the sitter we wouldn't be too late."

"Call me later, Cat, and fill me in on what happens," Josie added with a wink.

"We'll walk out with you," Kevin announced, taking River's hand.

As they exited through the kitchen, Rick heard the muffled voices. He was tempted to join the two women. What if Shayne hadn't talked Finch out of leaving? Finch had more sense than that, didn't she?

"What's got into you?" Cat asked.

"Nothing. And why am I suddenly the one you're all focused on? Finch is the one in trouble."

"You sound like Colt when we first met," Cat told him. "I seem to remember you laying a few lectures on him about being overprotective."

"You guys are crazy. It's not like that at all." It wasn't. Colt had fallen head over heels for Cat. He'd been afraid to let her out of his sight. "Colt was in love with you. There's nothing going on between me and Finch. She's Shayne's friend, for God's sake."

"And that makes her off limits?" Troy rose, his one eye drilling into Rick's. "Do you think any of us would have objections if you were interested in her?"

"I'm not, so it's a moot point."

"Bullshit." Leave it to Cat to shoot the first straight arrow. "You're easy to read when it comes to her. You're almost always at her side. If you're not, you're watching her.

"Okay." He crossed his arms over his chest and pressed his back into the sofa's cushions. "Let's say I am interested in Finch in more than a professional way. It wouldn't make a damn bit of difference because she doesn't like anyone associated with law enforcement, especially me."

"That's not the way I interpreted it." Gib crossed an ankle over his knee. "She admits she had an issue with *some* officers. I didn't hear her sweep them together into one category."

"Well, you haven't spent as much time with her as I have. Besides, with her history, what would it look like for me to be seeing someone with her background?"

Cat shot out of her seat. Colt grabbed her quickly, his large hands clasping her tiny waist before pulling her into his lap. "Somebody needs to slap the crap out of him," she snapped, fighting to get out of Colt's arms—and Cat looked like she had every intention of being the one to do the slapping.

"He's digging for excuses to support his argument, Cat. He knows better." Colt directed his attention at Rick. "If you want to talk yourself out of your attraction to her, we can't stop you. But I'm putting you on notice. I will beat the shit out of you if you so much as suggest that her history makes her any less an equal to one of us."

What *had* possessed him to make the unwarranted and ugly comment? Finch's history had nothing to do with his argument against getting close to her. He wasn't ready for a relationship. Just because his friends had found someone special, he didn't mean he needed a partner. At least not one with her temper and a disdain for his profession. Regardless of what Troy had said, she was Shayne's friend, and that made her family. What happened if the two of them got together and things didn't work out? He suspected it wouldn't be pretty. His friendships meant too much to him to risk a personal relationship getting in the way.

"She's attractive and smart, but there are a number of

reasons a why it's not a good idea for me to get involved with her."

"Would you care to elaborate?" Cat asked, now snuggled against her husband's chest.

"No, I…" Everyone's attention pivoted from him to the area behind him. Shit. He caught the faint hint of a fragrance he now associated with Finch. How much had she heard?

He prepared himself for wrath or tears. He saw neither. Shayne whispered into Finch's ear. Her expression remained neutral, but he caught the slight nod of her head.

Troy walked over to his wife, pulling her into his arms. "Drop her off at the office tomorrow," Troy addressed Rick. "Steve will be there all day. I'll be back when I'm done at the marina."

Rick nodded, but his eyes didn't leave Finch. Had Shayne worked some kind of miracle with her? He could only describe her expression as thoughtful. He didn't know what to make of it.

Gib brushed against Rick's shoulder. "Stop being an ass. You're both adults," he murmured before proceeding toward the kitchen. His golden ponytail swung over his shoulder as he turned toward his friends. "If you need me, call. I'll be out on a shoot in the morning but should be done by lunch."

"We'd better get going." Rick crossed the room. Finch hadn't said a word, which was both good and bad. There was no argument about spending the night at his place. That was good, but silence from a woman, he'd learned, wasn't necessarily a good thing. He quickly decided he preferred verbal expressions of anger to the silent treatment. He'd had a few relationships. None of them serious enough that he spent this much time analyzing them.

"Let me check outside before you take her out of here," Colt said. His hand disappeared above the massive refrigerator before reappearing with one of his Glocks. Rick waited by the door with Finch. Neither speaking. With any luck, the rest of the night wouldn't be any different.

18

———

inch propped pillows against the headboard and crawled under the covers of the queen size bed in Rick's spare room. She grabbed the pad of paper from the nightstand. Her intention was to jot down questions she kept asking herself. Doing so could trigger a memory—something important.

The problem was her mind kept wandering to the man in the room next to hers. The trip to his place was, thankfully, quiet. She'd spent her time dwelling on the comments Shayne had made and the bits of conversation they'd overheard as they'd exited the kitchen. It was driving her crazy.

Was Rick attracted to her as Shayne had insinuated? He had a hell of a way of showing it if that was the case. Then again, she wanted to slurp him up. She was doing her best to hide it. The two of them were so wrong for each other. Hell, maybe he hadn't gotten laid in a while. She certainly hadn't. Would that solve the problem? Get it out of their system, assuming that was the case?

How mortifying would it be if she slipped into his

room, made the suggestion, and he refused? Nope. Not going there.

Fuck him. Well, not literally. That would be a mistake. What she needed to do was focus on something else.

Staring at the blank page, she resisted the urge to throw the writing pad across the room. Temper, temper, she reminded herself, exhaling deeply. She grabbed the pen she had tossed on the bed and began scribbling thoughts that popped into her head.

Questions… Why did Tony lead her to the boat? What did they intend to do with her? Was Tony a party to this or was he duped, as well? Where was he? Was he dead? Running? Was all this a huge misunderstanding?

She scratched through the last question. Getting kidnapped—which felt like an extreme description—and then being run off the road made it more than a simple misunderstanding. Her vehicle had been tagged. Someone must have her confused with someone else. She had no family. Nothing of monetary value. There were no secrets to uncover.

Looking at the sheet of paper, she focused on it. Mentally wandering and wondering wouldn't get her anywhere. She started another page, listing the names of people she knew. It was going to be a long list considering how many places she'd lived, but she had to start somewhere. Tony Gambino topped the list and led her back to her initial question. Why did he lead her into that trap on the boat?

She'd gotten along with Tony. He'd always been polite —talkative, but polite. Since the other massage therapists were usually busy in one of the treatment rooms, she saw him every time she stepped out into the lobby to greet a client. He did most of the talking whenever they interacted. She didn't like answering questions regarding her past. Come to think of it, he'd asked quite a few. As she recalled their conversations, she chewed on her fingernail. She hadn't seen them as interrogations. Probably because he shared information about his family, which would then lead back to hers. She considered herself a master at avoiding that subject and turned the questions back on him. Now that she gave it some thought, he'd made more inquiries into her past than anyone else she'd known since being on her own.

Tony had never pushed her. She'd simply considered him inquisitive and nosey. Was there a reason behind all those questions? She penciled in *personnel file* next to his name. The guys assumed he'd gotten her email address from her personnel file. Assuming he did, how did he get access to it? She scribbled a note to call Mrs. Gonzales to see if Tony had requested the information or had access to employee files for any reason. She couldn't imagine either was the case and Gonzales hadn't mentioned it during their earlier conversation. Still, she should ask.

Tony was shaping up to be the bad guy, but then why the warning message? Or was it a threat? If so, why bother? The incident on the boat and being run off the road were big enough threats.

Pen to paper, she started listing what she knew. Assuming he'd been telling her the truth, Tony's family was originally from New York, but he was raised in Tampa. That was the one safe topic of conversation. They were both familiar with the area, which confirmed that part of his history as far as she was concerned. She listed the car he drove, a description of him—things Rick and his friends already knew.

She finished with Tony, then began to list others who populated her small world, starting with Mrs. Gonzales then adding her co-workers. The area to the right of the names remained mostly blank. She didn't really know any of them. That had been the reason she convinced herself to accept Tony's invitation. It was past time she'd made friends, or at least tried. Had she mentioned that goal to him? Had she inadvertently initiated the plan for her own abduction?

Her mind was wandering again. She had no way of knowing what Tony was thinking. Her head hurt, her back ached—her body was telling her it was time to call it quits for the night. Being a massage therapist, she was good at reading the signs the body was giving off, but her mind wasn't having it.

Tired of twisting and turning, she crawled out of bed. Rubbing the back of her neck, she felt the knots twisted there. Too bad there was no one to massage it for her. Like a bolt of lightning, her mind flashed to her host. Was Rick asleep? Was he thinking of her? Had Shayne imagined things? Or worse, was she playing matchmaker?

There would be little sleep tonight. Her body was warning her it needed rest, but she hadn't hit the wall yet. When she did, she'd sleep.

She wandered over to the window. She wanted to open it, yearning for a breath of fresh air instead of the artificial environment created by an air conditioner. Unlatching the lock, she raised the window.

She inhaled the whiff of jasmine that drifted in with the night air. Her shoulders relaxed on the exhale—then went rigid as the door to her room opened.

"Is everything okay?"

Her heart lodged in her throat at the unexpected interruption. As she turned to face her host, that same heart now hammered against her breastbone. Wearing sweatpants and no shirt, Rick's broad shoulders almost encompassed the entire doorway. Wisps of blond hair dusted his chiseled chest before disappearing below the elastic waist-band and into the netherworld. A world she urgently wanted to explore. She tried to swallow, but her mouth went dry. He was a work of art. A model for a sculptor.

"Are you all right?"

Instead of yelling at him for scaring the shit out of her, she simply stared. His expression changed from one of concern to knowing, then to interest

Now it was her turn to be anxious. Retreating a step, she bumped into the windowsill.

His bare feet were silent as he crossed the tile floor. His arms caged her in as he reached behind her and shut the window. Her nostrils filled with a new fragrance—one that was totally male and unique to this man. His focus was no longer on her eyes, but on her lips. Speaking was impossible. Thinking was just as hard. His stare was unnerving, but not frightening. Still, she lowered her eyelids, hoping to break the link between them. Instead, she felt his warm breath on her cheek. Her eyes snapped open.

"Tell me if you don't want this," he whispered.

Still mute, the tip of her tongue darted out to moisten her lips. Apparently, that was the answer he needed. What breath she was holding escaped as his mouth covered hers. Her worries disappeared at his touch. All she wanted was to feel—feel the warmth and rawness in his kiss. She leaned into him, closing the little distance that remained. When his tongue teased her cupid's bow, she let out a small gasp. It was enough. He slipped his tongue between her lips. His hands, a mixture of strength and tenderness, slid up her spine. His fingers raked her hair as he deepened the embrace. They were so close a wisp of air would have trouble passing between them.

Beer, salt—and heat. She could smell, taste, and feel them all, but mostly she felt heat. It engulfed her, melding her to him. His lips brushed across her cheek until they reached her ear where he lingered, suckling her lobe. She extended her neck, giving him full access. The warmth traveled south, pooling between her thighs. She moaned.

"Am I hurting you?" he asked, pulling away.

"No. Don't stop." She hardly recognized the smoky, demanding voice. When was the last time she'd wanted to be with a man this badly? Had she ever? She tightened her hold on to him when he took another step away from her. "Please?" she asked.

A small smile softened those strong features before he lifted her into his arms.

She gasped as she was literally swept off her feet. That only happened in movies, right? Apparently not because it was happening now. She studied his strong features, etching this moment in her memory forever. If she could freeze time, this would be the moment.

She drifted downward until her back rested against the mattress. He traced the bridge of her nose with his fingertip until he reached her lips, then tenderly brushed them with the pad of his thumb. Her heart quivered as his tongue teased the corner of her mouth. This was all new to her. In her limited experience, men didn't take the time to do much more than slip on a condom. She floated on the gentleness of his touch. Selfishly she took all he was willing to give, soaking it up greedily.

"You're not dressed for this," he said, whispering against her lips. "Raise your arms."

Electrical sparks danced across her skin as his fingertips grazed her sides. He stopped short of removing her shirt completely. Instead, leaving it tucked under her chin, her arms raised. As he lowered his head, her eyes drifted shut, anticipating the pleasure that was to come next.

He rolled his palms over her breasts, teasing her nipples as he did so. She shivered.

"You like that?"

She nodded, arching her spine, inviting him to take what he wanted. He accepted. Taking one breast into his mouth, he tweaked the nipple of the other. A hand slid lower over her belly. How many hands did he have—and why did she care? When he reached the band of her sleep shorts, he stopped. Seriously? Afraid that he'd changed his mind, she opened her eyes just a hair. He was shucking his sweats. He apparently slept commando because there was nothing else for him to remove. His chest was a gift from the gods, but the rest of him was even more impressive.

She wanted this. She wanted him, but doubts crept in. Her experience in making love was limited. Considerably less than his, she'd bet. She'd only embarrass herself and disappoint him.

"You're thinking too much." He sheathed himself, then completed the act of pulling her t-shirt over her head.

"Am I that easy to read?"

"No. You're actually pretty damn hard to get a handle on, but you were going to pull that shirt down, weren't you?"

Hell. He'd caught her before she'd even realized what she was doing.

"Relax and enjoy," he chided her.

"It's been a bit one-sided. I've been savoring your attention and not reciprocating."

"That, my lady, is a compliment." Lowering his head, his tongue circled a sensitive nipple. She writhed, silently asking for more. He scraped the nipple with his teeth before turning his attention to the boxer shorts she'd slipped on. In one quick move, her shorts and panties disappeared.

He traced a moist line between her breasts and over her abdomen until he reached her navel, then circled the divot in her belly with his tongue. He was so intimately close to her she felt the intake of air as he inhaled her scent. Then he was mounting her.

Slipping his hands under her thighs, he lifted her bottom off the bed. She was already wet and waiting. She clinched as he entered her. It was his turn to groan. He leaned back, sliding away. She locked her legs around his waist and drew him toward her until he was buried deep inside her.

Her body had been humming. Now it was burning. Hips rising, she moved in a rhythm that had her soaring higher and higher until she reached a peak above the sensory clouds. He shuddered, his thigh muscles tightening as he let out a loud growl. She followed him over the mountaintop.

As her breathing slowed, the situation became awkward. He'd collapsed onto the mattress next to her in silence. What was she supposed to say? Thank you? They'd both enjoyed the comingling of their bodies—or hadn't he? The silence lingered, growing heavier as the seconds ticked by. A minute ago, she was sucking in air. Now, the invisible weight on her chest forced every ounce of oxygen from her lungs. She no longer felt the heat of his body. He'd distanced himself—physically and emotionally. She shivered.

"You're cold."

"It's the air conditioning," she lied. A cold front had quickly settled in the room.

"It's time we both got some sleep." He rolled off his side of the bed. After a quick trip to the bathroom, he swiped his sweats off the floor. He paused in the doorway, backlit by the light from the hall. She couldn't see his face. She didn't think she wanted to.

"Can you be ready by seven-thirty? I need to get to the station early. I'll drop you off at Steve's on my way."

He didn't wait for an answer. The door clicked shut. She buried her head in the pillow. What the hell had she done?

19

What the hell had he done? Rick stared out the kitchen window, a mug of steaming black coffee in his hand. Showered, shaved, and dressed for work, he was ready to leave. He wanted to leave. Now. Alone. To skulk down the steps and forget the woman in the guest room. No. Run from the woman was more like it.

What had possessed him to make love to her last night? Because she was sassy, smart, and attractive. He was drawn to her. She hadn't rebuffed his advances. Instead, she welcomed them. Was he that bad at reading women, or was it only Finch who gave him difficulty?

Regardless, he'd crossed a line with her. She was Finch. Shayne's friend and, therefore, family. You didn't screw family—literally or figuratively.

Looking at the guestroom door, he knew he wouldn't avoid her much longer. She should have been awake and ready by now. He held on to the ridiculous hope that if she was sleeping soundly, it meant she wasn't making as much of a big deal out of last night's encounter as he believed it deserved. That stung. What was wrong with him? He couldn't have it both ways.

He'd lied when he'd told her he was needed at the station early. His hope was the sooner he got to work and away from her, the sooner his desire for her would fade. Right now, he wanted to pick up where they'd left off last night. Just the thought of her made his groin tighten. Shit.

Tossing the remaining coffee into the sink, he rinsed the cup and stowed it in the dishwasher. Shayne would wonder where they were by now. Coward that he was, he called Troy instead.

"I'll be by in a bit."

"Why?" Troy asked. "Did you forget something?"

"What?" But he knew what. He threw open the door to the guest room. It banged as it hit the wall. Finch's bed was neatly made. She was gone. When? In the middle of the night? No. He never slept that soundly. He would have heard her if she'd left last night as he'd gotten very little sleep. She had to have let herself out while he was in the shower. Had she been so desperate to escape his presence that she'd walked to Steve's? The compound was less than two miles away. Not a hard walk, but not one a target should make on her own.

"She's there, isn't she?"

An ominous silence filled the line. "I have the distinct feeling I'm going to have to kick your ass when I see you," Troy finally answered.

"Is she okay? Does she look okay?" Rick ignored Troy's threat.

"Why? What did you do? Is there a reason she felt the need to slip out on you? That's what she did, didn't she?"

"I'll be over in a minute." Rick grabbed his keys, wallet, badge, and weapon.

"Don't." There was a firmness to Troy's tone that had him stopping before he reached the door.

"Why not?" He owed her an apology. Succumbing to his desire for her was bad enough but running for cover as soon as the lovemaking was over had been inexcusable.

"Because you don't want to see me right now, and she apparently doesn't want to see you, or she would have waited for you this morning."

"You're making assumptions." Rick was already in his truck. He was going to talk to Finch regardless of Troy's objections.

"Assumptions based on observations like the smoldering looks you've been sending her way. The insistence that she stay with you. The fact that she snuck out on you this morning. They all add up to one thing." Troy paused. "We trusted you to take care of Finch, not take advantage of her. I expected better from you, Rick. I really did."

Rick sat silently behind the wheel. He expected better of himself. What drew him to Finch—what magic was he unable to resist? She was irritable and a bit too sensitive, yet feisty and strong. Sexy, although he didn't think she saw herself that way.

She hadn't pushed him away when he'd held her. And, God, she'd felt so good in his arms. Had he mistaken her need for comfort as an invitation? He didn't think he was that dense. She was a willing participant, at least until the fog of lust cleared and he'd realized he taken a bite from the forbidden fruit.

"I'm headed your way. Don't get in mine," Rick said.

"Give her a break today."

"Don't give me orders. If she doesn't want to see me, she can tell me herself. She's an adult."

"Thank God for that," Troy muttered.

"That was below the belt, Troy." Rick's hands tightened on the steering wheel. Is this what his error in judgment had cost him? The respect of his friends.

"It was," Troy agreed, "but I'm not in the mood to apologize." The phone went dead.

Rick suspected Finch would be in the garden with Shayne, so he bypassed the front of the building where he'd run into Troy or Steve—or both. Instead, he took the drive that separated the photography studio from the building that housed the garden center and security business. It was a chickenshit move.

In an even more cowardly move, he slipped through the side gate. He heard voices coming from the front of the garden. Troy and Shayne. If those two were together, where was Finch? If she was inside, he'd have to suck it up and get past the two. He could handle Troy. Shayne would be a different matter. No doubt her husband was making her aware of his conversation with Rick.

One apology at a time. Finch came first—he hoped. Turning a corner in the maze of plants, he spotted the gazebo. Finch sat at the table with her laptop. Fingers dancing over the keyboard, headphones covering her ears, she wouldn't see or hear him approach, which worried him. She was totally oblivious to her surroundings. Troy didn't have eyes on the security cameras right now. Was Steve manning the visual feed? If he was, he'd have spotted Rick by now. Best get this done—and fast.

His palms were sweating. He blew out a long, heated breath. Was it the woman or the investigation that had his nerves on edge? He'd been in battle before his years with the Chicago Police Department, yet he couldn't remember a single incident that made him feel this far out of his comfort zone or unsure of himself.

He circled the structure to avoid approaching Finch from behind. Having already caused enough damage, he didn't need to be frightening her. When his foot landed on the single step leading up to the platform where the table and chairs rested, she slowly raised her head. Her expression quickly changed from surprise to neutral. She showed no emotion at his appearance—neither positive nor negative. He'd have preferred anger to her dismissive posture.

"Why did you leave this morning?" he asked as she removed her headphones.

Finch's head dipped to one side as she opened her copper-kettle eyes wide. "Seriously? You have to ask?"

"Do you always run from your problems?"

"Do you?" she snapped. "I wasn't the one to leave the room like an escaping convict."

"Touché. I owe you an apology." He was glad there weren't microphones attached to the cameras that covered the place.

"I don't need or want your apology. I realize I can't break all ties with you since you're working this case, but from this point on, I'm only a case to you. Nothing else. Got it?"

Ouch. That hurt as much as a slap in the face. He deserved it.

"If that's what you want."

"Isn't it what you want? You couldn't have left the room faster if it had been on fire. And I don't intend to be another late-night booty call to satisfy your needs."

"You didn't make any effort to push me away," he reminded her, his nerves raw.

"My mistake. It won't happen again." She swiped her headphones off the table. "Is that all you wanted?"

"What are you working on?" he asked. Damned if he wasn't trying to stretch out his time with her.

"If you must know, I'm going through the documents that we didn't find at the apartment. Not a very pleasant walk down memory lane, but it fills the time while I wait for my credit cards to arrive."

"Then what?" Did she plan on leaving the island?

"Don't worry. If you need me, you'll still be able to reach me." With that, she slipped her noise canceling headphones on.

Suppressing the urge to rip the gear off her head, he reached over to remove them. She beat him to it.

"How do I get rid of you?" she asked, tossing the headphones on the table.

Rick glanced over her shoulder, surprised Troy or another member of the group hadn't made their way through the garden yet. "Look. I said I'm sorry for leaving you like I did."

"Are you also sorry you entered my room in the first place?"

His jaw tightened. The best thing to do was lie. It had been a mistake, but he wasn't sorry for the lovemaking. He should be, but he wasn't. "No," he admitted. "Just for the asinine way I acted afterwards."

"If I accept your apology, will you go away?"

"We haven't finished talking."

"There's nothing to discuss. We both made a mistake. Is it possible for us to go back to disliking one another? I was more comfortable with that."

He was reading too much into her comments? Because going back to disliking him meant there had been a break-through—one he'd thoroughly fucked up. He shouldn't be pursuing her. Troy was right but seeing her again, all logic went out the window.

"Your plan is to leave here, isn't it?"

"Yes. As soon as I get my car. And I'll talk to Shayne, so don't try using that guilt card on me again. You don't want to be near me, and I can't imagine another victim of assault being assigned around the clock watchdogs. I don't want special treatment."

"Your car is a wreck." It was all he could think to say.

"It's in one piece and may resemble an escapee from a junkyard, but it can be driven. Troy checked."

Damn Troy. "But…"

She reached for the headphones again. "I'm going home. I can't stop you from looking into this mystery, and I'll do what I can to help, but I want to go back to my life."

"You were abducted, then run off the road and almost killed." How did he make her understand the danger she was in?

"The accident was probably the result of a crazy, pissed off driver."

Rick was looming over her now. His temper flaring. "You know that's not true."

"I'm tired of arguing with you. Unless you're here in an official capacity, please leave."

She managed not to flinch when he slapped his hand on the table. "You're my responsibility."

"The hell I am. I'm not even a resident of this lovely community. You have no authority over me or responsibility for me." She glared at him.

"After last night…"

"After last night, I want you to take your pretense of caring and leave." This time, she shoved the earphones in place and returned her attention to the screen. She was flushed. Her temper was burning as hot as his, but she was channeling inward.

"We're not done," he all but shouted as he headed to the office. Why the hell was her acceptance of him so damned important? Last night—hell, even this morning— he couldn't wait to get away from her. Now he wanted to be with her, and she wanted nothing to do with him.

"I ought to knock the crap out of you," Troy said as he cleared the jungle.

"Go ahead," Rick said. "I've done some dumb shit in my life, but I may have topped them all this time."

"What else did you do?" Troy stepped toward him.

"Enough," Shayne snapped at both men.

"She can't hear us," Rick told her. "She's got those humongous headphones on. Does Steve have eyes on her?" he asked Shayne.

"What do you think?" Troy crossed his impressive arms over his chest. At least his hands weren't fisted in Rick's direction.

"You boys need to stop the macho bullshit. Finch is an adult. She can make her own decisions."

"What are you thinking?" he asked, trying to figure out the peculiar smile on Shayne's face.

"That she won't be alone." She grinned.

"I told her you'd be planted on her doorstep. That threat isn't working any longer."

"You're not going to stay with her," Troy warned his wife.

"Men," she swore. "Will you both be quiet for a minute?" She took a breath and nailed Rick with her sharp, narrowed eyes. "I don't know what you did to piss Finch off…"

"He slept with her," Troy growled.

"He did what?" Gib asked as he exited the building through the screen door. His gray eyes homed in on Rick. Josie was right on his heels. Great.

Josie bumped Gib with her shoulder. "Why is Finch off limits?" she asked, a bit of sparkle in her eyes. "Didn't you pack condoms for Troy when he and Shayne went into hiding? And weren't you the one who suggested strongly to Steve that he have 'make-up sex' with me after we fought?"

Gib stared at her. His mouth open like a guppy.

"I don't think you have room to be judgmental in that department," Josie added.

"The affection was obvious," Gib defended himself.

"Then you're missing the obvious here," Josie shot back.

"Now wait just a minute." Rick raked his fingers through his short hair. This was getting out of hand. "If you're suggesting I'm in love with Finch…"

Both Shayne and Josie gave him a smirk. Rick snarled. That was the trouble with happily married women—they believed every man and woman in their orbit should be as well.

"Really?" Gib asked, his gray eyes assessing Shayne and Josie. "I usually catch that sort of signal. I noticed the attraction, but…"

"You haven't spent that much time with them," Shayne said. "And I know Finch pretty well. I need to find out what pissed her off, since lover boy here isn't talking."

"Could be he's just bad in bed," Josie laughed.

Rick ground his teeth. Doing anything else would land him in more hot water, and it was already hot enough.

"C'mon." Josie tugged on Shayne's sleeve. "Let's get her talking. Besides, I have information that needs clarification."

"Then Troy and I should be there." Rick started to follow.

"Not this time, boys. We'll bring you up to speed later." Josie flicked a grin over her shoulder as she and Shayne locked arms and ambled down the path toward the gazebo.

20

---

inch's head hurt. Massaging her forehead with her fingertips, she tried to forget her visitor. It hadn't been necessary for her to be that nasty. She'd blown things out of proportion. She was acting like a silly school-girl. Get over it—and him.

She returned her attention to her documents. Reading reports submitted by her foster families was embarrassing. She'd been a bigger ass than she'd remembered. It was a miracle she didn't land in juvey long before she did. What would have happened if she had? She could flip a coin, she supposed. Depending on the counselors and facility, she may very well have found herself on the streets and actually breaking the law instead of being stupid and unknowingly tagging along while a crime was committed.

Taking a break, she changed the music flowing through her headphones from rock to classical. The knot in her neck began to unravel. She closed her eyes and let the music and tropical breeze carry her away from her past—from her encounter with Rick, and the threats against her. Inhaling the sweet fragrance of the garden, her shoulders relaxed. It was no wonder Shayne preferred her work in this wonderland than her former job tending bar.

As the memories abated, an overwhelming tiredness took hold. She wanted to put her head on the table and nod off. There'd been no sleeping last night after Rick's exit. At the sound of his shower running this morning, she grabbed her meager possessions and slipped out. Another childish move.

Resting her head in the palms of her hands, she almost dozed off. She needed to get to her own place. A good night's sleep and she'd be able to think clearly. She certainly wasn't spotting any red flags going through her papers.

A hand on her shoulder startled her. She flung the headphones on the table as she pushed away, ready to run.

"Whoa. Whoa," Shayne said.

Finch pressed a hand to her chest, trying to catch her breath. "Shit."

"You okay?" Josie asked.

"I will be. Give me a second. I didn't realize I was so jumpy."

"You have every right to be," Josie said, taking a seat across as she tossed her long, dark hair over her shoulders. "Sorry. We didn't mean to scare you."

"Even if it was possible to hear you," she said, pointing at her headphones, "I'd have had the same reaction. My mind was elsewhere."

"I have an idea where it was," Shayne said. "What did Rick do to piss you off? He'd never force himself on you so, come on, girl…spill."

Finch was certain she'd turned several shades of red. Shayne and Troy had figured out that she and Rick had shared a bed last night. She'd overheard them discussing the subject rather vigorously. It was the reason she'd clamped on the headphones as it was another confirmation that she'd screwed up.

"I'd rather not discuss it. It's not important."

"It is if he hurt you. If I'm going to tear of couple of strips off his hide, I need to know why," Shayne explained. "Spit it out so we can get to work. Josie has a few questions for you."

"I was a fool."

"In what way?" Josie asked.

"I read more into the interlude—for lack of a better word—than I should have. I shouldn't be mad at him. I've had sex before, but I never had anybody leave like that."

"Like what?" Shayne's eyes narrowed.

"Like I charged by the hour, and he didn't want to be hit with another fee. I felt like a damn hooker. He got what he wanted and left."

"That doesn't sound like Rick, does it?" Josie searched Shayne's face.

"No." Shayne smiled. "And I don't think it's what you think it is, Finch. I think he was scared."

"C'mon. He's a cop. Former Special Forces. Why would he be afraid of me?"

"Not of you. Himself."

"Huh?"

"He needs to work out his feelings—feelings I think he's afraid to admit he has. Give him a break and a little time."

"I don't care what his problem is." Finch ran her hand down her face. The subject wasn't one she wanted to discuss. "I'm leaving as soon as I can. And don't even think about parking your ass at my place." She pinned Shayne with a looked she hoped would seal the point. "You know damn well I wouldn't have this kind of protection if it weren't for you and your friends."

"And you should take advantage of it," Josie scolded her. "We're bad asses. And the guys aren't half bad either."

"Thank you. I don't plan on turning my back on that part. I'll deal with Rick, but only in his capacity as a detective on this case."

Both women laughed. Finch didn't see the humor in any of it. "Can we move on to what you wanted to ask?" She tapped the folder Josie had laid on the table.

"Okay. We'll drop it for now. First, let's talk Tony."

"Have you located him?"

"No," Shayne answered. "Troy and Steve are still working on tracking him. The FBI doesn't have any reason to look for Tony. He's not wanted for any crime."

"Like trying to kidnap me."

"Unfortunately, not," Josie agreed. "I know Rick believes you, but he can't open a case on your word alone. The Lee County Sheriff's Office isn't looking for him for the same reason."

"Plus, we don't know if it was Tony behind the wheel of the car that tried to run me off the road." If it hadn't been for the vehicle assault Rick witnessed, who knows who would have believed her? She needed to put on her big boy pants, stop allowing herself to be distracted and concentrate on the problem of who wanted to harm her. Until she did, she'd be looking over her shoulder.

"You got it," Josie confirmed. "That leaves us to do our own research. And, if I do say so myself, I'm one hell of an investigative reporter."

"So Shayne has told me. Did you actually take down a sitting State Attorney?"

"It was a team effort."

"And she saved Troy's life on the same day." Shayne grinned, squeezing Josie's hand.

"Is it always so intense around here?" These women

awed Finch. They also gave her a sense of belonging—for the first time she could remember.

"Not usually. We're pretty normal, but it can occasionally get lively here." Josie smiled and reached across the table, taking Finch's hand in hers, completing the circle. "Now, let's get back to Tony."

"What do you want to know?"

"You said he lived in Tampa before he came here?" Josie opened her notebook.

"It was one thing we had in common. He was familiar with the place. It was a connection. I guess that's why I trusted him. I don't know…"

"I'm still digging and have feelers out, but so far I can't find a Tony Gambino in Tampa. Did he mention where he worked or lived?"

"No." Why hadn't she asked? Because it was always tit-for-tat with personal questions, and she avoided them. She glanced at her laptop. "Do you think it would be worth a shot to email him?"

"I understand he was in contact with you, and that could turn out to be an interesting tactic. Let's discuss that with the guys before we go there," Josie suggested.

"I want to have another go at my FBI friends." Shayne smiled. "Maybe they're not sharing all they can. I'll twist their arms again and see if I can squeeze more out of them. They prefer to stay on our good side as they occasionally request some *off the books* assistance." ·

Shayne had put finger quotes around her *off the books* remark. What the hell sort of things did this group get into? Despite her curiosity, she didn't have the energy to ask. "Is there anything else?" Finch slumped into her chair. She was running out of steam.

"I'm going to ask you to take one of those DNA tests." Josie raised her hand, stopping any objection Finch was ready to make. "I know you're not interested in your birth parents. I can understand that, but your ancestry may hold a clue."

Finch shook her head. She didn't want to deal with digging into her parental history while all this shit was going on.

"Take the test, Finch," Shayne encouraged her. "Josie will keep the results to herself if you don't want to see them. We're working blind when it comes to your family history. This could help."

"Won't they know I'm looking for them?"

"Only if we want them to." Josie reached out and took Finch's hand again. "One day you may want to know. You may need to know for medical reasons. Think of it as a *break glass in case of emergency* type of thing."

More like taking a step into hell, but she nodded in agreement. "If it has anything to do with this mess I've dragged you into, only then will we discuss it. Agreed?"

"If that's what you want," Josie said. "I purchased a kit at the drugstore, hoping you'd agree. We can mail it tomorrow if you take the test today."

Finch had believed her life was settled until a couple of days ago. A good job she enjoyed. Her own place. It wasn't much, but it was normal. Growing up she'd just wanted to be normal. Now, she was reaching into the history she wanted to forget. On the upside, she was making friends. She subtracted points for allowing herself to trust Rick with a small portion of her heart. That still hurt, but she was a big girl. She'd get over it. Right now, she had more important things to worry about than that asshole.

"What about my child welfare records? You said they'd been accessed. How is that possible?"

"Anyone can access records through the department's website, but certain information is restricted because of the child's age. My contact at DCF said there were two requests for your records last year. The most recent inquiry was eight months ago." Josie flipped to another page.

"Can you tell what they were looking for?" Shayne asked.

"There was no way to tell if the interested party was homed in on one particular period or a particular foster home."

"Another dead end." Finch opened her laptop to check the time. She missed her watch. "Where the hell are my credit cards? It's going on noon."

"You aren't seriously planning to go home and back to work, are you?" Shayne asked.

"I want to feel normal again. I need to work."

"It's not safe, Finch. Not yet anyway. If you don't want to stay with Rick, we can make other arrangements. Stay with one of us or Gib. He's got plenty of room to spare," Shayne suggested.

"That would be an excellent idea." Josie's mouth curved up in a wide grin.

"You said he was a rogue."

"He is," Shayne agreed. "But he'll be a gentleman as far as you're concerned."

"I'm not sure how to take that." Finch eyed the two women.

"Gib doesn't poach," Josie explained.

Finch did not know what that was supposed to mean, but Shayne and Josie both had a conspiratorial look in their eyes. "I don't know what you're talking about, but I want to go home. I want to sleep in my bed. I want to feel safe again."

"You don't feel safe with Rick?" Josie's smile disappeared as she tucked the papers into a file.

"I think she means secure. She's comfortable in her old

world," Shayne said, turning to Finch. "I get it. I was there before Troy. No matter how much you want it to stay the way it was, your life is changing. It will not be the same after this. You're not going to be the same. Scurrying home is another form of running away."

Anger bubbled to the surface at her friend's words. Finch wasn't running away. She was simply reclaiming her life.

She wrestled between irritation and explanation. She didn't have time to decide which side to err on as a screen door banged shut and a vehicle raced into the drive next door. "Get inside. Now!"

21

*R*ick didn't want to leave Finch without first clearing the air between them, but it was probably a good idea to give her time to cool off.

As he pulled onto Periwinkle Way, he spotted the car. The vehicle was headed in the opposite direction. What caught his attention was its speed. It was crawling as it approached Colt & Gib's photography studio. It almost came to a stop in front of the building shared by Cat and Steve before the driver hit the gas. Instinct had Rick making a U-turn and following the car. The vehicle pulled into Bailey's Market at the end of the strip of road.

Rick recognized the man behind the wheel. Tony. He seriously doubted Gambino came to Sanibel to shop for groceries. Tony wouldn't be able see Rick from his position, but Rick had a good visual on the guy. Rick bet he wasn't contemplating buying a pot roast. His fingers tapped rhythmically on the steering wheel. He was thinking. So was Rick. How he'd found Finch was another question, but it would be obvious on Tony's pass by the building that she wasn't alone.

His target started his engine. Rick went with his instincts and headed for the compound. The SUV fell in behind him. He dialed Troy.

"Where's Finch?"

"Outside with Josie and Shayne. Why? What's up?"

"Get them inside. I'll be there in a second."

He took a sharp left off the main street, then a right into the alley that led to the rear of the buildings. He was out of the truck and hopping the fence as Gib and Troy appeared. Troy's weapon was at his side.

Shayne and Josie didn't have to be told to move. Each woman grabbed one of Finch's arms and pulled her from her chair and toward the building. Gib stepped in front of them. Troy and Rick took up the rear until they were safely in the break room at the rear of the business.

"What's going on?" Gib asked.

"You looking for a vehicle?" Steve shouted from the front waiting area.

"Mid-size SUV? Black?" Rick shouted.

"Yeah. It's making a slow pass out front. Single male driver."

"Can you catch him?"

"Seriously?" Steve joked, dashing out the front. If Steve hadn't enlisted, he'd have been on the NASCAR circuit. Rick's only concern was whether the driver would spot Steve's distinctive, restored Mustang GT.

Rick raced to the front. "I'm coming with you." He slid into the passenger seat, shutting the door as Steve took off.

"You want me to catch him?"

If any other driver had asked that question, Rick would have nixed it immediately. Periwinkle was a two-lane road and busy with traffic in both directions. It wouldn't be a problem for Steve.

"I want to know where he's going. At the very least, I want that tag number."

"Could be another stolen car. You think it's Tony?" Steve whipped out of the lane and passed a car, barely missing an oncoming vehicle. He didn't blink.

"It's him. He's figured out where Finch is."

"Call Josie. She was outside. Ask if she spotted a vehicle in the alley."

If the man was looking for a way to get to Finch, he'd have made a complete circle of the business. Rick scrolled to Josie's number and dialed. After the third unanswered ring, his stomach dropped. Since his phone was on speaker, Steve heard the call roll over to voice mail. He cut across traffic, pulling into a restaurant parking lot, then immediately forced his way into traffic, heading toward the compound.

"Maybe she's in the bathroom," Rick said, reading his friend's mind.

"With this shit going on, she'd take the phone with her. Gambino was a diversion."

Rick agreed and, damn it, they'd fallen for it. "Troy and Gib are there." He was already dialing Troy's number, but the same sick feeling hit him when Troy didn't answer. Rick debated calling for official back-up, but without knowing what the situation was, he didn't have cause—or time. He made one quick call.

"There may be trouble next door," he said as soon as his former commander picked up. "We should be there any second, but you're closer."

"Who's over there?"

Rick heard a desk drawer slam shut, followed by a door. "Josie, Shayne, Finch, Troy and Gib—and possibly one or more unknowns."

"Roger. Leaving the line open," Colt said, but communication ceased. Rick heard the rustle of fabric as the phone was stuffed into a pocket.

As they approached the two businesses, Steve let off the gas and coasted into the lot of *Island Images*, doing their best not to announce their arrival. Steve opened his glove box and pulled out his weapon. Rick unholstered his. Both men slipped from the vehicle, leaving the doors ajar.

Rick took the front as Steve headed toward the rear of the building. He'd just slipped around the corner, his back plastered to the stucco wall, when his phone crackled to life.

"Stand down," Colt said. "We're clear."

With a sharp whistle, Rick alerted Steve. As they entered the building, Steve went directly to Josie, who was leaning against the breakfast bar. Rick didn't miss the gun on the countertop. Shayne was wrapped so tightly in Troy's arms it was a wonder she was able to breathe. Colt was on the couch next to Finch, his gun on the coffee table in front of him. Gib was digging through the first aid cabinet.

"What the hell happened?" As much as Rick wanted to take Colt's place, until he knew what was going on, he needed to be ready to move.

"One at a time," Rick interrupted, when everyone started talking at once.

"It's my fault," Finch raised her voice before anyone could speak. Her face was pale, but her voice was steady. "All this cloak and dagger stuff. The risk I was putting everyone in…I'd reached a limit. I stormed out the door."

"And no one stopped you?" He was staring at Troy and Gib.

"Gib and I were right behind her. Shayne ran past us." Troy was pressing his wife to his chest. "Don't you ever pull anything like that again."

"What happened?"

"A guy popped out of the shrubbery and grabbed Finch. Initially, he pointed the gun at her, but he pivoted, turning the gun on Shayne. He warned us if we took another step, Shayne would get the first bullet." Anger and fear laced Troy's voice.

"How the hell did he get past the security cameras?"

"Because I wasn't watching the feed," Troy barked. "I was watching Finch. I can't be in two places at the same time, and you and Steve took off."

"God, I'm so sorry." Finch had her head buried in her hands.

"Where did he go?"

"He's gone." Troy's tone was dripping with frustration. "There must have been a vehicle waiting for him at the end of the alley. They took off before I rounded the corner, damn it. I heard a powerful engine head toward Periwinkle. Sounded like a big-ass truck. You need to call it in."

"Call what in? You don't have a description. I can't have the department stop every truck on the island. Start at the beginning."

22

_S_he was a mess—both mentally and physically. Her reckless actions had put everyone in danger. After Rick and Steve took off, the others had huddled around her. Instead of feeling secure, Finch had felt trapped and terrified. Like a child running away from home, she'd wanted out—and she'd done just that without thinking. Despite the catastrophic results, the desire to bolt was still strong. Her friend had almost been killed on her account which only increased the urge to escape.

"I need to get out of here," she said to the room. "I can't put any one of you in danger again."

"Let's make that the second item up for discussion," Rick said, taking the seat next to her. "First, I need to know what went down here."

"Troy told you most of it."

"Not all of it. Did you recognize him? Was he from the boat?"

"I never got a good look at the man on the bridge, but I'd say this guy was the same size and build." Rick took her hand. An hour ago, she would have pulled back. Now his warm touch not only gave her strength but anchored her. It also hurt.

"Ouch." She flipped her hand over and stared at her palm.

"You're hurt." He traced a finger over the scrapes on her palm. "Gib, let me have that first aid kit."

"Why do you think I was getting it in the first place?" He was already standing over Rick's shoulder.

"It's just a few scratches." She glanced at her other palm. Dirt was imbedded under that skin as well. One discovery led to another. Straightening her legs, she noted the tears in her leggings. She was a mess.

"How'd you get hurt?" She flinched as he swabbed the scrapes with antiseptic wipes.

"She head-butted the guy, then tackled me to the ground. He didn't know what hit him," Shayne told him. "She was protecting me."

Rick's large hand brushed over her hair. "You've got a lump there. You need to be checked out."

"No. I'm fine. I've been hit harder." She regretted the last sentence the minute it was out of her mouth. Sympathy was written all over their faces. Why did they care when she'd caused so much trouble?

"For a big man, the asshole moved like lightning the second she broke free," Troy said. "Gib and I were already rushing him, but I never had a clear shot. He had a plan to get out fast."

"Why grab me? He had ample opportunity to take a shot at me. What do they want with me?"

"That would appear to be the million-dollar question." Colt made his way to the refrigerator and pulled out a cold pack. He handed it to Finch. "For your head."

"Did he say anything?" Rick asked. "Think. A word or two may be helpful."

"Nothing until he threatened Shayne. I am so, so sorry." She bit her lip, trying to hold back the tears as she looked at her friend. Why didn't they understand she needed to leave?

"Stop it," Rick scolded her.

Were her thoughts that obvious? There was a time she was better at hiding her feelings. She was letting her guard down too much and too often.

"Here's the thing," Rick said in a softer tone. "The best way to keep everyone here safe is to figure this out. They've already tracked you here. There's nothing to stop them from returning, whether or not you're here."

"He's right," Colt said. "We're tied to whatever is going on from the minute Rick found you on that beach. Your leaving won't stop anyone from looking for you here or trying to use one of us to get to you."

"You didn't put anyone here at risk," Rick added. "The ones at fault are the people who tried to abduct you."

"I'm a firm believer that everything happens for a reason," Cat said. "We were meant to be a part of this. And you couldn't ask for more qualified people to help you figure this out."

"But…" Finch started.

"No 'buts'," Shayne interrupted. "You're safer with us and we're safe as long as we work together."

She hated that she'd brought all this to their doors, but she hadn't had control over what had happened after she'd been dragged onto that boat. Blaming herself for the state of things wasn't helping. Working with them might bring an end to this nightmare faster. Besides, taking off was running from her problems, not facing them. She'd done a pretty good job of it until now. It was time to get her feet back under her.

"Okay," she said. "What can I do?"

"You said you had a diary. It wouldn't hurt to look at that. Reviewing it may trigger a memory," Rick suggested.

"It's at the apartment. I need to get back there anyway. I need to make a thorough search for those papers." Finch got to her feet, signaling she was ready to leave.

"We'll regroup tonight," Steve said, pulling a water from the fridge.

"Let's plan on meeting at our place," Colt suggested.

"That would be best." Rick ushered Finch toward the rear door. "I don't think they've traced her to my home. I want to keep it that way."

It worried Finch, but they were better equipped to deal with the situation than she was. It was so damned hard to trust others, but it was obvious she needed to learn.

"I'll ride shotgun," Gib injected.

Josie stepped forward. "Let's get that ancestry test out of the way. I can still send it out today."

Finch didn't want to take that step, but she wasn't going to argue any longer. The sooner they figure this out, the sooner these people would be out of danger.

"Let's do it," she said, trying to put a positive tone to her agreement.

23

———

"How you doin'?" Gib asked as they drove through her Fort Myers neighborhood. Instead of riding the traditional shotgun position in the passenger seat, he was seated behind Finch. Rick spoke with his captain and reported what had happened while Gib had gone to retrieve the weapon he kept in the safe next door. It was common knowledge Gib wasn't fond of firearms, but they also knew he was proficient in their use and wouldn't hesitate to use them if the situation called for it.

"A little sore, but I'll live," Finch answered, twisting so she faced Gib. "I imagine Shayne is going to feel the brunt of it tonight."

"Troy will make sure she's pampered," Gib said. "Hey. Where did you learn to tackle like that? The Tampa Bay Bucs could use you. You were fast. Damn fast."

Rick glanced to his right to see Finch blush. She wasn't so tough after all. Leave it to Gib to bring out the softer side of her personality.

"My favorite foster home had a dad who was a high

school football coach. He didn't have any qualms about letting me take part when he practiced with the boys who'd been placed in the home. I wanted to stay there longer, but so many of the places had age limits. They were good foster parents."

"I'm glad not all were horror stories," Rick told her.

"No. Not all were like the Simpsons. Most were in what I call neutral territory. A few excelled and others sucked."

Regardless, she was constantly on the move. Never knowing an actual home. His family had always been close. Rick had left the Army early to care for his dad after a severe heart attack. He was glad for the last few years they'd had together.

"Do you know where Simpson is now?" Gib asked. Rick glanced in the rearview mirror. The lighthearted expression he wore so often was gone. Gib loved women, but he never disrespected them and would have words with anyone who did.

"I tried to put that one behind me," Finch answered.

Gib quickly dropped the subject. Finch's posture and tone told them both it wasn't something she wanted to discuss. Rick was aware Josie was trying to locate the couple. He'd be touching base with her. He seriously hoped she'd find the man as he wanted to visit the bastard.

They arrived at Finch's apartment after stopping by the office for the new key. The management had agreed to tack the cost of the new lock onto her rent at the first of the month. Gib and Rick sandwiched her between them as they went up the stairs to her unit. Taking the key from Finch, Rick unlocked the door. Gib kept her off to the side as he opened it.

He entered the apartment, making a quick sweep. There was no sign anyone had been in the place since he and Finch had left.

"Gib, if Finch doesn't have an objection, go through her desk, and see if you can find any legal documents pertaining to her history. That will free Finch to search the rest of the place. Grab your diary while you're at it."

"What are you going to do?" Finch asked.

"I want to catch a few of your neighbors. See if they noticed anything unusual going on. Your unit is isolated. I wouldn't think you'd have much traffic down this way."

"Mrs. Murphy lives downstairs. She's retired and home most of the time."

"I'll start there."

Rick made the rounds of the building quickly. Except for Mrs. Murphy, no one was home. The absence of tenants wasn't a surprise as it was a workday. Mrs. Murphy, unfortunately, had little to offer. She confirmed she'd heard noises the day after Finch's swim across the Bay but had assumed it was Finch.

The sounds she'd heard confirmed Rick's theory that someone had been in Finch's apartment, and it hadn't been Finch.

"Well?" he asked when he returned. Gib was helping Finch search the place. They were checking under couch cushions and kitchen cabinets. Unless Finch was losing touch with reality, they weren't going to locate the documents there. He'd known before they reached Finch's unit that they wouldn't find them.

"Nothing. The papers are gone," Finch confirmed his assumption. "My diary was where I always keep it. Nothing else seems to be disturbed."

Rick stared at the thick, tattered book. He had pictured the small, simple latched book kept by most teens. This diary resembled a dictionary. It was enormous.

"Your whole life must be in there—in detail."

"It pretty much is." The solemn look on her face told her most memories weren't all that pleasant.

"You ready to go?" he quickly added.

"Hang on." She vanished into the bedroom.

He glanced at Gib, who shrugged his shoulders.

Finch returned, clutching what looked to be a charm bracelet in her fist.

"You said you had nothing of value here." Rick was looking at the piece of jewelry.

"I don't think it's valuable—but it is a bit of a mystery. Since we're working on one, this might be part of it." It was all she said as they hurried down the stairs.

Passing through the automated toll booths on the way to Sanibel, Rick was relieved that the subject of staying at his place no longer appeared to be an issue. Finch and Gib had chatted about mundane subjects which seemed to put her at ease. Gib had a gift. Colt had introduced Rick to Gib, and they'd been friends ever since. He was a joke-ster, a ladies' man, and one of the best damn men Rick knew.

"What's with the bracelet?" Rick asked as they made the right onto Periwinkle Way. "Why did you think it was important?"

"I don't know that it is, but with all the questions Josie asked about my parents, they reminded me of this. The county estimated the date of my birth to be the day before the paramedics found me. Anyway, on my eighteenth birthday I received a charm bracelet with a single charm attached. I don't know where it came from. There was no return address."

"Was there a card or note?" Gib asked.

"Nothing."

"But it was addressed to you?" Rick pressed.

"Yes."

"I saw more than one charm on the bracelet before you tucked it into your pocket. Have you added to it?"

"I haven't bought any charms, if that's what you're asking. Every year, except for the past one, I've received a charm on, or around, my birthdate. Whoever was sending them always had my current address. I never figured out how they found me."

"You didn't receive one on your last birthday?" Rick asked.

"No. I'd just moved here. Maybe whoever sent the charms lost track of me or was tired of sending them."

Rick doubted the person suddenly lost interest after years of never missing the date.

"It's not a big deal. I never wore the bracelet, anyway."

"Do you remember the order you received each charm?" Rick asked as they pulled into the lot in front of Cat's and Steve's businesses. He didn't think Finch understood the possible significance of the bracelet and the charms. He was eager to get a look at them.

"They're on the bracelet in the order I received them."

"Do you remember any postmarks that would indicate where they came from?" Gib asked.

"Trust me. I checked. Not a single one was from the same city—or state, for that matter. The bracelet and charms give me the creeps," she said as Rick jumped into the truck.

"If they make you uncomfortable, why do you keep them?" Gib asked.

Rick had put his arm over her shoulder, directing her toward the front door of Steve's office. She accepted his emotional support with no pushback. He's surprised himself with the natural inclination to hold her close. Because of that closeness, he felt her shrug in answer to Gib's question. She'd received each charm on her birthday.

Had she ever received a birthday present? He'd bet not, at least not as an adult. She was right to believe there was significance to the charms. Whether they were connected to what was happening to her now was another question in need of an answer.

24

Finch felt strangely alone in Steve's office despite the fact he sat across the desk from her. Gib had left and Rick was at the station completing a formal report on her second near abduction. Was it her imagination or was Rick hesitant to leave? He probably hated writing reports. Troy had taken his laptop and retreated to the garden to work and monitor the security cameras. It allowed him to watch Shayne, who'd insisted on working today.

"I want to apologize for the ass I've been. I'm used to being on my own and I don't want anyone to get hurt because of me."

"We're good," Steve said, leaning back in his chair, "so stop worrying. Did you find the documents and the diary?"

"The documents are missing, which is weird. Why not simply pull them off the DCF site? Why steal them?" She shrugged. It didn't make sense.

"They may not have been aware they were that easy to access—in which case they aren't very bright—or they hoped you had more than official papers in the file."

"I didn't."

"And the diary? Did you find it?"

She reached into the large bag she carried and pulled out the book.

"Holy shit." Steve grinned. "That's a diary? It looks thick enough to be a dictionary."

"I wrote a lot. I call it a diary but it's mostly musings. A lot of my daily activities are in here, but I was never too explicit for fear one of my wardens would take it away. It contains enough information on each home, it should help refresh my memory. There's also a lot of daydreaming in here, as well. Besides my clothes, the bracelet and this diary were the only things I made sure stayed with me when I moved from home to home. I was so relieved when it was returned to me after I got out of detention." She stopped. "Sorry. I'm blabbering."

"You didn't know those kids were going to rob that house, did you?"

"No. I shouldn't have been that naïve. I'd lived with my share of troublemakers. While one of the boys was in foster care, the rest of the kids I was with were from good families." She emphasized the word *good*. "I was dumb enough to believe if you came from a nice home, you didn't pull shit like that. Learned a big lesson that night."

"Hard lesson to learn," he agreed. "Now, I've got a few more questions, if you're up to it."

"Shoot." She paused when he smiled again. "Wrong word. Go ahead."

"What can you tell me we wouldn't see in your DCF documents? Any issues with the other foster kids that shared homes with you? Major problems?"

"They came in all shapes and varieties. Some nice. Some not-so-nice. Most of them scared." Finch shrugged.

"And those who were in the Simpson house when the

bastard tried to rape your roommate? Did they get any blowback from Simpson? If they did, they could hold that against you."

Recalling that night and the months that followed, nothing came to mind. "Things quieted down until the night he broke into my room. The others had moved on by then."

"What about someone connected to the Simpsons. Someone who imagined they had a reason to get even with you?"

"Why would they? Nothing ever came of it while I was there and as far as I know, nothing ever did."

Steve planted his forearms against his desk, leaning toward her. "Simpson went to jail after you left the home."

That got her attention. She sat up straight. "None of my social workers told me that. For what?"

"Assault." Steve pulled the top sheet from a file folder and placed it in front of Finch.

She stared at the police report. "What would this have to do with me?"

"Simpson spent time in the county jail. He lost his job, and they lost their foster parent status, so that source of income dried up, as well."

"But I had nothing to do with that. They were still fostering kids at the time I left. I tried to warn the agency, but I don't know if it did any good." Finch twisted the hem of her blouse.

"It's beyond me how they ever got to be foster parents." Steve ran his hand through his hair, his frustration obvious.

"DCF doesn't have enough foster homes as it is, and there aren't enough people willing to adopt." In a way, she'd been lucky. Most of the kids were there because of family substance abuse or violence. Many were adamant that they'd return home. Finch didn't have any of those false hopes. She didn't have a home to return to and, therefore, didn't waste her time thinking her life would change for the better. The counselor at the detention facility gave her hope. She'd taught Finch to believe in herself. While she didn't have the money to go to college, she was able to pay her way through trade school and learn a skill. She might have easily landed on the streets with the twenty percent of the kids that aged out of the foster care system. By her standards, she was fortunate.

"So that's a dead end?" Steve asked, returning the sheet he'd given her to his folder.

"To my knowledge, I'd say so. There was an older son who had moved out of the house. He creeped me out. Fortunately, he rarely visited the house."

"In what way did he make you uncomfortable?"

"I don't think you'd understand, but your wife would. He'd slowly undress me with his eyes. I could feel the layers slip away as he stared at me. Like father, like son, I suspect. Thankfully, he wasn't there often."

Steve scanned his notes. "He's not listed as part of the household. Do you remember his name?"

"Yeah. They called him Tommy—which he hated. He reminded them often he was an adult and to call him Tom. I think Mr. Simpson did that because he wanted to get under his son's skin. I don't know why he bothered to visit. They always argued. Unless they forced us to eat a meal together, I stayed in my room when he was there."

Steve stopped entering data into the computer. "Has the DNA test gone out?"

Finch nodded. The subject still made her uncomfortable. What would she do if she found she had relatives? What if her parents had dumped her and kept her siblings —assuming she had any? She'd been fine—good, actually —not knowing. This mess had dredged up things she'd obsessed over as a child but had managed to get past as an adult.

"Why would you think my gene pool is part of this mess? You know access to my records is easy. Even if the information wasn't available online, all my biological parents had to do was contact the officials at the DCF to find me. They've had plenty of time and ways to contact me, but neither of them did. Why would they want to be part of my life now? To screw it up again?" She got out of the chair and went to the window. A storm was brewing, both inside and out. "I'm an adult. The idea of snatching me as a child isn't all that far out there but kidnapping a grown woman in order to reunite the family is far-fetched."

"I seriously doubt either of them would be behind the kidnapping attempts, although we shouldn't rule it out." He raised his hand to stop her retort. "If they were, I doubt it would be for sentimental reasons." Steve leaned back, resting his head in his interlaced fingers.

"Have you got a theory?" Finch studied him. Did this entire group think in terms of jigsaw puzzles? "What would trigger them now and not in the past twenty-plus years?

"I do not know. It's another thread to pull. You get enough threads you can put together a pattern."

Finch chewed on her lip. She was lost. She was having trouble following a single thread, let alone seeing any sort of pattern. The slamming of the rear door snapped her out of her musings. Steve's right hand moved swiftly, opening his desk drawer, and reaching inside. His hand rested there for the few seconds it took for the voices to reach them.

The instant they heard Shayne's laugh, Steve shut the drawer. Finch didn't doubt he'd been reaching for his weapon. She let out a long, slow breath.

"Did you guys solve the mystery?" Shayne asked as she and Rick walked into the office.

"I think we just muddied the waters," Finch answered as her friend plopped down in the chair next to her.

"No," Steve corrected her. "We made some headway. It takes time to piece together an investigation."

"Did the bracelet give you any ideas?" Rick asked Steve.

"What bracelet?"

"You didn't show it to him?" Rick asked her.

"We got involved. I forgot." She reached for her bag again. She stuffed the diary in it, then slipped the piece of jewelry from one of the smaller compartments, laying it on top of Steve's file folder.

"As I told Steve, I don't know if it's relevant, but beginning with my eighteenth birthday and up until this past year I've received a charm on what the authorities listed as my birth date."

Finch got out of the way as they all hovered over the desk to study the trinkets.

"You said the charms are in the order you received them?" Rick asked.

"Yes. The first ornament, a fire truck, is an obvious reference to my arrival on the planet." When she'd received it, she'd tossed the entire package in the garbage thinking it was a sick joke, but instinct and curiosity had her retrieving it. After examining the bracelet, charm, and package, she found nothing that gave her a hint as to why she'd received it or its origin. For whatever reason, she'd dropped it in a drawer instead of throwing it away.

"There doesn't seem to be any pattern to the charms," Shayne commented.

"Exactly. I don't see any theme," Finch agreed. "They

only grabbed this because you all keep pressing me on my lineage. I don't know if it can help."

Shayne had retaken her seat and reached for Finch's hand. She appreciated the support. The subject of her foster homes and even her time in detention didn't bother her as much as discussing the day she'd been abandoned.

"Are you thinking what I'm thinking?" Steve asked Rick, who now held the piece.

Rick didn't instantly respond. He caressed and studied each charm, passing them through his fingers as if they were rosary beads. When he returned to the first charm, he nodded. "They're a message of some sort or they're clues leading to one."

25

———

"That's crazy."

The rounded copper-colored eyes drew Rick in. He'd noted the stunning signature of her features often, but the shock and dismay of the revelation made them more pronounced.

"I agree it sounds crazy," he said, squatting down in front of her, "but the randomness of the charms that follow the first two, appear to make no sense. From what I understand about charms, they typically signify a specific event, location, or celebration. These don't. For an individual to track you down and send charms willy-nilly makes little sense. They're a message of some sort."

She glanced at the others in the room. "Listen to them," Shayne said. "Trust them."

"You said the first two weren't random. What did you mean? The first one is obvious. But the second?"

Rick rested the second charm on the pad of his index finger. "You don't recognize what this is?"

"I never examined it that closely. Are you saying the little squiggles on it mean something?"

"Don't look at the pattern inscribed on it. Look at the shape of the charm. What does that remind you of?"

The room remained quiet while Finch stared at the charm. He knew the minute the meaning hit her. A teardrop ran down her cheek. "It's a tear," she said, wiping her own away.

"I don't think she wanted to leave you." Rick took her hand. "I think that's what this is trying to convey."

"Well, she did leave me." Finch viciously wiped away another tear.

"And we don't know why. She may have been convinced she had no other choice and did it did it to protect you." Rick took her into his arms and pressed her head to his shoulder. She didn't struggle against his offer of comfort. Instead, she snuggled in closer. "The answer might be in the rest of the charms," he suggested.

Finch gathered herself and pulled away. Rick immediately missed her closeness. At that moment, he stopped fighting. He surrendered the battle he'd been waging to keep his emotional distance.

After wiping away any remnants of her breakdown, she tucked her hair behind her ears. He suspected showing weakness was not something she did often. She was tough —a fighter. Even in battle strong men broke down. He'd witnessed it. Every member of the team would attest to it.

"I can't believe I've had this all these years and never suspected, let alone cared, what they meant. I can't explain why I kept them."

She'd regrouped. Rick admired her ability to pull herself together so quickly.

"Do you know what the other charms mean?" he asked.

"I don't."

Rick looked over at Steve and Troy. "Any ideas?"

"On first glance? No," Steve responded.

"The lock and key are significant," Troy said. "There's a secret to unlock and it could be the other charms are keys to it."

"Somebody has watched *National Treasure* a few too many times," Shayne kidded her husband.

Rick took the bracelet from Steve's desk and studied it. "Are these in the same order you received them?"

Finch nodded.

"None of the charms have any significance to you?"

"The only one that struck a chord was the fire truck. I didn't dwell on the others."

"You might want to now," Steve suggested.

Rick held out the bracelet like a clothesline. A sphinx followed the fire truck and tear. After that, a seashell. Then a scroll, the skeleton key, a playing card, a bear, and a tiny replica of a laptop computer. The final piece was a heart-shaped lock.

"The lock was the last item I received," Finch told them. "I didn't get a charm last year on my birthday."

"Which means whoever was sending these is done or wasn't able to continue," Troy asserted. "The message or code may be incomplete."

Troy was right, but Rick wished he'd hadn't given voice to the second thought. Finch was still adjusting to the possibility that the annual gifts were from one or both her parents. She was so certain they'd abandoned her because she wasn't wanted or loved. Now there was the possibility she'd been wrong, and if she was, Troy had just suggested that the connection was truly severed. The tightened jaw and dull look in those beautiful eyes told him the insinuation had registered with her.

"Let's work with what we have in front of us," Rick said. "Where are we meeting tonight?"

"Why go anywhere?" Steve asked. "It will be tight, but we can all squeeze into the break room."

If everyone was available, it would be a tight fit. But Rick was glad to have them. He was particularly interested in River's take on the charm bracelet. She created the most imaginative and beautiful costume masks anyone could envision. Each mask told a story in its own way. He was hoping her artist's eye might recognize the storyline these charms were trying to tell, or perhaps she would be able to identify the source of the jewelry pieces.

They ordered food from their favorite Italian eatery. The aroma of spices, bread, and garlic permeated the air, announcing its arrival. Throughout dinner, the talk revolved around mundane subjects. Rick was glad for the respite for Finch's sake. She'd been dealt an emotional blow. Spending time amongst his friends with casual conversation appeared to relax her. The haunted look had vanished, and she'd even cracked a smile when Gib offered to run away with her.

After dinner, Steve retrieved the bracelet from his office safe, where Rick had asked him to secure it. He'd texted River before she left home and had asked her to bring her tools—equipment she used while working with small, delicate pieces. He passed the bracelet and charms to her.

"What do you think?" he asked. Everyone leaned in, waiting—hoping, he supposed—for River to have a eureka moment.

"I'm not an expert on jewelry," River stated.

"But you know more about baubles than the rest of us," Cat reminded her.

Rick had never paid attention, but none of the women in this tight-knit group were into jewelry. He'd rarely seen any of them wear more than their engagement and wedding rings. Was that an oversight on their husbands' part or was that their preference?

River placed the chain and charms under alight, then examined it under the magnifying glass she'd brought with her. "A few of these charms are expensive, while others are on the cheap side. My guess is that most were bought at different places."

"I remember each postmark was from a different part of the country," Finch commented.

"You didn't keep the envelopes, did you?" Steve asked.

"No. I didn't see a reason to. I almost didn't keep the charms."

"I don't think it would have helped much," Rick said. "Whoever sent these wasn't staying put long."

River examined the pieces again. "The scroll represents the Constitution. Look closely. Most of the stuff that represents text are no more than scribbles, but the first three words are clear. *We the People*."

River held up the charm. "Does that strike a chord?" she asked.

"All I know about the Constitution is what I learned in history class," Finch answered. "If it's a clue, I don't know what it means. I don't understand what any of them are supposed to suggest. I can't even tell you why I kept them."

"Intuition," Cat said, firmly.

Gib left the room, quickly returning with a pad of paper. "Why don't we list what we think each charm symbolizes? We agree the scroll is the Constitution."

"Good idea," Josie smiled at Gib. He gave her his signature wink.

"And we know what the fire engine and teardrop mean," Finch added, running her hands through her hair.

"We do?" River's head snapped up in surprise. "I

understand the fire engine signifies where you were found. What's your interpretation of the teardrop?"

"An apology of sorts," Finch answered. "The guys here think it may express regret."

Rick wanted to reach for her again, but she was doing a damn good job of holding it together. Now was not the time to interfere.

"That's a good possibility," Josie recommended. "So, what else do we have?"

"A key, shell, two playing cards, a sphinx, a heart-shaped lock, a bear and," Josie paused, looking closer at one of the charms. "That's a laptop computer."

"Can you tell which playing cards those are?" Gib asked.

"An ace of spades and two of hearts," River answered, studying the charm under the glass.

"Nothing about those cards stands out," Gib said. "You guys?"

They ran through the list of charms, each person making suggestions on the symbolism they associated with them.

"It may be left over from my time dealing with Intelligence or because I read too many thrillers," Colt said, "what if the bear points to Russia? It's a long shot, but the bear is one of their national symbols."

"Are you suggesting we're talking national intelligence information?" Kevin asked.

"I'm just throwing it out there. The computer would also fit that scenario."

"That wouldn't explain the cards, shell and sphinx," River pointed out.

"I have a theory," Gib offered, "but I don't know how it would fit in with Colt's."

"Go ahead," Rick prompted him.

"Las Vegas."

"How did you come up with that?" Colt pressed.

"The cards are obvious, and the sphinx may represent a well-known casino in the city. Shell games are a form of gambling."

"The sphinx may also refer to Egypt," Troy suggested.

"And the bear may just be a bear," Colt admitted.

"I believe whoever put this bracelet together was terrified," Rick said, without hesitation. "So terrified, the only way the person felt safe to document what they knew was to create this cryptic message."

"So cryptic no one understands them. What are the charms supposed to tell me?" Finch's forehead crinkled. "It can't be why I was left outside a fire station. A simple letter would have sufficed. Why would they be terrified?"

"You may have been abandoned because of the story these charms tell," Troy suggested. "That might explain why this is all so cryptic—to protect the sender and you."

"Then how was I supposed to figure out what they meant? It all seems so over the top." Finch raised her hands before they flopped back into her lap.

"Not when you throw in the attempted kidnappings," Rick pointed out.

"Are you suggesting my parents were involved in espionage?"

The silence that descended on the room told Rick they were all thinking the same thing. "We're suggesting this isn't simply an interesting puzzle. If it was serious enough for a parent to hide their child by abandoning her, it's not something small."

"But what?"

"If we can get back to the lock and key charms," River interrupted. "I'd say those two were purchased together. They have the same hallmarks—artistic touch for lack of a better word. And they appear to be more expensive than the others. There was care taken in selecting them."

"If they were purchased together, why send them separately? Years apart," Shayne asked.

River reached in her small took kit. Everyone's attention was on her hands as she attempted to separate the tiny key from the bracelet. "Shall we try it?" she asked, slipping the key into the almost invisible keyhole of the lock.

26

The little heart popped open with the tiniest of snicks. While he'd been half expecting it, Rick was stunned to see the miniscule microchip inside. River tipped the lock and let the chip fall onto her fingertip.

"Is this what I think it is?" she asked.

Colt raced to the small kitchenette and swiped a paper towel from the roll and grabbed a zip-lock bag from a drawer.

"Let me have it," Rick said, placing his large finger next to River's. Both their hands were still under the standing magnifying glass. The men all jockeyed for a position to view the item.

"Microchip," Colt stated. "This adds an additional layer of alarm."

"We don't have the tools to read it here," Steve admitted. "No telling what's on it."

"Which, I assume, was the point," Rick added. "Time to call the boys in Tampa."

"Do it now," Steve urged him, vacating his chair. "If there is any chance there are classified documents on that thing, I don't want it anywhere near this place." He headed toward his office. "I'm going to check the cameras. Colt. Troy. Kevin. You want to make a sweep of the grounds?"

"He's scaring me." Finch pointed to Steve's retreating backside.

"Precautions," Rick tried to calm her as Colt went out the front, pulling a gun from the waistband of his jeans. Troy had been carrying a gun since the incident earlier in the day. He went out the rear door with Kevin.

"The guys know what they're doing," Cat told her.

Rick left the remaining group and made his way to Cat's office, shutting the door behind him. The team had worked with FBI Special Agents Morgan and Hernandez on several occasions. He had both their cell phone numbers on his call list.

Hernandez answered on the first ring. "We don't have anything else on the Gambino guy," he said without fanfare.

"You wouldn't happen to know his whereabouts, do you?" Rick asked, since the agent had mentioned the man.

"We only investigated his history. Why? What's going on?"

"Long story, but we found a microchip. We have a suspicion as to what's on it, but we haven't the tools to confirm it. You do."

"And you wouldn't have called one of us if you didn't think it was important. You have my interest. Talk to me."

Rick filled him in on the details. Shayne had been the one to contact them regarding Gambino. She enjoyed getting under their skin and they'd owed her, but she hadn't given them much information. Rick spent the next thirty minutes in a back-and-forth conversation. Morgan and Hernandez were excellent agents. Rick trusted them. Fortunately, they trusted the team as well.

"I'll send an agent from our Fort Myers field office over. Where are you?"

Rick told him. He was glad they'd have it off their hands tonight.

"I want the bracelet, too."

Rick's instinct was to argue but having it out of their hands was a safer option. "As long as we can get it back. It's the only connection Finch has to her family. I don't want her to lose it, if that's the case."

The office door opened. Steve stuck his head in. "Is that Morgan?"

"Hernandez," Rick answered. "Why?"

"Josie overnighted Finch's ancestry test. Ask him if they can light a fire under the company to get the results."

"Did you guys find anything on your sweep of the compound? Are we clear?" Rick asked.

"For the moment." Steve shut the door behind him.

Rick passed the request along to Hernandez.

"You think this is all connected to Ms. Finch's history? If you want to put a stronger spin on the second abduction, Morgan and I can find a way to justify officially coming in."

"Thanks," Rick said. He appreciated the offer. "Let's see what's on that chip first. We may need your help later or you may have no choice depending on what you find."

"You said it was over a year ago that you received the heart charm. So why are they after Ms. Finch now?"

"Good question. We're still putting the puzzle pieces together. You'll call us as soon as you know something?" Rick tossed his pen on the desk. He shouldn't be frustrated. This wasn't his first complicated case, but it was the first one which involved Finch.

"I'll tell you what I can, but I don't know how much that will be. What you're suggesting may have national security implications. If that turns out to be true, any information I can share with you will be limited."

"We have people we care about and need to protect. I expect you to give me enough information to protect them."

"I'll do what I can," the agent repeated.

Rick disconnected the call. He shouldn't have been short with Hernandez. He was right. If this involved national security, the FBI wouldn't be able to share much. Rick headed back to the break room. They'd work with what they had, which was currently a piss-poor amount of information.

"Hernandez is sending an agent from the local office to pick up the chip and the bracelet," he announced when he joined the others. "I'm sorry Finch. It makes sense for them to examine it. They have equipment we don't have. We'll get it back. I promise."

"You can trust those two," Shayne chimed in. "They can be dicks at times, but we always work things out."

"It's no big deal."

Rick suspected it was a very big deal. If their theory that the bracelet and charms were from one of her parents was true, then it was all she had from them.

"Before the agent gets here, I want as many pictures of the charms and bracelet as possible," Rick said, pulling out his phone.

"Let me get my equipment," Colt said, rising from a stool at the breakfast bar.

Rick mentally kicked himself as his friend left the building. Colt and his camera equipment would capture every minute detail of the charms. You could count the number of feathers on a bird's wing in his shots. He glanced at Finch, the reason for his distraction. Distractions often proved deadly.

"And the DNA test? Any progress there?" Steve asked, pulling a bottle of water from the break room fridge.

"They're going to reach out to the company and ask them to fast-track it. Even if they agree, it will still take a few days."

Rick's eyes drifted to Finch. Every time her family was discussed, a darkness passed over her face. He'd been lucky. His parents had loved him and his sisters until the day they'd died. He couldn't imagine what it would be like to have never known them. Worse yet, to think they'd never wanted him.

The agent arrived in less than an hour. The hand-off was quick. While waiting, Colt had photographed each charm from every angle.

"Anything else we need to address this evening?" Rick asked. It had been a long day and the events of the day had to have taken a physical and mental toll on Finch. It had become natural for him now to gauge how she was feeling by looking into her eyes. They were pinched at the corners, yet some spark remained.

"Did the boys in Tampa say any more about Gambino?" Josie asked.

"Hernandez said they hadn't dug any further than the cursory check we'd initially asked them to make. Gambino has no obvious links with any illegal activity. Why? Do you have something?"

"Something. I talked to a journalist in Tampa. He recognized the name. The Gambino family is well known in the area. My colleague uncovered a small bit of news. There was a kerfuffle at the largest casino there a little over a year ago. No arrests. It barely made the papers, but he found Tony Gambino's name in the short piece."

"What happened?" Rick asked.

Josie opened a document on her phone. She hadn't

been kidding when she said he'd barely made the news. The story from the Tampa Bay Times stated one manager, Tony Gambino, got into a scuffle with a patron of the casino. The reason for the dispute wasn't known.

"You're right. This isn't much," Rick said, returning the phone to her.

"Not at all," she agreed. She passed the phone to her husband, who'd been hovering over her shoulder. "But Tony told his boss at the spa, he was taking care of a sick relative to explain his gap in employment. He never mentioned working during that time, let alone working at a casino."

"And if Gib is right," Finch said, "a few of the charms point to a casino."

"It doesn't have to be Las Vegas. Gambino was in Tampa," Kevin commented.

"There's one major casino in Tampa," Gib stated. "If whoever sent these wanted attention pointed in that direction, the charm would have been a guitar, not a sphinx."

"The sphinx points to Egypt for all we know." Kevin yawned. "It may make more sense to me after a few hours of sleep. Today was my second twelve-hour shift in a row. Give me a night to clear my head."

"Get some rest. If we find anything, we'll text you," Colt said as Kevin and River headed out the front.

"I still think I'm right about the Vegas angle," Gib repeated.

"There hasn't been any organized crime associated with Las Vegas in decades," Troy argued.

"He's right," Rick agreed. "They were literally run out of town."

"Regardless, if nobody objects, I'm going to make a few calls."

"Who do you know in Vegas?" Shayne asked.

"I have friends," Gib winked.

"Of course you do," Cat responded, a grin lighting up her face.

"Hold on," Rick warned him. "Let's start off close to home. Would you happen to know anyone at the Hard Rock in Tampa?"

"No, but I could."

Troy spit out his beer, setting off a round of laughter. Finch watched them all, her brows raised in confusion.

"Gib makes friends wherever he goes," Cat explained. "Particularly those of the female persuasion."

"I'm personable. What can I tell you?"

"How would you like to make a visit to Tampa? See what you can find out on Gambino and what he was doing at that casino," Rick suggested.

"Colt? You good without me for a day or two?"

"Go. But stay focused," Colt chided him with a grin.

"Why don't I call Mrs. Gonzales and press her for more information on Tony?" Finch asked. "He may have been in contact since we last talked."

"I doubt he'll be calling her again. He quit," Rick reminded her.

"What about his apartment? The police checked on him, but has anyone searched it?"

"Unless he gave you a key that would be breaking and entering." Rick was getting tired and edgy. "Let's call it a night. Like Kevin said, we can look at this tomorrow with fresh minds."

As they filed out of the building, Finch made a beeline for his truck. Her short, crisp moves, along with her clenched jaw and tight lips, telegraphed her mood. She wasn't happy. She hadn't appreciated him dismissing her suggestions. The first one wasn't likely to get them anywhere. In addition, talking to Gonzales might raise unintended flags. If it became necessary he'd move it up on the list of things to do, but he'd put it on the back burner for now. The idea of searching Gambino's apartment was textbook illegal. Despite Finch's contrary mood, she hadn't hesitated to get in his vehicle. A small success.

As she snapped her seat belt into place, he couldn't resist the pouty face.

27

Finch had no sooner settled into her seat when Rick leaned across the console and pressed his lips against hers. He nibbled at them, paying particular attention to the corners of her mouth. She didn't retreat but fell into the kiss. Hands tenderly caressed her neck, warming her skin. His tongue worked magic on her lips, neck, and throat. The simmering heat was turning into a full blaze. She needed more. No longer patient, she coaxed his head up then crushed her lips against his. Their tongues danced a frenzied tango. She wanted to take and be taken, but as she leaned in further, her seat belt held her back. Damn it. As she fumbled to unfasten it, there was a tap on Rick's window.

Colt was standing next to the driver's door. "I suggest you two take this elsewhere," Colt said as the barrier disappeared. "You're sitting ducks and I'm not staying out here all night to cover your ass—literally or figuratively."

Rick pushed the ignition switch as Colt stepped away. Finch swore there was a tint of redness creeping up Rick's neck, but it was dark, and the lights emanating from the dash might simply be causing the illusion. She averted her face from both him and his former commander, knowing damn well she was flushed. She was too old to be making out in cars.

What had changed between them tonight? Touching her moistened lips, she was surprised by her reaction to his kiss. The initial tenderness had quickly turned carnal. She'd welcomed both. If Colt hadn't tapped on the window, she had a pretty good idea where that kiss would have led.

Tucking her hair behind her ear, she snuck a glance in Rick's direction. There were no streetlights on the island, so it was pitch dark outside. The occasional oncoming traffic and the dash provided the only light in the vehicle. Rick kept his eyes on the road, his expression one of concentration. Had she been the only one affected by the kiss?

"Why?" she asked.

"Because you needed kissing."

A ghost of a smile crossed his face. At least he wasn't feigning ignorance.

"I'm not sorry," he added. "I was an ass last night. It won't happen again."

"What won't happen again? The kiss? The visit to my bedroom? Or the speedy departure?" Frankly, she was afraid of the answer, but she had too much to deal with to continue playing games.

"Unless you have an objection, the only thing I won't repeat is my cowardly retreat."

"You hurt me," she admitted. "Why did you do it?"

She felt his exhale as he pulled onto his property. He put the car in park and unlatched his seat belt. "We need to take this conversation indoors. Colt's right. We shouldn't be sitting out in the open. While it's highly unlikely anyone traced you here, I don't like taking unnecessary chances."

He came around to her side of the truck and hefted her out, then rushed her up the steps. Once inside, he locked the door and set the alarm.

"I should probably change that, since you obviously know it."

She didn't take offense at his reference to her early morning escape. He'd been smiling as he'd said it. What had changed his perception of her?

"You haven't answered my question," she said while placing her purse and laptop on the chair next to the door.

"Do you want something to drink?" he asked, flicking on the kitchen light.

"Are you always this good at avoiding questions?" She leaned against the doorjamb while he pulled a beer from the fridge. He held one out toward her. She shook her head.

"I'm a cop. I'm better at asking them." He twisted the cap off, then took a swig. A fortifying gulp?

"Then ask yourself the question, then answer it so I can hear."

He grinned. "That backbone grew some tonight, I see."

"It was out for repair," she quipped. "I need to settle this thing between us before I can deal with all this other shit. I can't tell one minute if you like me, despise me, or just plain lust after me."

He took her hand and led her to his living area. After taking another pull from his beer, he sat it on the end table along with his gun. He took both her hands in his.

"About last night... I wasn't expecting this attraction to you. It blindsided me. Then there was your relationship with Shayne. It felt out of line—like I was hitting on a family member."

She stared at him. He believed she was off base because she was a friend of Shayne? Finch didn't know whether to laugh or admire his sense of honor. "And my criminal record? Did that play a part?"

"You don't have a criminal record," he corrected her. "You were in the wrong place at the wrong time."

"I'm gathering you've eliminated all the reasons I was a pariah?" She tried to reclaim her hands, but he held on.

"You were never a pariah. Just unexpected. I constantly give the guys a hard time about falling in love as if I were exempt. I think I believed it—until you."

"Are you saying you're in love with me?" He wasn't saying that, was he?

"I don't know what I feel, but I know I want to be with you—that I don't want to run from that feeling any longer."

"Maybe you feel responsible for me. You found me on the beach. I am a friend of a friend—an obligation."

"If I didn't feel something here," he pressed her palm to his chest, "last night would have never happened. I couldn't admit that to myself then. I can now."

What she didn't verbalize was that the feeling was mutual. She'd have kicked his ass out of the room at his first move if there had been nothing more than heat. She'd wanted him then. She wanted him now.

He was braver than she was because she had no intention of admitting her growing feelings. It would make her too vulnerable. It had taken years for her to erect barriers to protect her heart. Rick had made a crack in that barrier, but she wasn't ready to let it crumble altogether. Not yet.

She'd gotten this far since leaving foster care by taking baby steps. Major leaps weren't in her repertoire. That didn't mean she was too afraid to open up a little—to believe just a little.

"Could we continue where we left off before Colt interrupted?" She brushed the back of her hand over his cheek. It was rough. His hair was so light, she could only feel the stubble.

Encircling her wrist with his fingers, he raised her hand to his lips, pressing them into her palm. "I'd like nothing better."

Rising to his feet, he pulled her into his arms. He didn't give her time to think, instead falling into a full-fledged assault on her senses. His tongue darted between her lips. She welcomed it. Running her fingers across his scalp, she urged him closer. She whimpered when he pressed his rock-hard erection against her. His lips wandered, lightly grazing her jawline until they reached the lobe of her ear. Her skin warmed—a warmth that flamed into a heat that settled between her legs. His kisses were soft and teasing until he reached the curve of her shoulder. He nudged away the collar of her blouse, allowing him to suckle her sensitive skin.

It was a heady feeling to know his body was hers for the taking. Nuzzling his neck, Finch began an exploration of her own. There was so much to explore. He was big, tall, and solid. Her hands crossed the plains of his shoulder blades, then slid lower until they reached his waist. Yanking his shirt tail free, she slipped her hands under the material and raked her nails against the solid muscles of his back. His waistband halted her exploration, frustrating her. Fumbling at the button on his jeans, Rick's hands clasped hers.

"Let's take this to the bedroom."

"Yes. Please." She wanted this man. It scared her—this need, this want. Fear began to creep in. Didn't she have enough to deal with without getting involved with this sexy cop?

Linking his fingers with hers, he led her toward his bedroom. Her steps slowed. He noted her hesitation.

"You're thinking too much."

"Am I? What if you were right? What if you regret getting involved with me?"

"I'm thinking you're afraid you'll regret it." He cupped her shoulders. "We'll take this slow. We want each other. That much is obvious. I want to explore every inch of you. I want to feel your heat. If you don't feel the same, say so now. It's your choice."

She dropped her forehead to meet his chest. "My life is one big clusterfuck right now. What if I'm looking for security and using you to attain it?"

"I don't think that's your style. Have you made a habit of sleeping with men when you're under stress?"

"Hell, no." And she'd just answered her own question.

"Stop thinking about the world for a while. Let's create our own." She pushed aside her fears and let Rick take her to a world where only the two of them existed.

His fingers danced across her face before pulling her in for another kiss. "I'm going to take my time with you tonight. You deserve so much more attention than I gave you last evening."

"Our time together last night was wonderful," she said. "It was the exit that hurt."

"I was an idiot. Forgive me," he whispered as he unbuttoned her blouse, then unsnapped the front clasp of her bra. He pushed both pieces of clothing aside. "I'll make it up to you," he breathed against her tender skin.

After paying homage to each of her breasts, he undid the zipper of her jeans and pulled them lower, along with her panties, until their reached her ankles. As she stepped out of them, he stopped her, holding her feet in place.

"Let me do it," he said. "Sit. Please."

She did as he asked, placing her bare bottom on the edge of the bed. Instead of instantly pulling her clothing free, he began to blissfully massage her feet. Her surprise at the tender gesture was quickly replaced with pleasure. She melted into the mattress, knowing she would gladly languish in his ministrations all night. But other parts of her body were tingling, demanding attention. She wiggled her ankles, sending the message. Speaking, she feared, would break the sensual bubble that surrounded them.

He laid a kiss on the top of each foot before he finished disrobing her. He then guided her to her feet, so he could toss the covers aside.

Adjusting her position on the bed, she reached out to catch the hem of his shirt, but he quickly removed the garment himself. Propping herself up on one elbow, she felt no shame in watching him.

Lordy, he was magnificent. From his silver blond hair and ripped torso to his lean waist and what lay south, he was a sculpture, and he was hers for tonight.

Rick opened the drawer of the nightstand and pulled out a foil packet. She reached for it. "Let me do it," she said, repeating his phrase.

She took the condom, but instead of sheathing him, she wrapped her fingers around the impressive appendage and stroked it. Rick groaned, his head falling back against his shoulders. A little reverse torture was only fair. Beads of liquid formed at the tip. Boldly, she leaned in, she flicked her tongue, tasting him. He flinched, but didn't move away, giving her permission to continue the exploration. This was a new frontier for her, but she would not let that stop her. Lavishing her attention on the act, she teased, tasted, and suckled.

"Enough." He stepped out of her reach. "You're killing me."

"I'm not finished," she grumbled. Her body had been humming. It was still humming. "Was I doing it wrong?"

"Savannah, honey, I don't think I could stand better, but we're both going to enjoy this time together."

"I was enjoying it." She grinned, reaching for him again.

"You're a devil." He sidestepped her hand and grabbed the condom off the bed. He didn't offer it to her, instead he sheathed himself. "Perhaps another time," he added, pressing her against the mattress. "Let's finish this together."

He stroked the moist area between her legs. "You really enjoyed that, didn't you? You're ready for me."

Hell yes, she was ready. "Stop being a tease." She was on the brink, and he wasn't working fast enough.

"I'm just getting started," he responded with a smirk before slipping into her.

At first his movements were slow, measured. Then, as he rocked harder, every nerve in her body cried out. She was so close. He reached between them, touching the most sensitive spot.

"Now, Savannah. Together."

And they did.

Afterward, they lay exhausted, entangled in one another. As she drifted off to sleep, she whispered, "You called me Savannah."

28

───────

*R*ick didn't want to wake her. She had to be exhausted from their night of lovemaking. They'd gotten very little sleep, drifting off occasionally only to wake and begin again. He didn't regret a minute of it.

He'd called her Savannah last night. It had slipped out but had showered her with warmth. Savannah was softer on the tongue—more fitting of the intimate moment. She'd noted it but, this time, hadn't corrected him—she simply snuggled into his chest. When had she started going by Finch, and why had she stuck with it? It didn't matter. Savannah fit her softer side. A side she tried hard not to show.

Gib had texted early, letting Rick know he was leaving for Tampa. The casino was open twenty-four seven. His friend would find someone to talk to before the place started popping tonight. Gib was as intuitive as he was charming. The two traits were especially helpful in getting information out of people. Most didn't even realize they were parting with useful info.

Rick was betting the microchip, and bracelet would provide the biggest clues. He'd push Morgan and Hernandez later today if he didn't hear from them. He wanted this issue a priority with the agency. The mystery was at least a decade old based on the timeline the charms were received—even older if the theory that her parents had abandoned Finch to protect her. For both those reasons, the FBI might conclude there was no immediate threat despite their urgency to get their hands on the items. Rick wanted answers sooner rather than later.

He stepped out of the master bath and into the bedroom. The scent of sex still hung in the air. His king-sized bed was empty, which was just as well. It negated the chances of him joining Finch had she still been in it.

The shower in the guest's bath was running. His heart settled at the sound, knowing she was there. He dated his share of women. If the interest was mutual, they would share a bed, but they were always gone before morning. He intentionally dated women with busy lives. It kept things from getting too close—too entangled. Savannah Finch had changed his thinking. Knowing she was here was different and right. He appreciated her kick-ass attitude and the way her mind worked. She'd built a life from ashes. So many people would have stayed in the ruins instead of struggling to make a better future for themselves. She was so much more than a beautiful woman.

"Good morning." She smiled as she entered the kitchen. Those copper-colored eyes reflected the morning sunlight. "What's the plan for today?" she asked, helping herself to a cup of coffee. "I want an assignment. I've let you guys carry the load."

He kissed her. Her lips warm from the sip of coffee she'd taken.

"I have cream and sugar if you want it."

"I learned to drink it black, but thanks," she said, taking another sip from her mug.

And what had that learning experience entailed? How had her tastes—her wants—been tailored by the places she'd been forced to stay?

"Well?" she prompted.

"We're headed to Steve's."

"Won't my presence there put people at risk?"

"We've got it covered. Josie and Cece will be with River and Kevin today at their place. Colt will have Cat attached to his hip next door in his studio. She can use one of their computers to work on her garden designs. You and Shayne will be with me, Troy, and Steve. The compound has good security as long as no one wanders outside. Clear?"

"What if someone takes a shot at me and hits one of your friends?"

Our friends, he wanted to correct her, but she was slow to trust, which was understandable considering her childhood. She was sharp. She'd figure it out. Instead, he addressed her worry.

"They've had plenty of opportunities to take you out. Instead, they've tried to abduct you. Stay inside and you should be fine. Safety in numbers."

"Aren't you working today?" she asked, shooting him a questioning look.

"I am. Just not at the station. I'm going to use Cat's office since she'll be with Colt." Rick had already talked to his boss, Pulaski. His captain was fine with the remote work. Pulaski's background was rumored to have included clandestine work for the government. Knowing the man, Rick didn't doubt it. It was probably about time he was brought up to speed on this case.

"I don't plan to sit on my hands all day." Finch's hands

rested on her hips. "This is my problem. I meant what I said. I want to work on this."

"See if Josie needs a research assistant or, if you haven't made it through your diary, keep working on that. It may trigger a memory that coincides with those charms."

Finch darted into the guest room. She returned with her laptop and the enormous book he still had a hard time thinking of as a diary. That should keep her busy all day. He didn't know a single woman in their tight-knit group who would be willing to be left on the sidelines. Finch fit right in.

Steve was waiting by the front door when they arrived. He quickly let them in, then set the alarm. Shayne appeared and lassoed Finch, pulling her along to the break room. Troy joined Steve and Rick in the lobby.

"Anything I need to know about?" Rick asked.

"Everything is quiet here," Troy told him, handing Rick the second mug of coffee he had in his hands. "The break room resembles a potting shed. Shayne's going to work in there transplanting seedlings, so she won't have an excuse to go outside. Finch can work with her, if she wants. Shayne will keep her mind off things."

Rick took a sip from the steaming cup. "She's going to go through that thing she calls a diary. See if anything strikes a chord."

"Good idea. Josie is still reaching out to contacts who may have information on Gambino," Steve informed them. "I've got feelers out to a number of private investigators in Tampa and New York."

"Let's finish this up in your office," he suggested to Steve.

Steve's phone rang as he dropped into his chair. He glanced at the screen. "I'm putting you on speaker," he told the caller. "Troy and Rick are here with me." He placed the phone on his desk and hit the speaker button. "It's Hernandez," Steve explained.

"Something up?" Rick asked.

"Something. A start, and it's not looking good."

A silent question passed between them. "Out with it," Rick told him.

"Our forensic people are still working on the bracelet and charms, but the chip had some very interesting and disturbing information encrypted on it. The encryption wasn't sophisticated, but still good." Hernandez paused.

"Spill it," Troy snapped. "You planned on sharing info before you placed the call. Don't start playing games with us."

Troy still had an issue with the two FBI agents. The lack of information they'd provided when they'd asked the team to take Shayne under their wing had almost gotten both Shayne and Troy killed. Shayne used their guilt to squeeze information out of the agents on the rare occasions it was needed. She seemed to enjoy it. Troy, on the other hand, only tolerated them because they could be useful.

"The chip was encrypted using steganography. Microscopic pictures embedded with additional information."

Rick heard the low growl in Troy's voice. The agent wasn't against exploiting Troy's impatience.

"What's the bottom line?" Rick asked crisply, pressing his hand against Troy's chest, urging him to retake his seat.

"There are lists embedded in the chip. Names with dollar amounts next to them. A lot of names."

"Are we talking blackmail?" Steve asked.

"That's one possibility," Hernandez answered. "We haven't identified all the people listed. The dollar amounts associated with each individual is substantial."

"I want that list." Rick didn't try to disguise the statement as a request. "We've got the only connection to that bracelet, charms and chip."

"We can bring Ms. Finch in for questioning," Hernandez threatened.

"Bullshit." Rick was the one out of his chair this time, pressing his hands against the surface of the desk. "If you bring Finch in, then her stalkers go underground until you let her go—on her own."

"She won't be on her own. She'd have you."

If Rick could reach through the phone, he'd have the agent by the collar of his pristine white shirt. "If you bring her in, then let her walk, you're putting a target on her back, and you know it."

"Like you did with Shayne?" Troy spit out.

"Ms. Finch, apparently, already has a target painted on her. Shayne was different," Hernandez defended himself. "We didn't know she had knowledge of the bomber. Hell, she didn't even know it until after we relocated her there."

"You sent her to us because you were aware there was that possibility, and knew we'd step up to the plate to protect her. Don't you dare try that shit again," Rick warned him. "If you want our help in the future, you play straight with us now."

There was a huff of resignation at the end of the line. "If we need to talk to her, we'll come to you. I cannot promise it will stay that way."

"What has your antennae up?" Steve asked.

"We're running the names through the system now, but we recognized a few of them right off the bat. This isn't looking good."

"You didn't call to give us that minimal amount of information. Elaborate."

"The individuals appear to be government officials,

politicians, or contractors. At least one had top security clearances. We'll know more soon. It's hard to say how far back this list goes, but a couple of those I recognized are dead."

"Are any of those deaths suspicious, besides simply being on the list?" Rick asked.

"Don't know enough yet to say."

"I want the names, Hernandez," Rick reiterated. "We have people here to protect. You wouldn't know about this if it wasn't for us."

"If I didn't know your intelligence background, you wouldn't be getting a single name from me. I'm trusting you. Don't make it a mistake." He paused. "These aren't to be put in an email, text or any form that can be resurrected electronically. No internet searches. Nothing. Understood?"

Rick began writing as Hernandez gave him the names. Steve did the same. Back-up was always good. He recognized a couple of them. It was no wonder Hernandez was jumpy and a miracle he was willing to share.

"No results on the DNA yet?" Steve asked after they'd finished the list.

"The company just received the sample. They've agreed to fast-track it, but it will be a few days. I'll call you when we get the results."

"Thanks," Rick said before Steve disconnected the line. Hernandez and Morgan were sharing more than they should. For that Rick was grateful.

"What do you guys make of these?" Steve tapped the paper with the list of thirty-two names. "I say we give them to Josie and let her have a run at them."

"No doubt Josie will be eager to jump on this, but I don't want her in the line of fire for simply asking questions."

"She'd have my balls in a wringer if I made that decision for her."

"Assuming you can't talk her out of it, let's split the names amongst us three. It will be a lot faster. We're only reaching out to people we know since we can't Google our way through the list. If we come up blank on one name, hand it off. We each have different sources. Be discreet and find out who they are and what they do."

"Troy?" Rick turned to address his friend. "Can you work on the foster homes? Josie has the list. Contact the ones you can and if they're willing to talk, ask them if they remember anything unusual happening with regard to Finch."

"They'll be tough nuts to crack. Particularly, if they're good foster parents. I'd be suspicious of any calls asking details of one of their charges."

"Dig deep and find your old, charming personality. Besides, we're not looking for details of her time with them. Just anything out of the ordinary for a foster kid. Did she have any visitors beside social workers. Did anyone repeatedly call asking questions? I'm assuming a good foster parent would shelter the child and report it. Take a look at her state file again, too."

"Got it. I'll also put in a call to the detention facility to see if they'll open up. If something out of the ordinary happened, it should be in her records."

"Do we share the names with Finch?" Steve asked.

"I'll talk to her."

"Can we assume she's part of the team now?" Troy turned to look at Rick.

The question was intended as a confirmation of his relationship with Finch. He no longer felt the need to disguise it. "As far as I'm concerned, she is. Whether she wants to be is her decision to make."

29

———

Finch wasn't having much luck with the diary or charms. She'd made note of names as she came across ones she'd forgotten. On a separate sheet, she listed the charms and any way she related to them. The connections were imaginative, at best. She'd learned to play cards in detention. She'd hunted for shells on the beach. She owned a computer. Anyone could make the same or similar connections. Still, she kept at it until Rick entered the break room.

"Finch, can I see you for a minute?"

She glanced at Shayne, who shrugged her shoulders. And why would she think Shayne knew what was going on? She'd cleared the breakfast bar and had spent the morning using it to repot seedlings. Finch had declined the invitation to join her. She had nothing against getting her hands dirty, but she had a project of her own. One that hadn't gotten her anywhere.

"Sure. What's up?" She grabbed her notebook, diary, and phone and joined him.

The icy silence that accompanied them down the short

hallway gave her chills. What had they found out that Rick didn't want to discuss in front of Shayne? They entered a large office. He indicated for her to take a seat in one of the visitor chairs in front of what must have been Cat's desk. Plant catalogs were stacked on bookshelves behind the desk. Stunning photographs of native plants hung on the walls. Natural light flowed in from a long, transom-like window that ran the length of the room near the ceiling. Finch lowered herself into the chair. Rick surprised her, taking the chair next to hers.

"You're scaring me," she admitted. "What happened?"

"Sorry. That wasn't my intent." He squeezed her hand and smiled. "The FBI called. They still have a long way to go, but they did get names off the microchip." He grabbed the sheet of paper he'd placed on the desk. "Do you recognize any of these people?"

Finch glanced over the list, then shook her head. "I don't think I know any of them."

"Take another look."

She studied the list again. "A lot of the names are common enough. Johnson, Parker, Wilson. There's even a Smith on here. If I've met any of them, they're not registering."

"That's okay," Rick said, taking the sheet from her. "It was a long shot, but we had to ask."

"Do you have any idea what they have to do with me?" Everything was so much simpler before she'd jumped off the boat. That had been the scariest night of her life—and that was saying a lot. Now, with the added twists and turns that followed her swim for freedom, it had gotten a whole lot scarier.

"We don't see a connection, but we just got the list. The FBI is working on the names. We're working them, as well."

"Can I help? I'm not getting anywhere with my diary."

"Finish going through it. See if anything clicks. Besides, we're going through backchannels and personal contacts for the information on the people listed since we can't input the names in any search engine."

"Why not?"

"If we wanted the names, that was the agreement."

Her skin prickled. "That sounds ominous."

"Serious. Not ominous." He gave her hand a squeeze. "Don't let that worry you. They shared the names. That's a positive."

"Will you let me know if I can help?" Reviewing her diary felt like busy work, but she didn't have their contacts.

"Is there any way I can go back to work?" She wanted normalcy in her life, not to mention a paycheck. "I need to keep my job. I have bills to pay. You know? That sort of thing?"

"Based on the names we've identified, the individuals searching for you are likely connected to people with power. If they get wise to our line in inquiry, that's going to ratchet up the heat—increasing the need to get to you. Your co-workers could be caught in the flack."

She'd already known the answer, and understood the logic behind it, but worry had her asking anyway. She had a little savings, but not enough to keep her going for months. There was rent and utilities to pay. Thankfully, she didn't owe anything on her car, but there was insurance— assuming they didn't cancel her policy since the demolition derby episode on the causeway. Then there was the fact she was sponging off these people. She hadn't contributed to a single meal yet.

"I can't stay unemployed forever. Mrs. Gonzales won't keep my job open indefinitely. Which reminds me, I need to contact her. I assume I'm still employed." A sigh of resignation escaped. A sign of weakness, damn it. But it wasn't just the paycheck, it was the tips. They made up a good portion of her income.

"If you need money…"

"Don't. Please. I don't want charity. I lived off it for far too long."

"Think of it as a loan," Rick said. He pressed a kiss to her forehead then began kneading her shoulders. The tension eased.

"If I get desperate, I'll let you know. Fair?" Her eyelids grew heavy under his tender touch.

"You're stubborn," Rick stated, returning her attention to the subject.

"A learned trait, I'm afraid," she said, leaning into the massage. He understood the unspoken request and proceeded to work her muscles.

"It was a statement, not an insult."

She tipped her head back to look at him. Those blue eyes gazed directly into hers.

"Your youth shaped you. You're tough and tenacious. You're also caring."

"Caring? I've been an asshole from the time we met."

"You were worried about Tony after your dip in the water, knowing he may have been involved in the attempted abduction. You worry about Shayne and the rest of us getting hurt because you're here. You're special." He finished his little speech by laying a kiss on the crown of her head.

No one had ever said those things to her.

"You've spent so much time trying to prove yourself that you haven't taken the time to see what else lies underneath the surface. You need to give that some thought."

"Why the lecture?"

"You're also blunt," he laughed. "Because you needed

to hear it. Now, move before I decide to make love to you on Cat's desk. I don't think she'd appreciate it, and I've got work to do."

The entire conversation was confusing. Regardless, it had lifted Finch's spirits.

"Why are you wearing that silly grin?" Shayne asked Finch when she returned to the break room.

Her face warmed at the question. What were friends for if she couldn't engage in a little girl talk? "Apparently, I'm a distraction. Rick threatened to make love to me on Cat's desk if I didn't leave the room."

"I knew it." Shayne was bouncing on her toes. "You guys are perfect for one another. I've seen the way he looks at you. Is it mutual?"

That question banked the fire kindling inside her. "I don't know. He's different. He treats me different. Even knowing my history, he wants to be with me."

"I wish you'd stop selling yourself short. The fact that you were in foster care certainly isn't your fault. The mistake that landed you in detention was simply that—a mistake. You did nothing wrong. Any man would be lucky to have you. I'm glad it's Rick. He's a good man."

Shayne had pushed aside the planting materials and cradled her head in her palms. Finch pulled out a barstool and sat across from her.

"This is going to sound trite, but it's me, not him. There was a time when I was little that I trusted my feelings, but that eroded over time. I don't know if I can open myself to trust someone completely. That wouldn't be fair to Rick."

"It's hard. I didn't have the childhood you had. Far from it, but I didn't trust Troy when he made his feelings known to me. He was a known womanizer. A wham-bam-thank-you-ma'am kind of guy. He didn't want entanglements and I didn't believe he could love anyone as plain as me."

"You're beautiful," Finch scolded her friend.

"Thank you, but I wasn't fishing for a compliment. What I'm trying to say is that I didn't trust, and that lack of trust almost cost me the most wonderful thing in my life. Trust Rick. Trust yourself."

Was it possible Rick would turn out to be the most wonderful thing in her life? Getting out of detention and achieving her accreditation as a massage therapist had been her biggest moments. Pretty small stuff in the big scheme of things. Happiness had never been a goal. Whether or not she'd find it with Rick, she needed to stop floating along. Perhaps it was time to stop taking baby steps and make a jump. Her palms grew damp, but she gave herself points for not freaking out.

Finch returned to the search of her diary. Rick had given her a copy of the list. She had a hard time believing she knew any of them. If they were notorious enough to land in her diary pages, she'd certainly remember their names. Still, she started skimming the pages of her journal, keeping the names in mind.

30

———

Rick was on the phone talking with a friend and former Army intelligence officer when a call came in from Gib. He let it roll over to voicemail. This call was important. Jeremy was retired Army, but he still knew people who knew people—and he understood the importance of tight security. At one point, Jeremy stopped him and asked him to repeat a name and its spelling.

"Does that name mean something to you?" Rick asked.

"I'll get back to you. Give me the rest of the names."

By the end of the conversation, Rick was optimistic that the intelligence officer would be helpful in getting information on some of the individuals. What did they have in common? The team had little to work with and Rick wasn't counting on the FBI sharing more than they already had.

He scanned the list again. The dollar amounts next to their names could be anything—income, debt, investments —literally anything. But the crime of blackmail kept jumping to the forefront of Rick's mind. If so, why were they being blackmailed and who was behind it? And what did it have to do with Finch?

His phone vibrated. Shit. Gib. He'd forgotten about his call. Rick swiped the screen then hit the speaker button. "What?"

"About damn time you answered." There was no animosity in his friend's tone—just his normal, good-natured ribbing.

"I'm not sitting around waiting for your call. I've been on the phone. What do you want?"

"To tell you I told you so," he paused. "I'm headed to Vegas."

"What's in Vegas? Is Gambino there?" Gib had his full attention.

"I don't know, but I wouldn't be surprised."

"Stop being an asshole and tell me what you found and what's got you on a flight to Las Vegas." Rick pushed the list of names aside and grabbed his note pad.

"Gambino was here, but his employment was definitely unorthodox according to the lovely lady I spoke with in Human Resources. It's a real shame I have to leave town so soon," he mused.

"I don't want to hear about your missed liaisons. What did she tell you that has you on the move?"

"She was nervous and hesitant at first. A promise of a future dinner date got her to open up. I'll send you the bill."

Rick literally rolled his eyes. "And what did this promise get you—in the way of information, that is?"

"Gambino was at the casino. She didn't know him personally, but after the incident that Josie reported, Heather—that's her name—Heather expected to see Gambino be called into HR. The casino doesn't enjoy negative publicity, so a call to the principal's office, so to speak, is usually a given. When that didn't happen, she got curious."

"And?"

"The only thing in his file was an employment application."

"Nothing else? Working at a casino, they would have a background check at a minimum, never mind all the other crap you have to complete."

"There was nothing. She suggested they might have misfiled the documents, but since she wasn't supposed to be in there in the first place, she didn't look further."

"That still doesn't explain why you're on your way to Las Vegas. What was on the application?"

"Very little, per Heather. What stood out to her was Gambino's address. It wasn't local."

"It was Vegas," Rick finished for him.

"Yep, Vegas," Gib repeated. "Heather didn't remember a street address, but I don't need it. I'll find him or his trail."

"Who do you know in Las Vegas?" Why the hell was Gib so certain he'd be able to track down one man in a city that size?

"I said I had friends. I've got a plane to catch."

"You don't have luggage."

"Aww. You're worried about me. How sweet."

"Fuck you," Rick laughed.

"Save that for Finch. I'll check in when I know something." The line went dead.

If Gib said he knew people who would help, Rick had no reason to doubt him. His connections, which he kept close to his vest, had come through a number of times. This, however, was the first time Rick aware that those connections or friends extended outside the state of Florida. Gib's history was not an open book. He lived on the island before any of the team members had arrived. Colt was the first to make his acquaintance. They were both photographers and had become friends. Every member of the team was grateful to Gib. He'd pulled Colt from the pit of darkness he'd been buried in since returning from Afghanistan. The quintessential ladies' man, Gib possessed an innate ability to read people. He'd recognized the despair and guilt their former commander suffered. While others had tried, Gib, using photography as a form of therapy, had been the one to kindle a fire under Colt—to light the spark they'd all feared had been extinguished. Then Cat had arrived and finished stoking that flame.

For that reason alone, they respected Gib's desire for privacy regarding his past. It didn't mean none of them had been curious. Questions, either direct or inferred, were always quickly batted away like a home run into left field. He was a good friend and a good man who would do anything for his friends, including stepping in front of a bullet as he'd done for Cat. His past was his to share —or not.

Rick put in a call to Hernandez, but got his voicemail instead, so he reached out to Hernandez's partner, Morgan.

"I want to know everything you know or can get on Tony Gambino."

"We aren't your personal investigative service, Wilcowski. Hernandez told you we didn't find any connection to the criminal branch of his family."

"We may be looking in the wrong direction. He told his last employer he'd been taking care of a family member to explain his lapse in employment, but he was working at a casino in Tampa instead. The spa has his previous address as New York, but the casino lists it as Las Vegas. And why did a guy who held a management position at a casino in Tampa take a job as a concierge at a spa in Bonita?"

"Where did you get this information?"

"Same way we always do. We asked questions."

"I'll look into it, but you need stop your digging."

"Why? What have you found out?"

"I'm serious, Rick. Forget those names. This is deeper than any of us imagined."

"Someone we care for is a target. We don't walk away from that. We know how to operate with discretion. If we didn't, we'd be dead." Talking to the wrong villager. A slip of the tongue. It didn't happen because they were trained well and had a commander with a sixth sense.

"You need to stop. If you trip up…" Morgan warned.

"We won't." Silence followed the comment, so Rick continued. "Hernandez said he indicated he recognized one of the names."

"He did."

"And?" Rick pushed when Morgan didn't elaborate. Silence again. Rick checked his phone, making certain he was still connected. The green bar remained steady, and the seconds ticked by.

"Morgan?" Rick prodded, grabbing the phone from the desk and taking it off speaker.

"Still here."

"But not answering my question. Can I assume a non-answer is a can't answer?" Damn. Rick wished he knew which name had put Hernandez on alert. Was it the same one that had caught Jeremy's attention?

"If I were you, I'd make that assumption."

"Would I be correct?" The same stony silence filled the air. He wasn't getting an answer, which was as good as a 'yes'. "What can you share with regard to that list?" Rick tossed his pen on the desk as he got to his feet, frustration bordering on anger. He understood investigations took time, but his instincts told him they had little, if any.

"I can tell you a few of the people on the list are dead."

A crumb. "How many?" Hernandez had mentioned one person was deceased.

"Several. A couple for more than a decade."

"Which means whatever is going on has been going on for a very long time." Rick pinched the bridge of his nose. "Have you researched all the names?"

"We haven't done a deep dive, but we skimmed the surface."

"And you've found a connection you can't share, I assume." He waited a breath, but Morgan didn't respond. Patience. Morgan wasn't the enemy.

"When did the first person on the list die?"

"Thirty years ago."

"Shit. And the most recent?"

"June of last year."

"Were the deaths unusual?" Rick rocked back on his heels.

"I've told you all I can."

And he'd told him a lot—either by omission or in words. What the hell was going on for over thirty years and why was it now rising to the surface?

"What's your gut telling you?" Rick asked him.

"Pay for play." The line went dead.

Pay for play. Not blackmail. Something of value in exchange for the dollar amounts next to their names. Information? The fact that Morgan refused to discuss the names or what possibly linked them together told Rick they weren't random targets.

Lobbyists were known for making such payments in return for political favors, but Rick didn't recognize any of the names as politicians. Of course, he wasn't familiar with the names of every current and former member of Congress. Josie would know.

"Hey," he said. "How's the research going?"

"New York is a big city. None of the journalists I've reached out to have returned my calls."

"Switch to Las Vegas. Gib found Gambino listed Sin City as an address on his Tampa employment application."

"It's still a big city. But not as big. I'd best get started."

"And the names on the charm? Did you get anywhere with them?" Rick asked. "Did any raise eyebrows?"

"Unfortunately, yes. I was going to wait until I dug a bit more before I called."

"What have you got, Josie?" He pressed the tip of one of the colored pencils Cat used on her sketches into the pad of paper with the names on it. The point broke. He reached for a pen instead.

"There are at least two congressmen, a CEO of a defense contractor, a senate staff member…"

"I'm getting the picture. So far, each has a connection to the federal government either directly or indirectly. Am I right?"

"It looks that way. How'd you guess?"

"Because Morgan wouldn't talk. Couldn't talk," Rick corrected.

"I don't like this," Josie mumbled.

"I don't like this either. You need to stop working on those names."

"I'll be careful."

"I don't need Steve giving me a bloody nose because something happened to you." Rick didn't want Josie anywhere near this.

"You're not my caretaker. Besides, I know how to get information under the table," she argued.

"No, Josie. If we turn over the wrong rock, we have no

idea what might crawl out. Remember, you have Cece to factor into this."

"Like I'd forget. I'll discuss it with Steve. In the meantime, I'll switch over to Vegas. Did you know that some of these individuals are dead?"

"Yeah. Give me what you've discovered so far. I want to check with the local authorities and find out the cause of death."

"I haven't gotten through all the names, but I'll give you what I have."

Rick noted the information Josie had unearthed. She'd been busy based on the data she related. It still amazed him how she did it. She'd tell you it was how a good investigative journalism worked—a mixture of charm and tenacity. Whatever it was, he was glad to have her on the team.

"Please. Put the list aside and work on Gambino and any Vegas connections. There's something there."

"I'll do my best. How's Finch doing?"

"Good. She's got backbone."

"Can I assume the two of you have worked out your differences?"

Rick didn't fuel Josie's wishful thinking but smiled to himself. Things had definitely changed last night.

31

Finch opened the door to Cat's office where Rick had holed up. She was so excited she hadn't thought to knock. His back was to her. She came to a stop when she saw he was on the phone.

"We've made progress," he said to the person on the other end of the line. His head was down as he scribbled on a pad. "I'll let you go. Be careful—and give our little princess a kiss for me."

Her stomach churned hearing his sign off. He wasn't married. No one here would have hidden that from her. Did he have an ex-wife and a child? Was he still close to her mother? Did it matter? It was a good sign if he took an interest in his child. Because Finch had slept with him didn't entitle her to know his whole life's history. He had a right to his privacy, even if her life was an open book.

She was slinking out of the doorway as Rick turned to face her. His smile reached his eyes, which had instantly locked in on hers. Slowly, those blue eyes narrowed as he took her in. His light mood darkened.

"What's wrong?"

"Nothing. I didn't mean to interrupt—especially a personal call. I'm sorry."

"Personal?" He glanced at the phone, the question etched across his brow. "That was Josie."

"Josie?" Oh, shit. Of course. The little princess was Cece. She felt her skin warm with embarrassment. Why had her mind gone in the direction it had?

"What were you thinking?" he asked, rising to his six-foot-plus height.

"Good question," she muttered. "That I'd intruded on a personal call," she admitted. She took a step back as he took one toward her.

"Who did you think I was talking to?" He was smiling. Actually, he was wearing a very kissable grin.

"Who you talk to is none of my business," she answered, her back now against the wall.

"You're flushed. Your skin is a lovely shade of pink. I bet a minute ago those copper-colored eyes of yours were as green as a tarnished penny."

And he'd win that bet, so Finch kept her mouth shut. She chewed on her lower lip, making sure it stayed that way. The action only widened his grin. He nudged her chin until her lips parted, then he leaned in and took her breath away.

Jealousy fizzled as his mouth crushed hers. The kiss wasn't tender or teasing. It bordered on primal—and she fell into it. She ran her hands across his broad, hard chest—which wasn't the only thing that felt hard as steel. Moaning in pleasure, she pressed against him. Her hands ventured south seeking the buckle at this waist but need had her fingers shaking. His hands joined hers. Thank God he'd come to her clumsy rescue.

Instead of a rescue, he put some space between them.

"As much as I'd like to continue," he explained, "We'd

best save this for a more appropriate place and time." He kissed the tip of her nose.

"Jeezus. I'm sorry. I'm sorry," she said, tugging her blouse down, then smoothing the wrinkles with her hands.

"I started it. Rain check?" He grinned.

"Yes. The sooner the better." Slipping from her position between the wall and the solid male form in front of her, she stepped away. Thank God one of them had the sense to stop before she wrapped herself around his waist.

"I came in here for a reason. Plastering myself all over you wasn't it."

"Did you find something?" He returned to the desk.

"This." She followed him, handing him a piece of paper. It was small, about the size of a playing card and the thickness of card stock. "It was tucked between a couple of pages in my diary. I'd totally forgotten I'd received it."

They studied the item Rick placed on the desk. The white paper had faded to a soft yellow, but the drawing on it was still clear. Arabic lettering was captured inside a drawn heart.

"When and how did you receive it?"

"It came in the mail. Again, there was no return address." Her finger lightly traced the heart. "I didn't associate the card with anyone. I can't remember if I even associated it with my birthday at the time. I found it tucked into my diary near the date of my thirteenth birthday, though."

"But you never received another card? Nothing similar?"

"Not that I remember. I flipped through the rest of the pages, and that was the only item stashed in there." Finch dropped into the guest chair. "Seeing it again, I remember thinking the scribbles inside the heart were pretty."

"Do you know what they mean?" Rick snapped a picture of the drawing with his phone.

"I do now. I was able to identify it after downloading an app on my phone. It's Sanskrit for 'love'." She pressed her fingers into her eyes, determined not to choke up or let a tear escape. "This symbol specifically means a mother's love."

"I saw something similar to this on one of the charms. Let's see if Colt has worked his magic." Rick picked up his phone again, this time punching in a number.

"Hey. Have you developed the pictures of Finch's charms?" he asked his friend. "Can you enlarge the photo of the teardrop? We need to get a good look at the scrolling on that charm. Finch found a card in her diary that appears to have the same markings. Thanks."

"He'll have an enlargement for us shortly," he said, returning his attention to the card.

"Do you guys always drop what you're doing to help one another? I'm sure he has work to do. You all have work to do."

"We worked together as a team for years. It comes naturally to us. Colt understands this is a hot-button issue. He also knows I wouldn't ask if it wasn't important."

"Even if it is the same as the artwork in the heart," she said, "it won't get us any closer to whoever is behind this mess. It will only confirm what you suspected—that my mom, or parents, didn't want to leave me or regretted doing so."

Rick made his way around the desk and stood behind her. Once again he kneaded the muscles at the back of her neck. "You're right. It doesn't help with the mystery, but that doesn't mean the message isn't less important. Some-one, your mother would be my best guess, went to a great deal of trouble to let you know you were loved."

"Why the hell didn't they just tell me? Why not send a letter instead of a puzzle it's taken years to realize even existed?" She left the warmth of Rick's touch and wandered over to study one of the stunning photographs on the wall. "What if I'd never known?"

Realizing she had at least one parent who cared after years of dismissing them, even hating them, tore at her heart. Why would they leave her the way they had if they loved her? After recent events, logic told her it was for her protection. Did they have any idea what she went through as a child? What was so damned important that they'd risk leaving a child without knowing what would happen to her?

She felt the heat of Rick's body grow as he pulled her back—cocooning her against his warm chest. He rested his chin on the crown of her head.

"Whoever put the bracelet and charms together was brilliant. I don't believe you would have gone your whole life without knowing. I suspect there's a message waiting for you somewhere in your future or one that was missed."

She twisted in his arms and stared into his eyes. "Why? Why do you believe that? I'd stopped hoping to hear from any family since I was six or seven years old."

"Because of that sheet of paper on the desk. There had to be a reason they were forced to make the unimaginable choice. My instinct tells me your mother loved you too much to put you in danger."

"Why send the card? Why did I receive those charms?" She rested her head against his chest. "If they wanted to break all ties, why did they reach out to me?"

"I'm not a psychologist. I can only guess."

She pressed her head to his shoulder, inhaling his earthy, masculine scent. Her muscles relaxed and her heart melted. As she nuzzled her face into his chest, she discovered something she didn't know she'd been missing her entire life—comfort. This was what it felt like to be comforted. Perhaps there was more, but she settled on this new, unique feeling.

"Are you okay?" he asked.

"I'm fine." She nuzzled closer. "If you have no objection, I'll stay right where I am while you explain your theory."

He brushed his hand over her hair. "Sure."

"What's your theory?"

"One of your parents either unearthed or stumbled on the information. Whatever it was, it forced them to run. If the person, or persons, hunting them didn't know your mother was pregnant, they wouldn't have had a reason to look for you. Running with a child would have put them, and you, in danger. Whatever they discovered must have been explosive, because I can't imagine making the decision to hide their child in the foster care system unless they believed it was the only way to keep you safe."

"That's so hard for me to comprehend. How much worse could my life have been with them than it was in those foster homes?"

"They're the only ones that can tell you why they did what they did. But I think whatever happened, or whatever they learned, scared them into that decision."

"Any theory as to why I was sent the charms? I didn't know they had any meaning until all this starting happening." She hadn't moved from his arms. Discussing her parents wasn't something she did. Why think of them when those thoughts only engulfed her in feelings of hurt and betrayal? Rick's strength, logic, and compassion maneuvered her through those feelings. "What if I'd never come to understand the charms were a message, as well as a puzzle?"

"Another puzzle we need to find the pieces for, but we'll do it—together."

There was a tap on the office door. "Sorry to interrupt." Colt paused at the entrance to the room. "I figured you'd want to see this sooner rather than later." He held out a large photograph.

"Is that the enlargement?" Rick reached for the photo.

"Yes. Does it match your drawing?"

Colt joined them as Rick placed the photo next to the card Finch had found. The photo was strikingly sharp.

"They match." Instinct had told her they would. Still, a band around her heart tightened. Had her mother loved her so much that she'd let her go?

32

Finch's shoulders sagged. Rick could feel the weight they were bearing simply standing next to her. She'd gone from hating her birth parents for abandoning her—to the possibility that they loved her more than most. A sharp and difficult turn to make. He reached for her, but she stepped away. Her spine straightened and her shoulders went rigid. The wind had been knocked out of her, but she bounced back quickly.

"What's the significance of the drawing?" Colt asked, his eyes assessing Finch.

"Love," she answered. The word came out on a whisper. "Specifically, a mother's love."

"It's Sanskrit," Rick explained.

"Which would mean whoever sent the charm went to a great deal of trouble to find it or have it made. I suspect its custom-made."

"Did you enlarge the other side of the charm?"

"I did, but the maker's name has been scratched off. No help there."

"Get both pictures to River. She buys pieces for her

one-of-a-kind masks from a variety of vendors, including jewelers. If we're lucky one of her suppliers will recognize the work."

"Will do. Are you okay?" he asked, turning to Finch.

"Getting there." She gave him a half smile. "Adjusting to the fact I may have been wrong my entire life."

"I have no doubt you'll make it." Colt gave her shoulder a little squeeze. "Shayne wanted to come back. Do you want to see her or Cat?"

"I'll get with them shortly. I need a minute."

Colt tapped Rick on the arm. A tilt of his head signified he wanted to speak with Rick alone. He glanced at Finch, who was now tracing the lines of the Sanskrit message.

"Let's give her those minutes," Colt said in a low voice. "I need to talk to you."

Rick faced Colt in the hallway outside of Cat's office. "What's happening?"

"I got a call from Gib. He just landed in Vegas."

"Jeezus, did he beam over there?"

"Got his friend's private jet and made a few calls on the way." Colt propped his shoulder against the wall.

"What did he tell you?" Rick looked up to his former commander, both figuratively and literally. Colt was a good four inches taller than any man in the unit.

"He's got a line on Gambino."

"Seriously? Does Gib know where to find him?"

"Not yet. He's working on it."

"Damn. I swear that man has ESP. Who the hell does he know who can find that kind of information?"

"One thing I've learned about Gib is that he enjoys keeping his secrets. I don't expect we'll have to wait too long before we hear from him again."

"Not at the rate he's moving." Gib never ceased to

amaze him. "Josie is, metaphorically, digging in the desert, as well."

"It's a big town, but only one primary industry. No doubt there's a hell of a grapevine between the casinos. If Gib or Josie tap into it, there's a good chance they can find information on Gambino and what he's involved in."

"We'd better hope Gambino isn't wired to the same grapevine, or he'll know someone is stalking him." Rick glanced at the door. He hated for her to be alone while digesting what she'd learned, but the woman had guts and asked for time. She didn't need him, but he hoped like hell she wanted him.

"Anything else interesting happen today?" Colt asked.

"I talked with Morgan earlier. There was a lot of innuendo, but not a lot of concrete information. My interpretation of the short and convoluted conversation was it involves government subjects. He wants us to stop researching the names from the list, but he came short of making it an order."

"Interesting," Colt said, raising an eyebrow. "Did he give you any clue of what we're looking at?"

"He used the term 'pay to play'. Considering his tight lip, my next leap is an exchange of information or favors for money. Since it looks probable this involves people in or close to the federal government, it would be a safe bet that we're dealing with trading dollars for information. Las Vegas would be the perfect place for that type of operation. People throw a lot of money away they can't afford to lose."

"Espionage? Over a thirty-year period?" Colt shook his head. "It's hard to imagine an operation going on for so long and no one noticing."

"I admit it's far-fetched, but I don't have a better theory—not yet, anyway." Rick paced the hallway. "Tony

Gambino can't be the one behind this. He's not old enough."

"Unless it's a family business," Colt suggested. "One that's passed on to the next generation."

"You mean the Gambino family?" Rick paused. "Our friends in Tampa can't find a connection between Tony and the rest of his family…"

"It's an obvious connection, though," Colt interrupted. "I guarantee you they're taking a second look now. I'm going to finish my spread for the magazine so I can dedicate myself to this. Let's meet again tonight," he added as he walked toward the front door. "With any luck, we'll have something new to kick around."

Finch was still fixated on the photographs, or pretending to be, when Rick reentered the room. She glanced over her shoulder. Those copper-colored eyes were now clear. There was no sign of tears.

"If one of these pictures comes up missing, don't send anyone to my place looking for it." She winked. "They're stunning."

"They are that," he agreed, walking toward her. He gathered her close. She settled against his chest in what was becoming a familiar posture. As she relaxed, it lifted the tension from his shoulders. "Are you doing better?"

"Yeah. It was a bit of a shock to find out what you believed your entire life might not be true. I fooled myself in to thinking I'd put my parents out of my mind—that they didn't deserve my attention or even my anger. To find out it's possible I was totally wrong takes a bit of getting used to. Not to mention the guilt."

"Guilt is a heavy burden to bear. Let it go now. Colt can tell you about the weight of carrying it. It serves no purpose but to eat at you. If they loved you, your parents wouldn't want that." He touched his cheek to the top of her head.

"And if they didn't?"

"You would still be wasting your emotional energy. There's no reason to feel guilty. You were an abandoned child, regardless of the reason, that hurt. You didn't know —couldn't even imagine—a scenario where they left you because they wanted to protect you."

"Do you think they're still alive?" She slipped from his arms and turned to face him. If there was such a thing as a hopeful look, she was wearing it. Damn.

He slowly exhaled. He had no way of knowing for sure, but he didn't think she'd ever meet her parents. There'd been no contact in over a year. No charms. No notes. Nothing. Whoever was behind the messages had either gone to ground or was no longer able to send them. His instincts told him it was the latter.

Anger clawed at the pit of his stomach. Why hadn't her parents reached out to someone else—anyone else? The FBI. Homeland Security. Hell, even an investigative journalist like Josie, who would have notified the authorities. Instead, they'd sent the information to Finch, who didn't understand the message she was receiving. The act had also made her a target. Rick wished they were alive because he very much wanted to know the reason behind their actions.

"I don't know," he answered. It wasn't a lie. "Once we get the DNA results back, the FBI will run it through the NamUs database."

"NamUs?" She cocked her head.

"It's a database that matches DNA with unidentified persons." He'd intentionally not used the word 'remains'— it felt too harsh, but she was smart. She understood what he was saying. It took a second for the sadness to replace the previous hopeful look.

"You believe they're dead, don't you?" She didn't wait for his response, dropping into the nearest chair. "I feel like I'm on an emotional rollercoaster."

"Let's wait until it slows down before we get on that ride," Rick suggested. He was sorry the inquiry into the bracelet had planted that seed of hope. "We're still missing a lot of information."

He crouched in front of her chair and took her hand. "We'll figure this out. I'm sorry if I got your hopes up only to shoot them down."

A smile—small, but bright enough to add a hint of sparkle to those beautiful eyes—graced her face.

"It's okay," she said. "You don't control my world. I've learned to live with bad shit in the past. It may take a while, but I'll get back to the surface. The difference this time is I'm not swimming alone." She squeezed his hand.

Rick touched his lips to hers. She lingered with the kiss before pressing her palms against his shoulders and nudging him away. "We don't want to get our engines started again, and we have a lot of work to do yet."

It was the first time she'd openly acknowledged herself as part of this team. Accepting that she had friends and support was a major step. He admired the shit out of her.

"What else did Colt have to say?"

"Gib is in Las Vegas. He has information Gambino has ties to the city. Josie is also working the Vegas angle. She's looking for any history she can find on him." He leaned against the desk. "We'll go over everything tonight."

"Tony never mentioned Las Vegas to me. Just Tampa and New York."

"Tony's work history appears to be in casinos. Which adds additional questions. Why was he working with you at

Spa Terra, and why didn't the facility examine his work history?"

"Should I try calling Tony again? Maybe he'll talk to me, assuming he answers." She reached for the cell phone they'd given her.

"Let's wait until we hear what the others have discovered," he suggested, pushing away from the desk. "Are you done going through that encyclopedia you call a diary?"

"A social worker gave the book to me when I was eight or nine years old. She suggested I write things down, especially if I was unhappy. I was unhappy a lot. She said it would help. I guess her experience told her foster kids needed to do a lot of writing." Finch stood. "It helped. Putting my fears, sadness, or anger on paper acted as a release valve. There were days it saved me."

Rick swept his hands over her hair, resting them on her shoulders. "I'm glad," he said, laying a whisper of a kiss on her forehead. "Do you still write in it?"

"Occasionally."

"Am I in it?" he asked, giving her what he hoped was a seductive grin.

She chuckled on her way out the door. It was good to hear her laugh.

33

Rick kept his eye on Finch as they ate dinner. He'd been worried she'd slip back into the darkness that had engulfed her earlier. She appeared to have rallied and while the laughter she'd floated on as she'd exited Cat's office was gone, her eyes remained bright. She fit right in.

"Updates?" Rick asked, scanning the room. He'd squeezed in next to Finch on the couch. The sofa was positioned against the wall under the south-facing windows. They had drawn all the blinds for safety reasons.

"I got a few 'fuck offs' from a couple of the foster parents," Troy volunteered. He sat in one of the chairs left by the previous owners of the property. Shayne was snuggled in his lap. "Most remembered you," he said to Finch.

"I imagine I wasn't easy to forget. I wasn't the most accommodating foster kid."

"There weren't a lot of negative comments, so maybe you weren't the bad ass you thought you were. I suspect they're used to troubled kids. The only ones I didn't reach were the Simpsons. I haven't been able to locate them, but I'll keep looking."

"Hopefully, they haven't reincarnated themselves in another state and are fostering kids again."

"I doubt it." Troy looked at Finch. "Not with his history."

"What else have we got?" Rick asked.

"I found the maker of the teardrop charm," River volunteered. She and Kevin sat side-by-side on high-top stools in front of the breakfast bar. Kevin had pulled the stools together, so they were touching. His arm hung over River's shoulders.

"Good going," Colt said. "I figured that would be a long shot."

"Your picture was a lot of help. Even though the maker's mark is obscured, there was enough visible that one of my vendors recognized it. An independent artist makes charms and other pieces of jewelry. He sells them online and through a small storefront in Colorado."

"Do we know who bought it?" Rick asked.

"That's where it comes to a dead end. The artist recognized the charm as one of his custom pieces, but he didn't remember who ordered it. Unfortunately, he is very tidy when it comes to record keeping."

"Unfortunately?" Finch asked. "I'd think that would work in our favor."

"By tidy, I mean he keeps records only as long as the law requires. If the charm had been purchased more recently, he'd have the sales record. Sorry."

"You've got nothing to be sorry for," Kevin assured his wife. "You did a hell of a job." He pressed a kiss to her cheek.

"It's unlikely the buyer used his or her real name and contact information—not with all the precautions we've seen them take," Rick noted. "It was another long shot. Good work, River."

"How far did you all get with the names on the list?" Colt asked. Rick's former commander sat at the other end of the small, floral upholstered couch. Cat sat on the stuffed arm of the piece of furniture, her bare feet tucked under Colt's massive thighs. Only someone as petite as Cat could resemble a pixie perched on a bed of flowers.

"The boys in Tampa haven't reached out to me again. I can understand why after digging into the names." Rick paused. "Did you see a pattern, Steve?"

"I'll say. The individuals I've identified all have a connection to the government in one fashion or another. One is a military contractor, another a staffer for a U.S. Senator—a senator who serves on the Intelligence Committee—and a few lesser players. All are in spitting distance to people in power." Steve leaned against the breakfast bar; his arms crossed. Josie occupied the remaining barstool in front of him.

"Pay for play…." Rick mused. Damn, this was getting ugly.

"What does that mean?" River asked.

"Paying or giving favors in return for information. I figured it was just flat-out blackmail when I first saw the names and dollar amounts."

"We all did," Steve agreed.

"What's the difference, and why do you all look so serious?" River asked.

Rick pressed his elbows against his thighs. "Blackmail is exchanging money to keep a secret. Pay for play works in reverse—exchanging money to receive information."

"Someone has a great deal of money," Troy commented. "We're talking millions of dollars."

"Has anyone considered a lobbyist?" Kevin asked.

"You said everyone identified has a relationship with the government."

"Lobbyists don't exchange favors with defense contractors," Josie pointed out. "Defense contractors are usually the ones doing the lobbying."

"Morgan and Hernandez have clammed up," Rick said. "I think we've got all we're going to get out of them. Do you guys remember Jeremy? Army Intelligence?" Rick asked.

"Yeah," Colt said. "What did he have to say?"

"Nothing yet. He said he'd be in touch, but he recognized one name. I'd swear it, but he wouldn't elaborate."

"That's not good." Colt ran his hand through his thick, black hair.

"That's what my gut told me," Rick agreed.

"It's not a good sign when someone with Jeremy's experience in intelligence recognizes a name and won't elaborate." Steve's stance was no longer relaxed. He'd moved from his position behind Josie and now stood next to her, his hand clasping her upper arm.

"I don't know if this will add another piece to the puzzle or muddy up the waters," Josie said, "but after Rick suggested I stop researching the names, I checked the causes of death on the ones we know have passed away. Two were suicides, one a car accident and one, apparently, of natural causes."

"Why did you say 'apparently'?" Finch asked.

"Because there are many ways to disguise a murder and make it look natural. If there's no reason to suspect foul play, no one would have requested an autopsy. The man was older. It wouldn't be surprising if it was a heart attack or stroke."

"This has been going on a long time," Rick agreed. "Stands to reason some of the targets would be older."

"Two suicides. Statistically, I'd say that was pretty high for the number of names on the list." Colt swiped the hair from his face again. Cat fussed with it, tucking the loose, black strands behind his ear.

"You guys have a theory," River said, with a hint of annoyance. "Want to fill the rest of us in on it?"

"Here's my take," Rick said. "Jump in if you have a differing opinion. In a nutshell, a person, or persons, unknown has been paying off gambling debts in exchange for information. Information that looks to be tied to our nation's defense or intelligence—or both."

"Thirty years of intelligence gathering, and no one got wind of it?" Cat slid onto Colt's lap, wide-eyed.

"Damn." Shayne was gawking at him.

"Yeah. Damn," Rick concurred.

"I know it's not our usual way of handling things," Steve said, "but I think we need to walk away from this one and leave it to the Feds. If you're right and, unfortunately, I don't disagree with your supposition, we're talking espionage. That's a job for the spooks. We're good, but we ain't that good."

"Nor do we want to know what they exchanged for that money," Troy added. "Steve's right. We need to leave this to the big boys."

"I'm so sorry I got you involved in this shit," Finch said, getting to her feet.

"Don't start apologizing again," Shayne warned her. "None of this is your fault."

"It keeps our lives interesting," Kevin smiled. "We'd get bored with the same routine all the time."

"If we use your logic, it's Rick's fault." Cat grinned. "He found you on the beach. Look, we can't always control what happens in our lives, but things happen for a reason. You're supposed to be here," she added, firmly.

"I can't understand why one of my parents would send this damning information to me. What if I hadn't kept the bracelet? No one would know what we know now."

"It would be nice to understand the reason behind that decision," Rick told her.

"I thought you agreed to drop it." Finch's brow creased.

"We'll let the government investigate the individuals, the money, and the information that was exchanged, but we still need to find out who's been trying to abduct you."

"I don't have any knowledge of this scheme, and I don't have the bracelet. Why would they come after me now?" Finch scooted her way to the edge of the couch. She was absently picking at her cuticles.

"Because they want to know what you know," Steve said.

"I don't know anything." She threw her hands up then dropped them into her lap.

"You do now," Troy pointed out. "Not the details, but you know there is a conspiracy of some sort."

"But I didn't know it when they forced me onto the boat. This still doesn't make sense to me."

"Their plans have changed, obviously. They went from a surreptitious search of your apartment to a kidnap plot. They must believe you know something that will harm them," Rick explained.

"Killing me would be simpler, wouldn't it?"

"Hush," Shayne chastised her.

"Based on their actions, we can surmise they want to know what you may know and if you've shared that information. They can't learn what you know if you're dead. Ouch." Colt rubbed his bicep where Cat had knuckle punched him.

"Sorry," Cat said, still scowling at her husband. "He's usually a bit more tactful."

"You said Tony started working at the spa two months ago?" Rick asked.

"About that time. I can't give you an exact date."

"Tony's home is in Las Vegas," Josie interrupted. "He owns a condominium there."

"But he has an apartment here." She glanced at Rick, a contorted look on her face. "The sheriff's office went there to check on him. He has a Florida driver's license."

"My contact, Victor, confirmed Gambino's primary residence is in Nevada," Josie eyed Rick and Finch. "I trust him. If he says Vegas is Gambino's home, you can make book on it—pun intended."

"Having property in Nevada doesn't mean he can't have an apartment here," Rick pointed out. "As for his driver's license, Florida allows an individual to keep a license from another state and still apply for one here. Snowbirds," he explained. They all lived here full time and understood the flight of people from the north when the snow started falling. "This is the first time I've actually known anyone who possessed licenses from two states."

"It makes sense," Troy said. "He couldn't get the job at the casino or spa without a local license. Almost every employer in Florida in requires one. They don't want to hire people who plan to take off as soon as the weather gets hot."

"How is Tony connected to this shit?" Shayne asked.

"What did your contact know about him?" Rick prodded Josie.

Finch fidgeted. Sliding her hands from beneath Rick's, she began twisting strands of hair around her finger. His instinct was to grab her hand and tell her to hold on, but he resisted. She was wired. She'd only feel trapped if he did. Instead, he rested his hand on her thigh, giving her an anchor if she needed one.

"Tony is well known on the Strip," Josie continued.

"Does he have a job?" Kevin asked.

"Victor hasn't been able to pinpoint an employer, but Tony spends a lot of time in various casinos chatting up high rollers."

"Marks." Rick instinctively knew the man was scouting for gamblers who would fit the requirements of his employer.

"Are you thinking what I'm thinking?" Colt asked.

"If you're thinking Gambino goes fishing for individuals who match the characteristics of those on the list, then we're on the same page."

"Then what is he doing here?" Finch asked.

34

It had all finally clicked. She searched the faces in the room. The men wore knowing looks. "The traitor—and that's what he or she is, a traitor—doesn't know what I know or who I might have told. There's only one way to find out. Interrogate me. Am I right?" she asked Rick.

The hesitation along with the worry written across the lines on his forehead answered her question before he spoke. "That would be my assumption," he said as he nestled her next to him.

At least he was honest. No one in the room overrode his admission. Her respect for them went up several notches. Her fear level climbed even higher.

"Espionage is punishable by death. Damn it. They must wonder if I have a fuckin' key that will lead to the ringleader. I'm guessing contacting Tony and asking him to reach out to whoever his boss is to proclaim my ignorance wouldn't help," she offered, half joking. Another part of her wished it was that simple.

"If our guess is correct, they won't stop until they're

stopped." Rick didn't mince words. Even after they first met, he'd been clear and straightforward. It was when they were dealing with intimate issues he became vague—even uncertain. In all honesty, the same went for her.

"Why are we assuming the incident with Tony and the information on the bracelet are connected?" Finch asked. "Do they have to be tied together?"

"The chances of you being in possession of information related to government secrets, being the target of two attempted abductions, not to mention the incident on the causeway, are astronomically slim. Yeah, I think they're connected."

Rick didn't sugarcoat it.

"He tried to run me off the road and into the bay. That doesn't fit your scenario. No one would get information out of me if I was dead."

"Maybe they're trying to scare you. You'd be an easier target on the run than you are here with us," Troy suggested.

"Makes sense," Colt agreed. "When that didn't work, they came after you here."

"Why haven't they tried again?" Finch was aware of the trickle of sweat making its way south between her breasts. Her heart skipped a beat at the memory of the confrontation in the garden.

"They may simply be waiting for another opportunity," Rick suggested.

Honesty wasn't always a good policy, she decided. Nothing like being a target.

"Do we know where those two bozos are?" Kevin asked. "Has there been any sign of the boat?"

"As far as the two assholes go, we've got nothing to work with except the sketch River drew and we haven't gotten any hits on it," Rick explained. "I suspect they're laying low—for the time being, at least. Or they were expendable. They were obvious fuckups."

"Troy and I contacted the marinas in the area." Steve lifted Josie off her stool. "None of the dock masters have seen a boat matching the description we have."

"We told them the boat may try to slip in at night and help themselves to whatever they need. They'll pass the word to other marinas along the coast. I'm hoping one of them will catch them on a security cam," Tony added. "We've left our number just in case."

"We need to get home," Steve said, as he and Josie made their way to the door. "Call if you need us."

There was a twinge of envy as the two exited. She hadn't missed the gentle touches or the way the two looked at one another. Looking at the other couples in the room, they appeared to share the same devotion to each other. What would that feel like?

"Has anyone heard from Gib recently?" Rick asked, scanning the room.

"Other than the text I got earlier today, I haven't." Colt stood in one fluid motion, sweeping Cat into his arms as he did. She hugged his neck, placing a kiss on his cheek. "Vegas never closes, but it doesn't start hopping until dark."

"You don't think he's hurt, do you?" Finch's gut knotted. He'd gone on a hunt for information on Tony and Tony was definitely in the bad guy's corner.

"We'll hear from him when he has something to share," Rick said. "But if it makes you feel better, we'll call him in the morning."

"It would," she answered. "You said he didn't have the training you guys did." Despite their training, she was worried for every man and woman in the room. She understood their logic in wanting her to stay close, but she'd live with the guilt for the rest of her life if one of them was injured or, God forbid, killed.

"I'll contact Morgan or Hernandez," Rick said. "Let them know the people on the list are theirs to chase and fill them in on what we know. We'll concentrate on Tony."

"THIS FEELS SO STRANGE." Finch gazed out the passenger window as they made their way to Rick's. Despite the subject matter of the evening, she'd felt at home tonight.

"What feels strange?"

"Huh?"

"You said something feels strange," Rick repeated as he reached his home. "What's bothering you?"

"Sorry. I was thinking out loud." She unbuckled her seat belt then twisted in her seat until she was facing him. There was a hint of worry in his expression. She wanted to kiss his brow and relax those worry lines. "I've never been with people like you. You look out for one another unconditionally. You trust one another explicitly. Trust doesn't come naturally to me, but I trust you and your friends."

He nibbled at the corners of her mouth. Ripples of heat shot through her. She tried to pull him closer, but he nudged her away.

"Let's take this inside," he said, brushing his forefinger across the ridge of her nose.

As she reached for the door handle, Rick tapped her on the arm. "Wait until I get to you."

"You said they didn't know where you lived." Nerves crackled across her skin at the possibility that they'd traced her here—to his home.

"You can never be too careful."

His implication was that if there was someone planning to ambush them, he'd be between her and a bullet. Fuck that. As soon as he was out of the truck, she opened her door and bolted for the stairs.

"I'm in a hurry," she quipped in response to his swearing. She heard his heavy footfalls as he rushed after her. The little game of chase had her laughing—until the crack of a gunshot split the night air.

35

*R*ick knocked Finch onto the landing at the top of the stairs the instant he heard the rustle of brush next to his home. The shot followed a nano second later. He felt the heat as the bullet clipped his right bicep. He plastered his body over hers. They were sitting ducks on the platform, but he'd dropped his keys as they hit the deck. The chances of getting safely inside were non-existent, regardless. To get in the house, they'd have to make themselves targets. The security light above them made the situation worse. It spotlighted them.

"Stay down," he ordered Finch. Keeping her covered, he took aim and shot out the light. They were showered with tiny shards of glass, but they now had the slight advantage of darkness on their side. The slats in the railing didn't give them much cover. They'd never make it down the stairs to the truck.

Another bullet clipped the wooden railing and lodged itself in the front door inches from them. Rick was grateful the guy wasn't using an automatic weapon. They'd have been torn to shreds by now. He briefly considered why their sniper hadn't gone that route. Did he want them dead, or was he trying to frighten them off?

Sirens wailed in the distance. Although his home was relatively isolated, he was close enough for another resident to have heard the shots—an unusual event on Sanibel. He cocked his head, listening intently. This time, the rustling of shrubbery wasn't subtle. Of course, the asshole wasn't sticking around to face the mass of officers who would descend upon them at any minute.

He pulled his phone from his pocket and hit the contact number for the station. He'd continue to shield Finch until the cavalry arrived. His assumption that they were safe here had almost gotten her killed. "Are you hurt?"

"I'm good," she answered. "You're not. You're bleeding."

Glancing at her bare arm, he could make out the dark spots where droplets of his blood had settled. Ignoring the sting, he focused on the call, relating information to dispatch. They would relay it to the responding officers. As soon as he saw the strobing lights approaching, he eased off Finch and settled on his stomach at her side. He kept his eyes focused on the surrounding area. The gunman was probably halfway to Fort Myers. The small department wouldn't have had time to set up a checkpoint leading to the causeway. Even if they did, it wouldn't be reasonable to stop every car leaving the island. He didn't have a description of the shooter—or shooters—or their vehicle.

"We need to stop the bleeding," Finch snapped, pushing against his weight.

He pressed her gently against the wooden surface. "Stay put until the area is clear. It's only a nick." Damn. He'd managed to get through several tours in the Middle

East without getting shot. Instead, he gets winged on his doorstep.

"How the hell did they find us?" he muttered.

"I'm sor…"

"Don't say it." She was going to apologize for putting them in danger. He didn't want to hear it. They'd opened a can of worms. He should have never assumed they wouldn't find her here.

As vehicles filled the area, he rolled to his feet returning his gun to its holster. He turned to help Finch, but she was already sitting, her feet planted on the step below her.

"Need help?" he asked, slipping his left hand under her arm.

"Let me sit for a moment. I don't think my legs will hold me."

Footsteps thundered up the stairs. It did not surprise him that his captain was leading the responders.

"Are you sure you weren't hurt?" Rick tenderly brushed his hand over Finch's head. "Sorry I had to tackle you."

"You saved my life. I'm guessing they've moved on from the kidnap phase of their plan."

"It would seem so." And what exactly did that mean? He didn't believe there were two different factions after her.

"There are times when I think I should politely ask you all to move off this island," his captain commented as he reached the top of the stairs. "Life was a lot quieter on Sanibel before you and your friends arrived."

"You'd be bored without us," Rick quipped. His left hand covered his bleeding arm.

"How bad is it?" Pulaski asked.

"Flesh wound." He grinned. "Never thought I'd say that." And it hurt like a bitch.

"And you?" Pulaski addressed Finch. "Are you all right, ma'am?"

"Just a few bruises, I think. My old ones were fading, so it was about time to replace them."

Rick helped her to her feet, admiring her wit, and internal strength. "Finch, this is Captain Pulaski. Captain, Savannah Finch."

Pulaski nodded at the introduction. "Let's get that arm attended to, then you can fill me in on what happened."

"We need to talk privately," Rick told him. "There's some big-time shit going down that I'm certain the Feds don't want us to share."

"You guys really know how to step in it, don't you?"

"Trust me. We don't go looking for it."

The powerful rumble of Steve's Mustang could be heard before the vehicle came into view. He parked along the street. Colt's jeep pulled in behind him.

"You two get with the paramedics." Pulaski pointed to the open rear doors of the emergency vehicle. "I'll see what we've found. If you don't need to be transported, we'll meet after you're patched up."

"I should have security footage. If they left the cover of the overgrowth at any time, then we should some have pictures."

Pulaski nodded.

"Is LCSO on their way?" Rick didn't want the local sheriff involved in this mess. The fewer people who got wind of what was going on, the better.

"I told them to stand back until they heard from me, but we're going to need their help. There's only so much our department can do."

Sanibel PD was capable but small. They would need the help of the Lee County Sheriff's Office forensics at a minimum. They'd have to be careful sharing information considering what they'd stepped into—to use Pulaski's words.

"We need to talk before I give a formal statement to the County," Rick told his captain as he hopped into the EMS unit. He reached out with his good arm to give Finch a hand.

"Then, unless you're bleeding out, stick around." Pulaski walked away, shaking his head.

"What the hell happened?" Colt and Steve stood at the open doors of the EMS unit.

"Why the hell didn't you call one of us," Steve demanded.

"We were busy dodging bullets. Besides, apparently I didn't need to call you. You're here."

He took a quick look at Finch. The technician was checking her pupils. His pulse ticked up. "Did you hit your head?" Had she banged her head against the landing when he'd tackled her?

"No. I'm fine."

"She has a scratch on her cheek. It's just a precaution," the medic responded.

"Are you going to tell us what happened?" Steve repeated the question.

"We were ambushed. Two shots. They came from the shrubbery over there," he indicated with a nod of his head. "Pulaski wants a meeting when we're finished here. He needs to be in on this," Rick added.

"Do you want us to join you?" Colt asked.

"What?" He was watching the paramedic clean the cut on Finch's cheek. He hadn't meant to hit her so hard.

"Do you want us there?"

"No. You guys can't add anything to this clusterfuck. You need to put the others on alert. It appears the game plan has changed."

36

Steve had found Rick's keys, so Rick was able to follow Pulaski to the station after the medics had finished with them. After they arrived, his boss directed them to the small conference room, then left them alone.

"Are we under arrest or something?" Finch was nervously scanning the small room.

He'd noted her hesitation as they'd climbed the steps to the elevated building that housed the police department. Rick had assumed that her body was feeling the effects of being tackled on the stairs. He should have considered that she'd have a negative reaction to being in a police station, given her history.

"No. Are you okay?"

"Just peachy. I have such fond memories of being in police custody."

"You're not in custody. The captain needs to know what's going on. We can speak freely with him without fear of accidentally sharing classified information."

"I don't understand."

"Pulaski is probably cleared all the way up to the White

House. It's a long story which is part speculation and part fact. Don't be afraid to talk to him. He's a good guy. He'll glean out any information that's not intended for the public records."

"Like the information that was on the charm?"

"Yeah. Like that." She was picking at her cuticles again. She'd be biting her fingernails next. He reached for her hands and was painfully reminded of his injury. "Shit."

"You should be at the hospital." Her voice was sharp with worry.

"I'll be fine. Next time I'll duck faster." He smiled, but the expression wasn't returned.

"I think it's time I left the island. Hear me out," she spoke over his objection. "You said to your friends the plan had changed. I got the message. Whoever was shooting at us wanted me dead. They're no longer interested in snatching me."

"We can still keep you safe. I let my guard down. I won't do it again." He swiveled the chair so he was able to reach for her with his left hand. She pulled away, the action hurting him as much as his wound.

"I don't blame you for that, but if I hadn't been with you, you wouldn't have been shot. Your earlier arguments against me leaving don't hold water anymore. It would be safer for you and your friends if I left."

"And where the hell would you go?" Rick was pissed now. She didn't trust him to keep her safe.

"Why is it your problem?" She shoved away from the table as Pulaski was returning to the room.

"If you guys are having a lover's spat, save it for later. Sugar and caffeine," he said, setting two vending machine bottles of Coke on the conference room table. "You need them both along with these." A bottle of aspirin appeared out of his hip pocket.

Finch beat him to the aspirin. Uncapping the bottle of pills, she placed three on the table in front of Rick, then loosened the cap on one of the soda bottles, sliding it next to the pills. Her crisp, abrupt movements spelled anger. She'd returned to being the obstinate, defensive woman he'd found on the beach. He needed to get her alone and talk sense into her, but his boss was waiting.

Pulaski placed his phone in the center of the table. "Start at the beginning. I'm going to record this on my personal phone. I'll cleave off any intelligence information."

"You know what this is about?" Rick asked.

"Not all the details. Let's just say I got a heads up. Now you two tell me everything you know—and then tell me you're going to stay out of it."

Rick filled him in, stopping occasionally to check with Finch to confirm his retelling of events was accurate. Pulaski peppered her with a few questions about her past but focused mostly on events that occurred since the trip she'd taken on the boat with Gambino.

"Any idea why their objective has changed?"

Rick glanced at Finch. She'd been calm. Too calm, in his opinion since the questioning began. Distant.

"I'd rather not speculate," he finally answered. He wasn't going to verbalize that his best guess was that Gambino was cleaning house. He feared a fraction in Gambino's group. The team was still trying to confirm Gambino's role in all this. Other than the boat trip and his convoluted history, there was no direct link between him and the information discovered on the charm—at least not yet. If he was involved, however, getting rid of Finch would sever that link.

"What if they were aiming at you?" Finch shifted in her chair. Fisting her hands, she dropped them into her lap.

"You were the one that was shot. Maybe they wanted you out of the way so they could get to me."

His gaze traveled up to meet those beautiful eyes—eyes that now welled with tears. Shit.

"Well?" Pulaski asked, eyeing Rick. "Is there any possibility he meant to hit you?"

"No," Rick said, stabbing Finch with a look. "I know where she was in relation to the bullet's trajectory. I got hit because I was tackling Finch to the landing."

Finch shoved her chair away from the table. "I need to use the ladies' room."

Rick stood, ready to escort her.

"We're in a police station and I'm capable of using the bathroom on my own."

Rick would have ignored her surly tone and followed her out the door if his phone hadn't vibrated. Gib. It was about damn time.

The din of noise in the background had Rick distancing the phone away from his ear. "Where the hell are you?"

"Where do you think I'd be in Las Vegas? A casino. The Luxor to be exact. I'd step away to a quieter spot if I didn't have my eyes on someone."

"I'm with Pulaski. Is it okay to put you on speaker?"

"Go ahead." Despite the noise, Gib's voice came through loud and clear. Rick placed the phone on the conference room table and hit the speaker icon.

"Hey, Captain," Gib said.

"I assume you have some information to report, Mr. McKay?"

"Call me Gib," he said. "I haven't finished my survey, but I'm beginning to see a pattern."

"What sort of survey? What kind of pattern?" Rick leaned over the phone. What the hell was Gib doing?

"I was able to locate an individual who is familiar with Gambino. Tony appears to spend a lot of time at various casinos chatting up big losers. My contact described him as a military drone seeking out a specific target."

"What are you getting at?"

"That I think it's time for the professionals to be conducting interviews."

"Would you care to elaborate?" Rick pushed.

"I was directed to two gamblers who are regularly seen with Gambino when they're in town. One works in the aerospace industry. The other for a U.S. Senator. Both of them are way over their heads in gambling debts."

"He trolls for marks," Rick stated, knowing that was exactly what the man was doing.

"Or Gambino keeps his thumb on individuals he already knows are willing to trade their gambling debts for information," Pulaski surmised.

"Both would be my guess," Gib agreed. "I tried but didn't get much out of them. I played the part of a whining, big loser. Neither of them suggested a way out of my predicament. The only information I got from them were their names. One of them is on the list."

"Get rid of that list." Rick almost jumped into the phone. "This investigation is going to the Feds on a silver platter as fast as we can get it to them."

"How'd you get them to tell you about their gambling debts?" Pulaski asked. "It's not the kind of thing most losers share."

"They didn't. I got the information from a friend."

"The investigators are going to want the name of your friend," Pulaski warned him.

"Not a problem. I'll touch base with a few other sources and see what they know."

"No, you're not," Rick told him. "This part of the

investigation has gotten too hot. Let the Feds handle it. You can give them any names that will help in their investigation."

"Let me see what else I can discover about Gambino. I'm here, after all."

"Am I not making myself clear? Leave it alone," Rick ordered his friend. "Finch was shot at this afternoon."

"Was she hurt?"

"Bumps and bruises. We hit the deck pretty hard."

"Damn. Is she there?"

"She's in the ladies' room." Rick glanced at his watch. What the hell was keeping her? Was she sick? People reacted to stress in different ways. "I'm going to check on her."

"Fine. I gotta run."

"Gib…"

The phone went dead.

Pulaski shook his head. "Don't worry about him. He's smart enough to know when it's time to leave. I'll talk to Morgan and Hernandez. You go check on Ms. Finch."

Rick listened at the door of the women's bathroom for any sounds emanating from within. It was quiet. He tapped on the door. "Finch? Are you in there?" Silence.

"I'm coming in." It was late. Unless a female officer was in the station, the chances were slim another woman would be occupying the room.

His stomach twisted as his quick inspection of the small lavatory proved it to be empty. As he raced to the front desk, he dialed Finch. Pick up. Pick up. God damn it, pick up.

"Did a woman leave here?" Rick asked the officer on desk duty. The phone in his hand continued to ring.

"I'd say ten minutes ago. She said you guys were done with her."

"Fuck." Rick's feet couldn't move fast enough. He disconnected from the unanswered call as he hit the bottom step. He dialed Troy. His friend answered as Rick was surveying the parking lot. Her beat-up, piece of shit car was gone. He hadn't expected different, but his gut still twisted.

"What's going on?"

"Finch is gone. She walked out of the police station while I was on the phone with Gib."

"And you didn't stop her?"

"She was supposed to be in the ladies' room. I don't have time to argue with you. Can you trace the phone you gave her?"

"No. It's a burner, remember?"

"Shit." He'd been hoping for a miracle.

"Why did she run out on you? Did you piss her off again?"

"Same argument. She believes she's putting us all in danger. Getting winged tonight by that shooter put an exclamation point on her logic." How would he find her? She was a target and on her own.

"Did she take your truck? We can track that."

"She took that wreck of a car you told her was safe to drive." He immediately regretted the remark and its harshness. "Sorry. Let me talk to Shayne. She may have an idea where Finch went."

"I'll raise Colt and have him check next door in case she ducked in there."

"What's wrong?" Shayne asked when the phone was handed off. "Is Finch all right?"

"She hasn't called, I take it?" He took the stairs two at a time. He needed to let Pulaski know what was going on then run to his place, but seriously doubted she'd retreat there. She'd want to put distance between all of them as quickly as possible.

"No, I haven't. What happened?" Shayne's voice came across as both scared and accusatory.

"She's reverted to worrying she's put us in danger. She snuck out of the station. Do you have any idea where she might go?"

"On the island? No. I heard Troy call Colt to ask him to check the nursery. Does she have wheels?"

"Her car, despite its damage, is still functioning."

"Can't you put out an APB or whatever you guys call it?"

"She's not wanted for a crime."

"What if they kidnapped her again?" Shayne argued.

Rick doubted they were interested in taking her alive now. That shot was aimed at her head. He didn't share that information with Shayne.

"If we can't track her phone, can we track her credit cards? They were delivered here yesterday. She'll need gas or food."

"Good idea." And one he should have considered. "Mention the cards to Troy and try calling Finch. She may answer for you."

"I hope so."

Rick found Pulaski in his office busily tapping away at his keyboard. No doubt, putting together the 'official' report—one that wouldn't include confidential intelligence information.

"Finch has taken off. If you've got any ideas up your sleeve on how to find her, I'd appreciate the help."

"I'm to assume she doesn't have a phone or a tracker on her car."

"A phone, but it's untraceable." They'd made certain of that. "You saw her vehicle. It's easy to spot." Rick glanced at his phone again hoping Shayne or Colt had found her.

"You know we have no legal reason to stop her, right?"

"Understood."

"If you or your friends do anything to skirt the law in order to find her, it better not wind up on my desk."

The words echoed behind him as he shut the captain's door. He needed to get home. Finch knew the alarm code. How good was she at picking locks? Chances were slim that he'd find her there, but she may have felt she needed her laptop. Had Troy put a tracking device on her computer? He hadn't asked.

His place was void of police and forensic units when he returned. If there were any stragglers beating the bushes, he didn't see any signs of them.

Entering his home, he caught the faint scent of the woman he'd made love to the previous evening—the woman he'd had every intention of loving tonight. The stillness engulfed him. He'd walked in the door a thousand times and was always greeted by silence, but he'd never felt this hollowness.

Shaking off the unfamiliar gloom, he went to the guestroom where Finch had stored her things. The computer sat on the top of the dresser. Shit. Even if Troy had planted a tracking device on the laptop, it wouldn't matter now. She'd been in a big hurry to get off the island. Her car was a rolling wreck and would stand out on Sanibel or Captiva. It was also easier to get lost on the mainland, assuming that was her plan.

Except for the few items at his place, everything was in her apartment. That would be her first stop—and it would be his, as well.

As he pulled out onto the street, his phone buzzed. He

hit the speaker button on the steering wheel. "Did you reach her?"

"I tried a few times, but she's not answering," Shayne said. Her voice resonated worry.

"I'm headed to her apartment. Think outside the box. Is there anyone besides us she could go to for help?"

"She's never mentioned anyone but her co-workers and she said little about them. I think that boat trip was her first attempt at making friends. I honestly thought we were making headway—gaining her trust."

"Finch didn't run because she didn't trust us. Don't get that in your head. She wants to protect us. Where would she go?" He stepped on the gas as he hit the causeway bridge.

"I don't know. Her apartment or work. She never mentioned a place that was special to her. I'll keep trying to reach her. Rick? Find her before something happens to her."

37

———

inch hoped her damaged vehicle wouldn't draw too much attention. She didn't want to waste time explaining the condition of her car to authorities. Both her headlights were functioning. She wasn't able to guarantee the same about her taillights.

She didn't have a final destination in mind, but she had to get as far away from here as possible. No one near her was safe. She'd figure the rest out after she put some distance between her and the people she'd come to care for —especially Rick. Remembering his bloody arm made her stomach churn. It was her fault he'd been hurt. What if he'd been killed because of her? How did he expect her to live with that?

Finch didn't realize how tense she was until she released her grip on the steering wheel after pulling into a space in front of her apartment building. Her knuckles hurt and the tips of her fingers tingled as blood returned to them. She took a second to check the area before grabbing the borrowed purse and digging out the single key from an inside pocket. With a last look over her shoulder, she ran for the stairs.

Safely inside, she grabbed a large, blue beach tote from the closet and began stuffing it with clothing. Her small travel case was still at Rick's. She mentally slammed the door shut on the sadness that tried to creep in. After topping off her supplies with toiletries from the bathroom, she headed for the tiny kitchen.

She threw protein bars, tuna packets, and crackers into a reusable cloth grocery bag. Who knew when she'd get the chance to eat again? She opened the refrigerator, reaching for bottles of water and noted the food she'd be leaving behind. By the time someone came to clean out the place, it would be spoiled or covered with mold. Even with the eminent threat of discovery, her conscious wouldn't allow her to leave the ugly job for anyone else. She pulled the garbage can from under the sink and began furiously dumping the contents of the refrigerator into it.

As she knotted the ties on the bag of garbage, there was a knock on the door. It was close, but she managed to stifle the squeal. The blinds were drawn so she couldn't see out, nor could anyone see in. Her car was out front, though. Anyone who recognized it would know she was here. Eyeing the short hallway, she abandoned her efforts to dispose of her perishables. Instead, she reached for her tote and the sack of food, then headed toward the bedroom balcony.

"Finch? This is Marge Murphy. Are you okay?"

Finch stopped. Going out the front door was preferable to dropping off the balcony. She knew Mrs. Murphy well enough to know she wasn't getting past her either way. The lady had the eyes of a cat and the hearing of an owl. She sighed, peeked out the blinds to make sure Ms. Murphy was alone, then opened the door.

"What's going on?" her neighbor asked. "Your car looks like it was at the losing end of a monster truck rally. What's with your face? Does that cut need attention?"

"I'm sorry," Finch said, taking a step away. "I don't want to be rude, but I can't talk right now."

"Are you in trouble? Can I help?"

"No." The word had come out hot and angry. She hadn't meant to snap, but she'd already endangered too many innocent people.

Mrs. Murphy's eyes widened but quickly narrowed into laser focused slits. "You're running," she stated, glancing at the bags at Finch's feet. "Did that man you left with the other day hurt you? I thought he was helping you."

Of course, her neighbor would remember Rick and Finch's last visit to the apartment.

"Nothing like that. He's a good man. I've inherited a bit of trouble and I don't want anyone to get caught in the flack helping me—that includes you. I need to be going."

"Okay, but call if you need me." She waved a large mailing envelope. "I need a pen," she said, pushing her way into the apartment.

"I really need to go," Finch reiterated. She couldn't take the chance Rick or anyone else would show up while she was there. Her palms were sweating. She fought against the urged to run.

Mrs. Murphy scribbled something on the envelope, pulled the trash bag from the can Finch had abandoned. "I'll take care of this," she said. "You take this." She shoved the padded envelope at Finch. "It arrived yesterday. The postman left it at your door. I didn't want to take a chance on a porch pirate spotting it. I wrote my phone number on the back."

The envelope was too large for the small mailbox assigned to each apartment. Her box had to be stuffed to the gills with junk mail by now, but she pushed that worry behind her. She hadn't had time to deal with it before. She had even less time now.

"Thank you," Finch said, pulling the door shut behind them both.

"Come with me to my apartment. I want to give you something."

"I don't have time," Finch kept repeating.

"Then move your ass."

Finch almost smiled. If she lived long enough, she hoped to be a pistol like Mrs. Murphy.

"Step inside if you're nervous," she said, "but I'll only be a second."

Finch did slip inside the apartment but stayed close to the door. True to her word, Mrs. Murphy returned from her bedroom in a flash. "Here," she said, shoving a fistful of bills into Finch's hand. "You'll need cash."

"I was going to swing by the ATM." She figured that was the safest place to get cash in the event her cards were being tracked. It wouldn't surprise anyone she'd gone home. Using the nearest ATM wouldn't be a big, red flag. She'd figure the rest out later.

"This will get you a little farther. Now go."

Finch leaned over to give the feisty woman a kiss on the cheek. She regretted not getting to know her better. Now she'd never have the chance.

Finch battled against tears that threatened to fall as she pulled out of the complex's parking lot. She was finally surrounded by people who sincerely cared about her, and she was leaving them. It would be selfish to stay. And then there was Rick. Her feelings for him went much deeper than simply caring—and all the more reason to get away.

As she expected, Spa Terra was closed when Finch arrived, but she had the passcodes for the door and security system. Mrs. Gonzales had expected her to return to work, so Finch was going on the premise nothing had changed. There were items she'd purchased to use in her job. The spa provided equipment and supplies for the therapist's use—all of them good, but Finch had gone a step beyond. She'd purchased upgraded tools of the trade. She wanted the best for her customers. There would come a time when she'd have to start over. There wasn't time to dwell on that right now. She wasn't capable of looking further than one step ahead. Anything else would be overwhelming. Her immediate plan was to get her stuff and get out.

Walking toward the building, she didn't think it was possible to feel any sadder than she already did, but the weight of leaving a job she loved cast another shadow over her. She enjoyed working at the spa. While she couldn't call her co-workers friends, she got along with all of them. The owners took pride in the business, and Finch had built up a nice clientele in her short time at the spa. Then there was her promise not to quit via text. She didn't see where she had a choice any longer. Her life had spiraled out of her control.

38

———

*G*oddamn fuckin' crazy drivers. Rick smacked his fist against the steering wheel before he jumped out of his truck to see if anyone was hurt. Why the hell did someone need to be in such a friggin' hurry that they'd pass on a bridge which would widen into four lanes less than a quarter of a mile ahead? The driver had clipped a car as it ducked back into the single lane to avoid an oncoming motorist. That was all it took to set off a chain reaction sending several cars careening into one another—and creating a blockade. Fortunately, Rick hadn't been close enough to become part of the entangled mess, but close enough to watch the bastard take off.

He called it into the station. As he suspected, units from both the Sanibel PD and Lee County were already on the way. He confirmed the description of the vehicle responsible for the mayhem, then began making his way to the cars that hadn't escaped the pile-up. Most of the vehicles had minor damage leaving the drivers and passengers shaken, but uninjured.

The police and tow trucks made fast work of clearing the bridge. While he'd waited, he tried Finch's phone again. Nothing. No ring, no voicemail—nothing. Where was she? He was assuming she'd headed for her apartment. If she was taking off, she'd need clothes. His second guess was the spa. It could be a safe place to hide temporarily. Since it was after hours the place would be empty. She might also have personal items there she'd want or need. He was guessing—shooting desperately in the dark hoping to find her before anyone else did.

As traffic began to crawl, he hopped into his truck. He no sooner engaged the ignition and was inching forward when his phone rang. Gib's name appeared on the display screen.

"What's going on?"

"I got a message from a contact telling me that the last person who was asking questions about Tony Gambino didn't fare too well. He suggested I'd be safer back in Florida."

"What happened to the person who didn't fare well?" Rick already knew the answer.

"He landed in the morgue."

"Tell me you're on your way home."

"No need to panic," he argued. "I just thought it was information you needed to know. I can still open a few doors for the FBI. I know people here."

"Call Morgan or Hernandez. Fill them in. We have no idea who might be compromised by this scheme. Until we know otherwise, only share information with those two. Share everything you know, but first get the hell out of Vegas. Don't poke your nose in anywhere else.

"Gib," Rick implored. "I've never questioned your past and I'm not going to start now. I don't care who you know and why you think they can help, but this is way over our heads. We're dealing with a national intelligence issue and, as a friend, I'm asking you to get your ass out of there."

Rick heard the sounds of traffic and people passing by as Gib, apparently, pressed on. He didn't possess the skills and training the rest of the team had. He made up for it with his connections, loyalty, and uncanny ability to come up with whatever they needed, when they needed it. It was his way of contributing to the team. Rick pulled out a carrot and dangled it on a stick, knowing it would get Gib moving.

"We need your help here. Finch is missing. We're looking for her now."

"How the hell did that happen?" There was a snap in Gib's voice. He was annoyed. Rightfully so.

"I screwed up. Just get your ass back here. We may need your eyes and ears."

"On my way. I'll call our friendly Feds from the plane."

One of these days Rick would figure out Gib's connections and friends, but today was not that day.

AFTER WHAT FELT LIKE AN ETERNITY, Rick arrived at Finch's apartment building. He pounded on her door but there was no answer. It wasn't surprising since her vehicle was absent from the parking lot. For a second, he considered breaking in. He wanted to know if she'd been there and, if so, what she took. She may have left a clue to where she'd gone. Busting in, though, would draw attention, and that would only slow him down.

Returning to the ground floor, he made his way to the rear of the two-story building. Studying her small balcony, he considered ways to access it. Sliding glass doors were a snap to by-pass and because the rear of the building faced farmland, he would likely go unnoticed. There was a rain gutter attached to the side of the building. He doubted the flimsy metal would hold his weight. He was visually searching for an alternative path when Mrs. Murphy opened the door to her small terrace which sat directly beneath Finch's balcony. Blue tips accentuated her gray spiked hair. She was a small woman, but small didn't mean frail. Mrs. Murphy stood straight, her steely eyes cutting through him. She held a cell phone in her hand, ready to call for help if needed.

"I remember you from the other day. Are you looking for Savannah?" she asked.

"Yes, ma'am. I'm with the Sanibel Police Department," he reminded her. "She's in trouble. I'm trying to find her."

"That explains why she was so jumpy." Lifting the hem of her tie-dyed, racerback shirt, Murphy slipped the phone into a pocket of her yoga pants.

"You saw her? When?"

"I heard her come home just short of an hour ago. A package was delivered for her yesterday. Since I was holding it for her, I'd been keeping one ear open. When she answered the door, it was obvious she was frazzled."

"Did she say where she was going?"

"Slow down a second and I'll tell you what I can."

He didn't want to "slow down". He needed to move and move fast, but he needed whatever information Mrs. Murphy could share.

"I appreciate your help, but I need to catch her."

"Understood." Her shoulders snapped to attention.

He'd bet Mrs. Murphy was ex-military. She'd be an interesting woman to talk to, but now wasn't the time.

"She made it clear she was in a big ass hurry. There

was a large tote at her feet stuff with clothing. Items were simply crammed in the bag. There was a second bag filled with bottles of water and food—the kind with a long shelf life."

"Did she say where she was going?"

"No, but she was in a rush to get there. I'd have offered to let her stay with me—I have a gun and I know how to use it—but I knew what her answer was going to be, so I didn't bother."

"You're right. She wouldn't put you at risk. She doesn't want anyone else getting hurt."

Rick didn't miss the quick flick of those sharp eyes to his bandaged arm.

"Is that why she took off alone?"

"Yes, damn it." There was only one other place left to check. He started toward his truck, then stopped to hand her his card. "If you see or hear from her, call me. Please."

"You care for her," she noted, taking the card.

"Very much." So much it hurt. He couldn't lose her.

"I gave her some cash," Mrs. Murphy yelled after him. "It wasn't much, but she seemed relieved."

"Thank you." It was a kind gesture but lessened the chances of Finch stopping for gas and using her credit cards any time soon. He suspected Steve or Troy had found a way to track their usage. He didn't ask how. It probably was illegal.

He stopped, turning to face Finch's neighbor. "Do you know what was in the package you held for her?"

"I'm not that nosey. It was a large, padded envelope. No return address. It came by U.S. Mail."

Which meant there was no way to track it to the sender. That alone had his radar pinging. "Anything else?"

"She took the envelope with her. It wasn't bulky, or bulging. I didn't see any signs of tampering. It had massive amounts of postage. Whoever sent it wanted to make sure it got here. I wrote my phone number on it, hoping she'd call if she needed help. As for Savannah, she looked scared, confused, and sad all at the same time. You need to find her."

inch punched in the code to reset the spa's alarm. After the beep sounded, her hand hovered over the keypad. Something felt off.

Being the last one to leave most nights, she was familiar with the place after dark. Normally there would be a soft light emanating from the shelves where they displayed products for sale. The small glass counter under the register should have had similar lighting. Neither were illuminated. There were no sounds coming from the area of where the therapy rooms and offices were housed. That wasn't unexpected this time of night, but it added to the ccrincss.

She had the urge to call the police. And tell them what? The place was quiet? The light in the display cases had been switched off. They weren't going to send a unit to check on the lighting. The spa was closed, after all. What else should she expect? Paranoia was not a good thing. She was imagining shit—blowing crap out of proportion. She needed to keep her wits and her head on straight.

On her way to the spa, she'd decided to head south

instead of north. Find a place in the Everglades or the Keys to hunker down, calm down, and think things through. Anyone wanting to leave the state by car had to drive north, so heading the opposite way would, hopefully, keep her under the radar. Rick would probably figure it out. She half hoped he did. Running wasn't the brightest move, but fear was a great motivator. She was no Jason Bourne. How long would she be able to stay in hiding? Would she find herself on the streets that she'd tried so hard to avoid? Forcing her worries to the back of her mind, she focused on the here and now.

Instinct was urging Finch to leave, but it had taken her years to save and acquire the tools of her trade. Besides, she was here. She'd get them and get out.

She slipped through the doorway and into the spacious area where clients relaxed prior to their treatments. The Zen-like music that normally filled the room had been silenced for the evening. Water still trickled from the man-made waterfall built into the far wall. A soft glow from the recessed lighting above the feature, accentuated the playful way the liquid danced over the rocky surface.

Finch entered the hallway and noted a light coming from the end of the corridor. She bypassed her treatment room and headed toward the break room. It had windows. The light was a beacon for anyone looking for her. She'd turn it off and grab her stuff on the way out.

When she reached the end of the hall, a vision from an old slasher movie flashed into her head. Spinning on her heels, she pressed her hand to her chest in the insane attempt to keep her heart from slamming against her sternum. No madman stood behind her with a knife poised, ready to strike.

As her fear abated, her nose crinkled. Another sniff had her questioning the unfamiliar odor. It was strong, and definitely not pleasant. Had food been left out to spoil? Her gut said differently. She had a feeling her day wasn't getting any better.

Steeling herself, she took a step into the room. Her eyes shot to the countertop hoping to see a discarded meal or bag of fast food left behind—something simple to explain the sickening odor. No such luck. Instead, two men were sprawled across the tile floor between the vending machines and the counter. Chairs and tables were in disarray, apparently pushed aside as the bodies fell. She didn't know death had a smell until today.

Covering her nose and mouth with the hem of her blouse, she inched closer. Any thought that either of them was alive was quickly erased. The taller of the two men had a hole in the center of his chest. Blood filled the grout lines, channeling the dark red fluid away from the body. His skin was a sickening gray color. His face, however, was untouched. Despite his pale, distorted features, she recognized him as the man from the boat—the one who had yanked her off the dock.

She assumed the other man was the second half of the team. He was facedown on the floor, a few feet away from his partner. The back of his head was literally blown away. Bone, blood, and tissue spattered across the glass front of the soft drink machine.

She needed to get out. God. Why the hell was she sticking around? What if she wasn't alone? Hands trembling, it took several attempts to unlock the front door. She made it to her car before dropping to her knees, gagging. The business's alarm wailed over her gasps for air. It didn't matter now. She needed the police. The sooner, the better. And she wanted Rick.

The burner phone was still clutched in her right hand.

Surprised she hadn't dropped it in her frenzy to escape the scene, she dialed 911 with trembling fingers.

"What's the nature of your emergency?"

"They're two men. Dead. I found them." The words tumbled out of her mouth.

"Where are you? Are you injured?"

"I'm…" The words froze on her tongue when a cold metal cylinder was pressed against the base of her skull.

40

$\mathcal{R}$ick used his GPS to navigate a less traveled route to the spa. He didn't want to get bogged down in traffic again—not when Finch's life might depend on him getting to her. He was going on his gut. If she wasn't at work, he'd be forced to wait until one of her credit cards showed up on Steve's radar. He wouldn't find her trolling the streets of Southwest Florida. He'd stand a better chance of winning the lottery.

If he wasn't so worried, he'd have done a fist pump when he spotted Finch's Toyota in the parking lot of Spa Terra. His assumption that she'd stop by work to grab personal items had been right. If he'd guessed wrong, he'd have missed her altogether. Pulling into the parking lot, he could hear the spa's security alarm. The sound sliced through him like a sword. Something was terribly wrong.

As he took off toward the spa, a Lee County Sheriff's Office patrol car cut across his path and stopped. His detour around their unit was cut short when both doors opened, and the deputies pointed their weapons at him.

"Freeze!" one officer shouted. "Hands behind your head."

Rick didn't make any sudden moves, particularly since his weapon was clearly visible. He locked his fingers and rested them on his head, then moved to fully face the officers.

"Detective Rick Wilcowski, Sanibel PD. My badge is in my back, left pocket." He kept his hands on top of his head where they could be seen. The deputies studied him carefully before the sergeant nodded. "There's somebody in there who may be in trouble. We're wasting time out here."

"Take out your badge nice and easy."

Rick kept his right hand resting on top of his head as he reached for the identification with his left. The fact that he still wore his work clothes with both his name and the police department's insignia emblazoned on his polo shirt may have factored into the trust they were giving him. Clasping his forefinger together with his thumb, he shifted just enough so the two could easily see he wasn't reaching for another weapon.

The screeching alarm finally silenced. Timed out, he suspected. At least the rest of his conversation with the two deputies wouldn't be a shouting match.

Why had the alarm sounded in the first place? Finch should have known the code. If they had changed it since she last worked, she would have beat it out of there, yet her car was still here. She wouldn't have waited for the police to arrive. She'd be terrified of being accused of breaking in.

The sergeant tossed the ID and badge holder to him after giving it, and Rick, a good, hard look.

"What's your business here?"

"I'm looking for the woman who drives that car. She

may be in trouble." He dropped his hands and took off toward the building no longer caring if he was a suspect.

He drew his weapon as he approached the building. Fortunately, the two officers, Garcia and Taylor, didn't question his response or his assumption of the lead. Instead, they unholstered their weapons, as well. Tugging on the door handle, it did not surprise him to find it unlocked.

The deputies moved quietly, following him into the business. The door separating the lobby from the bowels of the establishment was open. That struck him as odd. The open door allowed them to see to the end of the long hallway. Light spilled from the last room on the left.

Rick and the two LCSO officers made quick work of checking each of the treatment rooms. At the end of the corridor, one deputy peeled off to inspect the office to the right. Rick and the sergeant moved to the left. The instant he noted the metallic odor, his heart sank. His feet moved on their own. His new companion stretched his long arm out, stopping Rick's momentum. The guy wasn't only tall but solid—and right.

Rick wasn't a rookie. You didn't rush into an unknown situation—but he'd been in battle long enough to recognize the acrid, rusty smell of blood. His singular focus was that Finch might be in there.

Nodding his understanding, they made a quick visual check of the area. Only after he stepped into the room did he allow the breath that had been trapped in his lungs to escape. Two men, bloodied and lifeless, lay sprawled on the floor near the front of the room. No one else was there.

"Finch!" he called out with the slightest belief that she was hiding within the range of his voice. "Savannah!" There was no response.

The sergeant's call for additional units barely registered. He needed to get past his fear and focus. He made his way to the victims. Tables and chairs had been knocked on their sides where the bodies had fallen. Rick didn't have to check for a pulse to know that both men were dead. No one could have survived their wounds. He recognized the guy with a bullet hole in his chest from the sketch River had done based on Finch's description of the man who struck her. His gut clench again. She could very well be in the hands of the bastard who had inflicted this damage.

"The place is clear," the second deputy said, joining them. "What the hell happened here?" he asked, taking in the room.

The smell of death permeated the space. There was no sign of a struggle other than the toppled furniture. After a quick visual inspection, Rick didn't see any damage to the walls or ceiling where a bullet might have penetrated. Two shots. Two men dead. Odds were they'd known their killer.

"We have a missing person," Rick pointed out to the deputies. "Savannah Finch's car is still outside."

"What makes you think she's not the killer?" the second deputy, Taylor, asked.

"Finch has never owned or fired a weapon." She was afraid owning one would only lead to trouble. "Whoever shot these guys was a professional. These were kill shots. She's been the target of two attempted abductions. Earlier this evening someone took a shot at her. My money is on one of these guys." He didn't have time to get into the details. The LCSO hadn't wanted to get involved in the incident on the boat. Not enough facts to open a case, they'd said. Now Finch was missing, and he was pissed they hadn't taken the attempted kidnapping seriously. Neither had he at the time, he reminded himself.

"Maybe she shot them in self-defense, got scared and ran," Sergeant Garcia suggested.

"She did not kill those men. Someone else had to have been here." It would also explain how the two men got into the spa. Finch wouldn't have let them in voluntarily. Had someone forced her to witness the murders? God, he hoped not. Whoever killed these guys must have Finch. Why? Did they think they needed a hostage?

There was only one person who was connected to both these men and Finch. Tony Gambino. He'd been involved in this mess from the very beginning.

The three men must have arrived in one vehicle, otherwise Finch's wouldn't be the only one left behind. Why come here? Unless they'd set a trap for Finch. Had Tony lured her in again?

There was nothing else to be found here. Finch was gone. He turned away from the two officers.

"Where do you think you're going?" Garcia asked.

"To check her car. She may have left something behind that can tell me where they've taken her."

"The car is off limits until the techs arrive. You know that."

He was ready for a fight, but before he could mount an argument to ignore protocol and search the car himself, the radios on both officers' shoulders sprang to life.

"Possible abduction in progress," the dispatcher's calm, clear voice sounded through their radios. "We have an open mic on a phone. Unable to track the location of the phone. The caller is a female. Suspect doesn't appear to know the line is open. Female is making it clear she's not a willing passenger." There was a pause. "Suspect has a gun."

"He must have Finch. She has a burner phone. They won't be able to pinpoint her using it. Ask the dispatcher if she's given any hint of location or destination."

"This is Sergeant Garcia. We may have an ID on the

caller. Has she said anything that would give away her position?"

"Caller mentioned a marina. Paradise, I think. The conversation is muffled." There was a pause. "The noise in the background has changed. I think they are out of the car."

"Send units to the Paradise Marina on Fort Myers Beach," Rick said, tossing his business card to the sergeant. "Let them know I'm on my way."

"This isn't your jurisdiction. You need to stay put."

"Like hell." Rick ignored the order and ran to his truck. He was a witness, at best. Not a suspect.

He took a second to buckle his seat belt only because the sounding alarm would interfere with the calls he had to make. As he tore out of the lot, his first call was to Steve.

"I need at least one of you at the marina ASAP. Someone has Finch. Her phone line is open and connected to 911. The Lee County dispatcher said she mentioned Paradise Marina. I'm on my way but I just left the spa, and they have a big head start." Sanibel was closer to the marina than Bonita. Rick was in his personal vehicle, so he'd have to do without lights and sirens. That didn't mean that he wouldn't break a few traffic laws on his way.

"You certain that's their destination?"

"She was sending us a message."

"I'll send up a Bat signal."

"Whoever has her, and my money is on Gambino, killed two men—my guess is they're the guys from the boat. You need to watch your back."

"Roger that," Steve replied.

Rick disconnected then dialed his boss.

"That BOLO from the County has something to do with you, I assume."

Leave it to Pulaski not to mince words. "Yes. It's

Savannah Finch. I was one step behind her. Someone else was one step ahead. I asked the sheriff to send units to the Paradise Marina. Can you follow-up on that? Looks like whoever took Finch killed two people."

"They're already on it. Rick…"

"What?" he asked when Pulaski paused. "What is it?"

"The open mic went dead."

Crap. "Did the dispatcher try calling her?" His tires left the surface of the road as he crested the Matanzas Bridge.

"She didn't and you know why. It would only alert her captor that she'd been in contact with the police. It may be as simple as her battery going dead."

Dead. Not a word he wanted to dwell on.

41

———

inch was sweating bullets—figuratively speaking. The semi-automatic handgun in Tony's lap was no joke.

She recognized the road they were on. Tony had driven the same route the night of the infamous boat trip. Why were they going to the marina? And why hadn't he killed her along with Beavis and Butthead? Tony had been silent since he'd forced her into his car. It had been parked behind a neighboring building which explained why she hadn't seen it in the spa's parking lot. His eyes constantly darted from the road to the rearview mirrors and back to the road again.

Finch struggled to free her hands, but it was useless. Tony had bound her wrists together with a large zip tie. Not tight enough to cut off her circulation but too tight for her to slip free of the restraint.

"We're headed to Paradise Marina. Aren't we?" Finch didn't know if the line to the emergency operator was still open or if they could hear what was being said. She'd slipped the phone in her pocket without disconnecting the

911 call. Tony apparently hadn't realized what she was doing when he'd come up behind her. It was the only thing in her favor since arriving at the spa. Troy had told her the phone couldn't be pinpointed, so she was hoping to pass along information about her location.

"Shut up."

"Who were those men, Tony? Why did you kill them? Was I supposed to die the first time you took me to the boat?" She kept talking—raising her voice with each question.

"If you were this talkative at work, the boat trip might not have been necessary. I needed information from you. I had a few ideas to make you talk, but those idiots had other plans for you. You're damn lucky I didn't let them get their hands on you. And you repaid me by jumping off the boat. I didn't see that coming."

"I never had any information to give you. I still don't," she lied.

"Bullshit. I want what your mother sent to you." He was convinced he needed her, or she'd be dead by now. His tone had her leaning hard against the door, putting as much distance as was possible between them. She glanced at the door's handle, then quickly dismissed the idea. Falling from a moving vehicle at this speed was a death sentence. She'd wait for a better opportunity and hoped one would come.

"I didn't know my mother. Why would she send me stuff?" Keep him talking.

"Cut the crap. A year ago, they finally caught up with the bitch and, surprise, surprise—she had a daughter. You. She sent you something. What was it?"

"What will it take to convince you? I don't have anything. Even if I did, I'd be an idiot to give it to you. I'd be dead as soon as you had your hands on it."

"There are easy ways to die and hard ways." The smirk told her he'd prefer the hard way. Didn't matter. The bracelet was in the hands of the FBI. What little she did know she didn't plan on sharing. She was dead either way.

"Why did you email me?" Square peg. Round hole.

"A bit of fun and a shot in the dark." He glanced her way but didn't wait for an answer. "There was the other possibility that you'd be less trustful of your knights in shining armor." He shrugged. "That didn't work, but I bet it scared you, didn't it?"

"Did you have fun killing those men?" she asked, ignoring the question.

"Clean-up on aisle one—or in this case, the break room." He laughed at his own sick joke. "Stupid jackasses. They got it into their heads you would be able identify them. If they killed you, we'd never know what you've learned and if anyone else had gotten wind of it." He shrugged. "I'd plan to kill the two of them after we were done with you, but their stunt on Sanibel tonight moved up the deadline." He laughed again. "*Dead*line. Get it?"

"What were you doing at the spa? Why were they there?" Finch once again wrestled with the binding on her wrists. Who the hell kept zip ties in their trunk? Apparently, people like Gambino did. If his first attempt at abducting her included restraints, she'd have never made it to shore. Hell, she wouldn't have even tried.

"I told them I was meeting you there and they could finish what they started. Imagine my surprise when you waltzed in. Fortunately, I'd already taken care of the two dicks or we wouldn't have been able to have this little chat."

"I have nothing to tell you." His hand sent her head slamming against the passenger window.

"We want to know what your mother told you. And

you're going to tell us." He made a quick turn onto the road leading to the marina.

"I've never spoken to my mother." She stopped fighting the bindings. The struggle was deepening the cuts into her wrists. "I don't even know who she is."

"Really, Mary Pierce?"

Using her foster name was a slap to her face. No one had called her that in years. And what did it have to do with her mother? "What do you know about my mother?"

"What do *you* know about your mother?" Tony snapped.

"I wasn't aware of her as anything other than an incubator until this past week." And Finch still didn't know how to process what she'd recently learned.

The seat belt snapped across Finch's chest as Tony slammed to a stop in the parking lot of the marina. He made his way around the front of the car, his gun fixed on her the entire time. Opening the passenger door, he grabbed Finch by the hair, yanking her out of her seat.

"Let me go. I can't help you."

His response was to shove her further down the dock. Water lapped at the pilings. She heard the distant sounds of traffic from Estero Boulevard. There were no sirens. Funny. She used to hate the wail of sirens. She'd welcome them now.

"You'd better hope you can. And keep your trap shut, or I'll shoot anyone who sticks their nose out to see what's going on." He punctuated the sentence by pulling the slide back on top of the Glock, loading the first bullet in the chamber.

She stopped talking, remembering the lady who lived on a boat nearby. Tony had just killed two men. He wouldn't hesitate to shoot an innocent bystander.

He pushed her. She kept her balance, despite the hard

shove. Had the 911 dispatcher picked up any part of this? She'd never stated her emergency. There hadn't been time. She had no way of knowing if pocketing the phone had obliterated the entire conversation.

Rick would be looking for her. She didn't doubt that for a second. He cared for her. Perhaps even loved her. She wanted to experience the emotion—to be with him while she explored regions of her heart that had grown cold over the years. If this thing went south—and it was quickly heading in that direction—there was a good chance she'd never see him again. She needed to change the status quo. But how?

The familiar boat was moored at the end of the dock. Had it snuck in as it had the last time? Finch assumed Tony and his co-conspirators would have expected the boat to be on a watch list. Why had she assumed that? The local authorities hadn't taken her escape seriously. According to Rick, no law enforcement agency had issued a report or requested the Coast Guard to look for a boat fitting the description Finch had given them. There had been nothing on the news. Anyone associated with the vessel would have assumed they were in the clear. What difference did it matter, anyway? The boat was here, and they were heading directly for it. Her chances of surviving a second outing were zero. She was not getting on that boat.

Finch lengthened her stride, inching away from him. Praying she'd judged the distance correctly, she pivoted—fast and hard, her arms extended. Her fisted hands connected with his, sending the weapon flying onto the wooden planks. His eyes followed the gun, giving her the second she needed to ram her knee into his groin. One hand moved to protect his privates. The other grabbed at her bindings. They both fell to the dock, landing with a teeth-jarring thud.

She hadn't been in a physical fight since leaving juvenile detention. One instinct came roaring back. There was no such thing as a fair fight. Not if you wanted to—and in this case, needed to—win. Finch had the advantage of fear on her side and a history that included protecting herself, particularly from assholes like Tony. She bounced to her feet, added another kick to her previous target then dropped one knee into his diaphragm, forcing the air from his lungs. She thought she'd heard a rib crack. Hard to tell over his grunts and groans.

Clasping her fingers together into a single, solid fist she swung her arms in another large arc. Tony's head snapped to the side. Blood spurted from his nose. Finch seized the opportunity to dive for the gun which had landed several feet away.

The rough surface of the wood dug into her knees and forearms. Ignoring the pain, she grabbed the gun. Rolling onto her back, she pointed the weapon at the wheezing man, who was struggling to stand.

"Move another inch, you bastard, and I'll put a hole through you big enough to see what's on the other side." Her arms had turned to jelly. Still bound at the wrist, her hands were slick with sweat and blood, but she kept a tight grip on the gun.

If looks were lethal, Finch would be dead, but Tony eyed the gun and Finch's expression. He didn't call her bluff. She'd never shot anyone, let alone killed a person, but after the danger this friggin' group had put her and her friends in, she damn well wanted to.

"Now it's your turn to talk. What the hell is all this about? What happened to my parents?"

His response was a cocky grin. She lowered the gun a few inches, aiming at the part of his anatomy that was probably still blue. "You're pissing me off. I don't think the cops will have a problem with me if my finger slips on the trigger."

She held his gaze and let him gauge her intent. She desperately wanted to put a bullet in this guy.

"We needed whatever your mother had been sending to you," he admitted. "There was nothing in the documents you kept. Look. I'm a dead man if I'm taken into custody. Let me go. I'll disappear. You won't see me again." The defiant asshole had lost his spine in a hurry.

"Answer the damn question then maybe I'll consider it." Wasn't gonna happen, but it was worth a try. "Why are you so sure I have something that came from my mother?"

"I don't know. My job was to get close to you—to learn what I could about you and your family. But you never mentioned them. It was like they didn't exist."

"They didn't exist to me. Why now? Why come looking for me now?"

"I don't know," he repeated. "I go where they pay me to go. I wouldn't be here if the…"

The squeal of tires interrupted them as a truck roared up to the end of the pier, followed by the thunderous pounding of feet.

"Finch! You can put the gun down, Finch. I've got him." Troy appeared at her side, his weapon pointed at Tony. "Place it carefully on the deck."

"Where's Rick?" she cried, looking over her shoulder. The sound of sirens registered. They were getting louder. Curiosity seekers were coming off their boats and onto the dock.

"Is he coming?" Her voice trembled as she set the gun on the wooden surface. She didn't care. She wasn't trying to be brave anymore.

"He should be here any second. I was closer." He motioned at Tony with his gun in hand. "I want you kissing the dock. Hands behind your head. Now," he ordered when Tony hesitated.

As soon as Tony complied, Troy drew a wicked-looking knife from his backside. "Let's get rid of these restraints."

It only took a quick slice from the sharp knife and her wrists were free. Not trusting her legs to hold her, she settled onto the rough deck, letting her aching hands drop into her lap.

"Smart of you to keep the phone line open. You gave us enough information to find you."

Sirens, screeching tires, and slamming doors, filled the air. Police crowded onto the dock yelling questions and giving orders. Finch blocked out the noises, closed her eyes, and wished for Rick. And then he was there, wrapping her in his arms, laying soft kisses in her hair. Tears flowed freely then as she leaned into him.

"I'm sorry I couldn't get here faster," he said, clasping her shoulders he held her at arm's length. "Are you hurt?"

"Her wrists," Troy pointed out.

"We need medics over here," Rick shouted.

"You have one hell of a lady there." Troy grinned at his friend. "She had the drop on Gambino despite her bound wrists. From the look of him, I think his balls are still halfway up his throat."

Finch watched as deputies pulled Tony to his feet and led him to one of the squad cars. She could see he was hurting from the lumbering walk and hunched shoulders. His nose was bleeding heavily. "I think I broke his nose."

"Atta girl." Troy shot her a grin before trotting toward the deputies.

"I was so scared," she admitted, leaning into Rick. If help hadn't arrived, she didn't know if she had the strength to go another round with Tony or had the guts to shoot him.

"You're safe now," Rick told her.

"Can you walk?"

Finch stared at the stunning, ebony-skinned medic. She hadn't heard her approach. Could she walk? Would her legs hold her if she stood?

"We can treat you better in the unit. This light," the medic added looking at the nearby lamppost, "sucks."

"I think so…"

In a lightning-quick motion, she was in Rick's arms and headed toward the EMS unit. He gently placed her on the gurney, then quickly made room for the paramedics.

"Will she be okay?" he asked from his position outside the open doors.

Worry lines etched his face and touched her heart. The big, tough cop didn't look so tough at the moment.

"She's lucky," the medic said, examining her wrists. "I think all she's going to need are a few stitches. We'll take her in to the ER. They'll call a hand specialist in to check her out."

"Keeping that phone line open was smart," Rick echoed Troy's remarks. "I was at the spa with two deputies when the radio call came in."

"You found the two men?" She swallowed hard.

"We did. I wish you hadn't had to see that."

"He killed them. He admitted it."

"I'm sorry. I tried to find you."

Finch squeezed between the two medics as soon as they'd finished wrapping her wrists, then squatted in front of Rick. They were eye level. She was steadier now. A few minutes ago, the short trek would have been impossible.

"This isn't your fault. It was a rash, hurtful move on my part. Yet you came after me despite that. If it wasn't for you, I'd probably be dead."

"I doubt it. Troy says you had things well in hand." He

pressed his lips to hers. "Promise me you'll never run away from me again."

"Never again," She promised, smiling at him.

"I hate to break up this love fest," an officer interrupted, "but we have questions that need answers."

"I need to talk to her first," Rick argued, "then she needs to be at the hospital."

"You're out of your jurisdiction," the deputy reprimanded him. "I have a few questions for her now. We'll finish after she's done at the hospital. You can talk to her after that."

Finch watched Rick's jaw turn to steel. He looked at Finch. "I'll make that call to Tampa." He waited until she nodded her understanding. Don't share with the locals.

The deputy appeared relieved by Rick's departure. It wasn't hard to understand why. Rick was a big man. He was also on edge and that edge was razor sharp. Finch sat on the floor of the EMS unit, allowing her legs to dangle outside the vehicle. Forcing her eyes away from Rick, she turned them toward the deputy, noting his name badge for the first time. David Wallace. He had one eye on Rick. Finch's mouth quirked up at the corner. It was probably her nerves, but it tickled her Rick made the deputy nervous. Rick had no authority over him, yet he was treading carefully.

"I'll be following you to the hospital. After you're cleared, I'll take you to the station. We need your statement and fingerprints."

And now she understood why the guy was so skittish. "Why fingerprints? I didn't shoot anyone."

"Look. Your boyfriend won't like it, but if he's any kind of cop, he'll understand."

Grinding her teeth, Finch debated if it would be worth kicking this jerk in his balls too. Not because he wanted to fingerprint her—been there, done that—but because of his insulting insinuation regarding Rick's capability as an officer. Asshole.

"We'll need your fingerprints to compare with those on the gun," he added.

Of course, they would. Her shoulders slumped at the realization of what was yet to come. It was going to be a long evening.

42

———

*D*eputy Wallace appeared to be a good investigator, but that didn't make him any less of an asshole. He was enjoying Rick's lack of jurisdiction, relegating him to the lobby of the LCSO central location. As a rule, law enforcement buildings didn't decorate with aesthetics or comfort in mind. This place didn't break that rule. The chairs were hard, worn plastic. The walls were an ugly shade of brown, covered with the department's logo, along with photos of men and women wanted for various crimes. They'd succeeded in making any visitor feel unwelcomed.

He paced the lobby, ignoring the deputy behind the glass. Instead, he kept looking at the door that separated the lobby from the rest of the building. Rick was tempted to piss off a few people and look for Finch. She was injured. She didn't need to be pounded with questions. Wallace was probably being a dickhead. Finch had street smarts, but this was different than being picked up for breaking and entering. The Feds needed to reach out to these guys—and soon. Finch could only tell them so much without jeopardizing a Federal investigation or making herself a suspect.

He'd received a firm no when he told Wallace he wanted Finch to ride with him from the hospital to the main sheriff's station. He wanted to make her aware of the boundaries of her discussions with the County, but he also wanted her by his side, even if it was only for the short ride. Instead, he'd been forced to follow them to the station. Troy stayed behind at the marina, doing a sweep of the place. The sheriff's office would do their thing. Rick and his team would do theirs.

Rick spent his forced separation from Finch on the phone. He'd received a call from Jeremy. It had been a courtesy call only. His friend explained he was unable to share what he'd uncovered. On the other hand, Rick shared everything they had with the former intelligence officer. Jeremy would pass it along to whomever he'd contacted regarding this mess. Rick also touched base with Morgan and Pulaski to fill them in on the events of the night and his call to Jeremy. They needed to coordinate their investigation.

None of what they knew revealed who was the head of the organization. Based on what he'd got from his abbreviated conversation with Finch, Gambino wasn't the one calling the shots. Rick never believed that was the case. He was too young and too inept to have pulled this off. He also didn't believe the person at the top was done with Finch. The sooner he got her out of here, the better. He wanted her on the island surrounded by people he trusted.

After speaking with Pulaski and then the Feds, Rick expected that to happen soon.

Less than an hour after the duo disappeared into the bowels of the building, Deputy Wallace strode out into the lobby, scowling like a bulldog. "I don't know who your connections are, but we've been ordered to cease questioning your girlfriend."

Rick wasn't fond of pulling strings but there were times it was good to have friends in high places.

"What's happening with Gambino?" Rick asked, invading Wallace's personal space. He suspected he already knew the answer.

"Same shit. The Feds are on their way to get him."

"You might want to delay writing up any report," Rick suggested. "It may save you a lot of paperwork because I doubt any of it will see the light of day."

"What the hell is going on?" Wallace's expression was a mix of anger and curiosity.

"Where's Ms. Finch?" Rick asked, ignoring the deputy's question.

"In the ladies' room."

"Not alone, I hope." Rick didn't wait for an answer, pushing past Wallace.

"No. That was also made clear. She wasn't to go anywhere without an escort. You're not going to tell me what's going on, are you?"

"I'm not at liberty to say." Wallace could spend the rest of his days wondering what the hell was going on. Rick didn't care.

The door to the lobby opened and a female deputy ushered Finch out. Wallace nodded to his co-worker then they both disappeared through the same door. Neither utter a word to Rick or Finch as they left. They objected to their jurisdiction being usurped. Tough shit.

"Are you okay?" he asked for what was possibly the hundredth time that day. He reached her side in two, long strides.

"Yeah. What happened to make me hotter than a stick of dynamite? One minute I'm being fingerprinted and the next minute I'm on my way out the door. I expected to be here all night."

Elbows bent, her hands were level with her shoulders. She reminded him of a doctor getting ready for surgery after washing his hands. Her wrists had to hurt. Lowering her arms to her sides would only increase the pain as the blood flowed south.

"Let's talk on the way to Sanibel," he said, leading her to the door. He took the time to scan the parking lot before exiting the building then rushed her toward the vehicle. He felt her tense as they walked. "It's okay. Just not taking any chances."

Turning right onto Six Mile Cypress Parkway he ran the yellow light at U.S. 41, then made a quick U-turn at the entrance to a city park on the other side of the busy highway. He waited. They'd been the last car through the intersection, but it never hurt to be cautious. The traffic light changed again, and traffic filled the road in front of them. No vehicles slowed or caught his attention.

"You're scaring me," Finch said to him.

"Sorry." He shifted to face her full on. Her eyes sparkled like polished copper reflecting the headlights of vehicles passing them. Reaching over, he pulled her closer until their lips were a hairs breadth away. "You scared me, too." He brushed his lips against hers.

"I didn't want you hurt. I don't want anyone hurt because of me."

"That's our choice to make." He kissed her softly. "I need you to trust me." Releasing his seat belt, he leaned over the console to deepen the kiss. He inhaled her scent. Tasted her sweetness. Both unique to her. He tucked the bright pink strip of hair that had fallen forward behind her ear. She was unique in so many ways. He hadn't appreciated it at first. If he was being honest, he'd initially held that uniqueness against her. No longer. He wanted to discover every idiosyncrasy she possessed and love her for what she was—assuming she'd have him. That would have to wait until this mess was behind them. There was still quite a bit of cleaning up to do.

"How are the wrists?"

"They hurt, but they'll heal. I'm glad I'm not driving, though. Holding on to the steering wheel would not be my idea of fun."

"Steve and Josie took care of your car. It should be at the studio. Kevin will be there with his medical kit if you need anything for the pain."

Rick brushed his hand over her hair, then lifted her chin to get a clear look at her face. A tear trickled from the corner of her eye. "What is it? What's wrong?"

"A bit overwhelmed, I guess."

"You have every right to be." He brushed the tear away with his thumb. "But you have friends. You have me to lean on if you need to." He was rewarded with a ghost of a smile.

"Thank you. Now," she said, gathering herself, her shoulders squared, "you're supposed to be filling me in on what happened. How'd I get sprung so quickly? I'm glad I wasn't there long. I didn't know what to say and what not to say."

"The higher-ups got involved. The information the FBI has been able to retrieve from that charm is damning. Gib, and a friend of mine, gave them additional data. It was enough to secure a move out of the local jurisdiction."

"Tony wanted whatever my mother sent to me. I assumed he meant the bracelet and charms." Finch settled into her seat. "He admitted he wasn't near the top of the food chain. Do we have any idea who is pulling the strings?"

"This investigation is way above my pay grade. The intelligence community will handle it from here on out. What we can piece together tells us an individual or organization has been wiping gambling debts clean in exchange for government secrets, then selling them to the highest bidder."

"Crap. And no one has any idea who is running this operation? Am I going to be looking over my shoulder for the rest of my life?"

"The people on the list are already being brought in for questioning. Statistically, one of them will talk. Whether they know the person at the top is a long shot. I doubt the ringleader would have direct contact with any of the marks. Every clue will get us closer. I promise."

"Do you believe my mother was involved?" She turned to stare out into the darkness.

"In all honesty, I don't know. Maybe she stumbled on to it or was initially part of it. In either case, she tried to share information with you. It would have been helpful if she hadn't been so cryptic. I'd like to know why she didn't contact law enforcement—or if she did and wasn't taken seriously? We can ask Morgan and Hernandez when they get here. You feel up to talking with them?"

"If it will help, but I don't know any more than I've already told you." She rested her head in the nook between the seat and the window.

"Relax. We'll be there shortly."

43

The parking areas at both businesses were packed with vehicles. Unusual for this time of night, but not unexpected. The entire team would be here in addition to their official guests. The only visible light emanating from the two buildings were the slivers that pushed their way through the plantation blinds of Colt and Cat's home on the second floor.

The driveway between the buildings was clear, so Rick used it to make his way to the rear. He took the only spot left—next to the alley.

It did not surprise him to see Steve and Colt headed toward them as he opened the door for Finch. The team always had each other's backs.

"I see our company has arrived," he said as they approached the steps leading to the living quarters.

"Pulaski is also here," Colt answered. "This is a big hornet's nest, but with the information from the bracelet and Gib's charming personality, it's coming together."

"Gib's here?" Even with the private jet, there was still a decent drive from Tampa.

"Troy picked him up at the airport. His presence was requested."

One of these days, he'd have to figure out how Gib seemed to be everywhere and anywhere he was needed. Today would not be that day. There were other priorities.

The ladies encircled Finch as soon as she entered the living room. It was obvious to Rick they orchestrated the mass greeting in a show of support.

"Are you hurting?" Shayne asked, carefully taking Finch's hands in hers.

"Not much. I was lucky."

"Let's take a look at them," Kevin said, joining the women. "I've got my kit in the master bath."

"The hospital took care of me," Finch told him. "I'm fine."

Shayne wasn't taking no for an answer. She took Finch's elbow and led her down the hall. "It will make me feel better if Kevin checks their work." Rick followed but was stopped as a large hand came to rest on his shoulder.

"We need you in here," Colt told him, indicating the living area.

"But…"

"Kevin and Shayne have it covered." Colt paused, waiting until the threesome disappeared into the large bath. "We need to talk before Finch returns."

Rick grabbed one of the dining room chairs, swung it around and straddled it. "Okay. Why did you want Finch gone for this conversation? I'd think she'd be pretty damn central to what we're here to discuss."

"The DNA results are in," Josie told him. "The FBI received the results first." Which obviously annoyed her.

"We had a warrant," Morgan stated.

The agent was explaining the intrusion into Finch's personal info. After decoding the charm on the bracelet, it didn't surprise him they wanted it ASAP. "I assume the DNA told you something?"

"After we received the results, we ran them through NamUs. We got a match," Morgan said.

"Two, in fact," Hernandez added.

Rick glanced at his friends. Apparently, they were already aware of the news based on their dour expressions. "Get on with it. Kevin won't be able to keep her in there indefinitely."

Morgan opened a file and pulled out the top sheet. "Six months ago, the remains of an unidentified woman were found in the desert outside of Las Vegas. Based on the decomposition of the body, they estimated that it was dumped there approximately six months prior."

"Dumped? She was murdered?"

"The coroner ruled it a homicide. There were other obvious injuries, but it was the blow to the back of her skull that would have been fatal. The case is still active, but unsolved. There were signs the individual was tortured. The strength of the DNA samples tells us it was Ms. Finch's mother."

He'd seen it coming, but it still hit him hard. How would the knowledge that her mother was dead—murdered—affect Finch?

"And the other connection?"

"You're aware of the human remains that have recently been exposed as water levels drop in Lake Mead? The second DNA match is a male found in a deteriorated oil drum. We estimate he was in the lake for twenty-five to thirty years," Morgan continued.

"Finch's father." Rick could do the math. The timing was right. He must have been killed about the time Finch was born.

"We're bringing in a forensic pathologist to do a thorough examination. There's a direct line from both individuals to Ms. Finch."

"Have you been able identify them? Do you know their names?"

"We're searching all DNA matches. So far we've got one hit. A good one. A first cousin. An agent contacted the relative and was told that her cousin, Anne O'Shea and her husband, Justin, disappeared almost thirty years ago. Mrs. O'Shea's mother is still alive. We're in the process of confirming the parental connection and talking to her."

"But you said she died a year ago. Where has she been for the past twenty-nine years?"

"That's going to take time to discover. We need to talk to Ms. Finch," Hernandez said.

Rick glanced down the hallway. "But you want me to break this news to her first."

"We argued she should be told privately," Cat said, leaning into her husband. "You and Shayne are closest to her, but we figured you'd want to be the one to tell her."

Rick got to his feet. "Are Kevin and Shayne stalling for time until I get back there?"

Colt nodded. "Kevin wanted to check the hospital's work and give her something for pain, assuming she needed it. The local has probably worn off by now. They should be finished, I would think."

When Rick entered the large spa-like bath, Finch was sitting on the lid of the commode. Shayne who had climbed onto the granite countertop was chatting with her friend. Kevin rested his shoulder against the doorway that led to the master bedroom. His massive forearms crossed over his chest. In unison, all heads pivoted in his direction.

"Did the doc's work meet your standards?" he asked Kevin.

"Her wrists will be fine as long as she doesn't lift

anything heavy while they're healing. We don't want her pulling the stitches out."

Shayne started to hop off the countertop, but Kevin took her by the waist and lowered her to the floor. After giving Finch a hug, she followed Kevin, silently departing the room.

"What's going on?" Finch asked the minute Rick blocked her exit.

"Let's go in here for a minute, Savannah." Rick indicated the master bedroom with a nod of his head. "We need to talk." The bathroom, however nice, wasn't the proper place to break the news to her.

"What now?" A spark of fear flashed behind her lashes.

He guided her toward the bed, by-passing the chair in the corner. He sat on the mattress, taking her hand in his. "It may not be easy for you to hear."

"What is it?" She scooted just far enough away from him so she could study his face.

"The FBI has identified the remains of a man and woman. The DNA you provided is telling us they're your parents."

He kept her hand in his as he related what the agents had told him. Her fingers had grown cold. Her skin paled. When he finished, she was staring at the floor, her expression blank.

"Are you okay?" Of course, she wasn't.

"I don't know." Her eyes were empty and dull. "I didn't know them. I didn't want to know them. Now I don't know how to feel."

How could she? She'd gone from hating her parents, to dismissing them, to digesting the possibility that she'd been wanted.

"Come here," he said, pulling her into his arms. "We'll

figure it out together."

44

———

Finch was still digesting the information Rick had shared when the agents began to pepper her with questions. When did she receive the note she'd tucked away in her diary? Hadn't she questioned who it was from? What about the charm bracelet and the charms that followed? Why didn't she question their origin? Why had she suddenly thought it was important and grabbed it as they'd vacated her apartment? Was there any other communication she wasn't sharing with the authorities? Every question was like a snap of a finger in her face.

That last question set her off. "Are you guys always such assholes?" Her earlier shock morphed into anger.

"I've told you all I can. I'm not hiding a damn thing. I want whoever is behind this to be stopped as much as you do, maybe more. They killed my parents and now they're targeting me. Don't you think I care that some bastard is getting their hands on government secrets and selling them? If I knew anything else, I'd tell you."

The agents glared at Rick.

"She has every right to know why her parents are

dead," Rick snapped. "Everyone here knows that much, and it won't be leaving this room."

"I think it's your turn to answer questions," Finch said, her elbows pressing into her knees. She raised her wrists to shoulder level again. "You're absolutely certain these two people are my parents?"

"Science doesn't lie," Morgan said.

"Then how the hell did I land in the Florida foster care system? They were in Nevada."

"We don't know," Hernandez admitted.

"What *do* you know?" Rick asked, anticipating Finch's question.

"Justin O'Shea was a reporter for the Las Vegas Review-Journal. A well-respected paper with a large circulation. It's still cranking out news which is a testimony in this day and age. It was the paper's editor who reported him missing."

Justin. Her dad's name was Justin.

"I know someone at the Review," Josie jumped off Steve's lap. "I haven't contacted him yet." She got to her feet. "I'll make the call."

"She's discreet," Steve assured the agents as they watched her leave. "She also can access info not always in your files."

"And my mother?" Finch's stomach fluttered as she addressed the agents. Was she finally going to learn about her mother?

"Anne Ward O'Shea. She was reported missing at the same time as your father. She was also a journalist at the paper," Morgan stated.

Anne. Justin and Anne O'Shea. She'd had parents. Of course, she did but for the first time in her life it felt real.

"And no one considered the simultaneous disappearances were odd?" Rick asked.

"We're giving you what we can," Hernandez responded, a bit defensively. "Besides, these investigations take time. There's a lot of digging to do and we still need a lot of answers. Our agents are beating the bushes in Nevada. The Las Vegas authorities are digging into the cold case. We're here to prod Ms. Finch's memory. To add to what we know."

"My apologies for being short. I'm tired, hurting, and a bit stunned."

Hernandez nodded. "Let's start at the beginning—a little slower this time. Tell us about the first package. I'd think receiving it would have raised your curiosity."

"It did. I remember that one more clearly than the others. The charms made me uncomfortable. I didn't move much after I turned eighteen, but I did move occasionally. Whoever was sending them always knew where to find me. It felt as if I was being stalked."

"Still, you kept them. Why?"

"I don't know except that somebody went to the trouble to send them to me. Most years it was the only recognition of my birthday I received. I liked to think of them as a birthday gift. Wishful thinking, I guess. I didn't understand the significance of any of them. They were a puzzle. I know that now, but how was I supposed to figure it out?"

"You'd need a key," Colt told her.

"Like the one on the bracelet?"

"No. Not a physical key. Notes or clues that would tie the charms together to tell a story. It could have been a poem, a flash drive, letter, or postcard. Was there anything you received that didn't have a return address or you thought was out of the ordinary?" Colt asked.

"Not that I remember."

"It may have been lost or intercepted." Rick suggested. "I still don't get why you? Why not go to the authorities?"

"I think I may be able to answer that one," Josie said, reentering the room.

"What did you find out, babe?" Steve asked, reaching out and pulling her back onto his lap.

"According to my source, O'Shea is legendary at the paper. He was known for going after hard stories. The paper has an award for investigative journalism named after him. My contact didn't know him personally. He wasn't there at the same time, but he says rumors regarding the disappearance have circulated for years. The general consensus is O'Shea dug a little too deep for a story and it got him killed."

"That still doesn't explain why Finch's mother sent her the items instead of contacting the FBI," Steve said.

"My contact gave me the name and number of another journalist, Lee Woodward, who is now retired. He remembered O'Shea. Said he was a hell of a reporter. Woodward knew he was working on something big but wasn't aware of the subject of the story. Whatever it was, it made O'Shea nervous, which was out of character. Normally, he'd get pumped up when he got his teeth into a juicy lead, but this time, Woodward said, he appeared fearful. Enough so that O'Shea was on his way to the FBI field office the last time Woodward spoke to him. He never saw Justin again," Josie added.

"There was no mention of a child?" River asked.

"Woodward wasn't aware O'Shea had, or was expecting, any children." Josie paused. "Based on the timeline we've put together, Anne may have discovered she was pregnant around the time all this started to percolate. Considering how skittish he was, O'Shea may have decided to keep that information to himself."

"Her husband's killers would have been looking for her to find out what she knew." Kevin was standing behind River, his hands clasping her shoulders.

"She ran. Somehow she ended up in Tampa." Morgan nodded in agreement.

"And, since no one knew of the pregnancy, she left Finch behind so that no one would be able link her to either Anne or her husband." Josie's voice cracked. "I can't imagine having to make that decision. I can't imagine the torment she went through, but I think I'd come to the same conclusion given the same circumstances. If my only choices were keeping Cece with me and putting her life in danger or letting her go so she could live, I know I'd make the same choice."

Steve pulled his wife close, laying soft kisses on her face. "It's a decision you'll never have to make."

"I know," she sniffled. "But Anne O'Shea didn't have anyone to turn to for help."

"Why the hell did she send the information to Finch— and do it eighteen years later?" Shayne asked.

"I think Josie answered the first part of that question. Where was Justin O'Shea headed when Woodward last talked to him?" Troy pointed out, lifting his wife into his lap.

"The FBI." Steve turned to the two agents. "I suggest one of you check with the Vegas field office and see if there was a file opened on O'Shea."

"If he reported what he knew to the FBI, wouldn't this shit have already been stopped?" Finch asked.

"Perhaps he didn't have enough information that led anywhere. It's not unusual," Morgan answered.

"A file still would have been opened," Pulaski countered. "Or maybe he spoke to the wrong person then paid for that with his life."

"Are you insinuating the FBI is involved?" Hernandez didn't try to hide his anger at the question.

"Not the agency, but an individual, perhaps," Pulaski suggested. "Considering what we're looking into, there's a good chance whoever is behind this would have been prepared for such a case. We're talking about human beings. All you need is one that could be threatened or bought."

"Who do we trust unequivocally in Las Vegas?" Hernandez asked his partner. "Have them check their records—quietly. O'Shea may have never arrived at the office or wasn't considered credible."

"My father was killed. I'd call that credible."

"I'm on it." Morgan left the room, punching in a number on his phone as he walked away.

"Let's get back to the packages." Hernandez returned his attention to Finch. "Most people would look for a return address."

"I did. None of them had a return address. Postmarks were from all over the country. The first one came from Virginia. I remember thinking I didn't know anyone in Virginia. I still don't. The packages never came from the same state twice."

"Do you remember which states?" Hernandez was busily keying information into his laptop.

"Colorado, Oregon, Michigan, and Florida. I remember those off the top of my head. There were ten charms in all. Ten packages. Which means I'm missing a few states."

"Did you notice any postmarks from Hawaii or Alaska?" Hernandez had remained seated at the dining room table. He continued inputting information into his laptop.

"I don't think so."

"Why are those two states significant?" Gib asked.

Finch had almost forgotten Gib was present. The normally effusive guy had been quiet, having ducked into a space near a large houseplant in the corner behind her.

"Getting on an airplane or crossing a border requires current identification or a passport, often both. The individual might have been afraid she'd be located if her information were put into a system."

"That would be one hell of a network to tie into all those systems," Steve commented.

"Oh. Shit. I almost forgot." Josie scrambled off of Steve's lap. "I'm surprised with all this talk of mail I didn't think of it sooner. You left an envelope in your car, Finch. I brought it upstairs for you." She dashed into the kitchen and returned with the grayish, heavy-duty envelope.

"I'd forgotten about it, too," Finch said, taking it from her hands. She'd been too eager to get away from her apartment. Mrs. Murphy had delayed her by taking the time to jot her phone number on the back of the square, self-sealing package.

"Can I see that?" Rick asked, extending his hand.

"Sure." Rick took the envelope from her, holding it by the corners. "You don't think…"

He turned the envelope over so that the address side was visible. "Does this writing look familiar?"

Finch stared at the large block printing, the excessive amount of postage and the blank spot where a return address would normally be printed. "It looks the same as the others," she admitted. "I didn't pay attention when Mrs. Murphy gave it to me. I just wanted to get out of there."

"You were scared," River said. "You were running. Any one of us would have reacted the same way."

By now the entire room had encircled Finch and Rick, including Morgan who'd returned from making his call.

Both FBI agents hovered over her and the package. Latex gloves covered their hands.

"We need to take that," Hernandez said.

"It's addressed to her," Rick argued. "You don't have the authority to take it away from her. Not, at least, until we know what's in it."

"Fingerprints," Hernandez warned, holding out a pair of gloves to Finch. "The outside has certainly been compromised, but the contents may have only had one handler."

Finch looked to Rick for confirmation. After a nod, she took the offered gloves. They were big but the real problem in opening the large envelope was her shaking hands. She finally managed it. She slipped a sheet of paper from the envelope then upended the remaining contents over the coffee table. A notebook, flash drive and another heart-shaped charm tumbled out.

After barely giving the items a look, she focused her attention on the paper in her hand. A letter.

'My dearest daughter.' Finch spoke the words softly. She was a daughter. She'd been claimed.

I've set it up so this will be sent to you should I not retrieve it in six months. I've dreamed of the day that I would hold you in my arms—to tell you how precious you were to me and your father. If you're reading this that chance will never come. I am so sorry.

45

"Can I finish it for you?" Rick asked. Her voice was cracking. It was tearing him apart. "Or would you prefer to read it in private?"

"Go ahead." She handed the letter to him then covered her face with her hands. "Everyone here will know the contents eventually."

The sooner they got this over with, the sooner he could take her home and hold her. He started to read.

Maybe I should have done things differently. I don't know. I still don't know. I did what I believed I had to do to protect you. Keeping your existence a secret was the only way I knew how to do that. I'm sorry my solution was so hard on you. I'm sorry I wasn't able to stop bad things from happening but coming back into your life would have only put you in danger.

It took me almost twenty years to realize the monster would never stop looking for me—that the organization would never stop functioning and it needed to be stopped. I turned the tables and began to gather evidence on them. I didn't trust the FBI after what happened to your father. Everything he unearthed and what I've been able to find is now yours.

On the same date this letter was dropped in the mail, a flash drive was to be sent to the FBI in Washington. I wish I believed they will act on the information, and you'll be safe. Since I can't be positive, I've kept your existence a secret from them.

The contents of this package and the charms I sent you contain the same information I sent to the FBI. Keep them safe. Use them as a bargaining chip should you need to keep the monster at bay. I pray it never finds you.

Please know your father and I both loved you. You were loved from the minute you were conceived. Our actions may not have reflected that. Initially, we didn't know what we'd uncovered. By the time we did, it was too late. It killed your father and ruined both my life and yours. One day I hope you'll forgive us.

I've enclosed the heart your father gave to me on our wedding day. The first heart you received expressed my love for you. You've always had our hearts, but now you can hold them in your hands if you wish. I hope you do. The other charms are explained on the drive.

I love you, Savannah. Yes, I know the name you selected. It's beautiful—just like you. I am so proud of you and my heart aches that I will never get the chance to tell you that face-to-face.

Be safe. I'm with your father now. I've missed that fearless, loving man every day of my life, just as I've missed you. I pray you get to know us through the pages of this diary.

Your loving mother.

Hernandez reached over and took the hand-written letter from Rick.

"Hey, wait a minute." Rick glared at the agent. "That's hers."

"It's evidence. This is all evidence," Hernandez said, waving his hand over the items on the table.

"That letter is personal. It has nothing to do with the investigation," Rick argued. "You heard it."

"Everything here, including the envelope is evidence. You know that, Rick. I shouldn't have to explain it to you."

"It's in her mother's writing. For God's sake. Let her keep it."

"It's okay." Finch placed her hand on Rick's thigh. "Everything will be returned to me, won't it? She said the three charms had nothing to do with the case. They were for me."

"Anything not classified will be returned," Hernandez agreed, his voice softening. "But I don't know how long it will take to get through this stuff."

"Let me at least make a copy of the letter for her." Rick was on his feet.

"Give me the Goddamn letter, Hernandez." Colt towered over the two men with his hand extended. It was already gloved. "I'll make a copy now."

"Be careful with it," the agent warned him. Colt was shaking his head as he made his way to his home office. Rick was grateful his friend had stepped in. Not many argued with Colt when he went into predatory mode. Cat was the only one to go head-to-head with him without qualm.

"And the notebook? Can we copy that, as well? The letter was clear. It's meant for Finch." Cat was standing where her husband had stood—her invisible claws extended.

"The piece of jewelry needs to be thoroughly inspected. Eventually, it will be returned. As for the notebook, it will have to be reviewed. If it doesn't contain classified material, it should be released back to you, but it won't be my call."

Rick started to object, but Finch took his hand. "It's okay," she said again. "I appreciate your help, but this scheme is more important than my personal relationship with my parents. I've been in the dark for my entire life, I can wait a bit longer to know what happened. The information should have been in the hands of the government long ago." A sigh escaped her lips.

Damn. He was so proud of her. She was willing to relinquish her first opportunity to hear her parents' story—to learn why they did what they did—because she understood the implications of what was at stake. He'd make damn sure the gifts her mother had left her were returned if he had to ride Morgan's and Hernandez's asses for the rest of their careers. Giving a side-eye to the agents, warning them off any objection as he snapped several pictures of the charm with his cell. It wasn't much, but at least she'd have that.

"Is Finch safe now that the FBI has the information they wanted?" Shayne asked.

"Depends," Troy answered first, "on whether they know that."

"True," Morgan agreed. "We have Gambino and by now they know that much. We got him out of LCSO custody as fast as possible, but he'd already made his call."

"I know how to make sure they know Finch no longer has it," Josie announced, a conspiratorial grin on her face.

"You do not need to be writing a story about this. Not yet, anyway," Morgan warned. "If they aren't aware of what happened here today, it will give us time to work our way up the ladder."

"And leave Finch a target?" Shayne snarled. "Fuck that."

"Don't worry, Shayne. I think that's wishful thinking on their part," Colt said, returning to the room. "The people behind this have lost track of Gambino. They going to assume he was moved to federal custody. They'll assume he's talking even if he's not. I hope you have him well guarded."

Hernandez jaw was set. He didn't argue.

"If that flash drive has concrete information on it, we should have an easier time of identifying the head of the organization even if he goes to ground." Morgan placed the original letter in a manila folder. "We don't know what Mrs. O'Shea sent to Washington, but nothing will be buried, I promise you that."

"The first thing I'd do is round up the people on that list," Steve suggested. "Otherwise, you may be losing a lot of witnesses if someone continues to clean house."

"Why would any of them talk to the authorities?" River questioned him. "If they have been selling government secrets, that's treason. What crime could be worse than that? I'd keep my mouth shut if I were them."

"Because their options if they don't talk are death by assassination, death by lethal injection, or flipping with hopes for a life sentence in a secure federal prison. It will be up to these guys," Kevin indicated the agents, "to convince them to pick door number three."

Hernandez and Morgan tucked the evidence they'd secured, into cases along with their computers. "We know our jobs," Hernandez announced. "We're done here—for now."

"Wait. Wait. Wait." Shayne chased after them. "You still haven't answered my question. Is Finch safe now?"

"For certain? No, we can't promise that, but it's unlikely. We have the evidence the organization has been searching for and, as Colt said, I wouldn't be surprised if they didn't already know that," Hernandez answered.

"The two men Gambino hired to abduct you are dead," Morgan added, stopping at the kitchen entrance on their way out. "With Gambino in custody, whoever is behind this operation should be packing up and getting out of town. Another reason we need to move quickly. If we hear different, we'll let you know. Stay on your toes."

"That's it? 'Stay on your toes'?" Cat was flushed with anger. "You can't guarantee she's safe."

"Do you want to request protection?" Hernandez glanced around the room. "If granted, they'll want to move her, and no one is going to share her location with you. Protective custody would be my preference but, since I know you, I assumed you'd nix that option. If you want us to request it," he paused, scanning the room, "we'll do it. That's no guarantee the agency will agree."

"Finch? What do you want?" Rick asked.

"What did the FBI office in Las Vegas have to say?" Finch asked the two agents.

"It was only a cursory search, but there's no record of Justin O'Shea contacting them. We're going to look harder, but we need to be circumspect." Hernandez told her.

"So, my father never got there—or, if he did, his visit was buried along with him."

Neither agent responded—their expressions dour, making Rick suspect the latter.

"There's no guarantee I'd be any safer with the government. I know it's not fair to you, but I'd like to stay here. I trust you." She paused. "It has to be your call. You need to think of the women and Cece."

"We women can speak for ourselves," Cat said. "Steve and Josie speak for Cece."

Steve pulled his wife to his side. Josie nodded. "As the parents of Cece, we want you to stay."

"We all do," Gib spoke up. Not a single one of Rick's friends voiced an objection.

"Thank you."

"If you change your minds, call," Morgan said.

Rick pulled Finch close as Colt locked the door behind them.

"Are we done for tonight?" Rick asked those remaining.

"I want to get Finch home." Home. He didn't want her anywhere else. It was time they talked about a future and whether she was ready for one with him.

"Go," Steve told them. "Send up a flare if you need us."

Rick eased Finch to her feet. She was still a bit shell-shocked after the events of the evening. She needed time to decompress which wasn't possible in a room full of people even if they were friends.

"Watch those wrists," Kevin warned her as he and River made their way toward the front where they had parked. "Try not to get them wet. Take a pair of Rick's evidence gloves, put them on and wrap tape around your wrists when you shower. Be careful what you lift. I'll check the stitches tomorrow. I'll take a look at your arm then, as well," he said to Rick.

As he and Finch passed through the kitchen, Cat handed them a bag. "Leftovers," she explained. "We have plenty and these should hold you through a couple of lunches."

The simple offer had Finch choking up as she gave Cat a hug. "Thank you. Thank you for everything." She was getting emotional over leftovers, proving she was tired and needed rest. They both needed a good night's sleep.

46

"Do you want one of us to follow you?" Steve asked as they headed toward their cars.

"We'll be okay. The two assholes from the boat are no longer a problem and Gambino is in custody. If there is still any interest in Finch, it will take a while to get reorganized and get here from Nevada," Rick answered. "Besides, didn't Troy install additional motion detectors at my place earlier today?"

"Sure did," Troy replied, hefting Shayne into his truck. Finch noticed he never missed an opportunity to touch her. After being buried under the wreckage of the country club bombing, she'd been a mess. Moving here and meeting Troy had changed Shayne's life. She glowed. Finch glanced at Rick, knowing her life had changed as well.

"It wouldn't be a bad idea to have one of us on guard duty outside your place," Steve pushed.

"With the upgraded security and patrols Pulaski has added, we're good," Rick assured them, then just as Troy had done a minute before, Rick lifted Finch onto the seat of his vehicle.

After sliding behind the wheel, he reached over and massaged her shoulder. "Are you hanging in there?"

"Honestly? I'm not sure. Relieved. Sad. Confused." She twisted against the seat belt he'd taken his time latching. He'd muttered she shouldn't be straining her wrists as he leaned over her to click the belt in place. She suspected he wanted the closeness. With all the shit that had hit the fan today, his last act made her sigh. "And happy," she finished.

"Happy?" His brow knitted together. "Why?"

"Because I have you."

"What?"

She would have been heartbroken by the question if there hadn't been that sparkle in his crystal, blue eyes, and a hint of a smile on his lips. "I do, don't I? Have you, that is."

"You do," he whispered, brushing his hand over her hair. "I planned to ask you the same question but wanted to give you time to digest everything you've been through. You just found out what happened to your parents. There's so much for you to take in, I didn't want to add to the mix until you were ready."

"It was clear from the letter that my mother loved my father deeply, yet they had so little time together. I don't want to spend my life missing you."

She undid the seat belt he'd latched and leaned toward him, brushing his five-o'clock stubble with her fingertips. "I want to find out where this goes. I love you. I'm not asking you to love me back, but to give me a chance—to give *us* a chance."

He tickled each corner of her mouth with feathery kisses before diving into a full throttle embrace. It was just a kiss, but so much more. It was an acceptance, a proclamation—and a promise. Wrapping her arms around his neck, she reeled him in.

"Your wrists," he murmured.

"They're fine. I was told not to lift anything. I don't plan on carrying you out of this truck, tossing you in its bed and making love to you—as delicious as that may sound."

"Did Kevin give you any pain meds?" he asked after a quick chuckle. He tucked an errant strand of hair behind her ear. She melted with each small touch.

"He did, but I didn't take it. I will if I need to, but I've had worse and survived."

His smile disappeared, replaced by worry that crinkled the corners of his eyes. "I'm sorry."

"Why? You weren't there. What happened, happened. It can't be undone. I learned from it. I'm not perfect, Rick." She leaned against the passenger door. "I'll never be perfect—and considering my history, I'm far from perfect for you. It scares me."

"The cab of my truck isn't the proper place to have this conversation, but here we are and here we'll finish it."

He'd stopped touching her which made her uneasy. She'd just reminded him that pairing up with her may not be the brightest idea for someone in his line of work. Would it harm his career?

"You've had good reason to be frightened most of your life, but the last thing you need to worry about are my feelings for you. I don't give a damn what happened in your past. You're a survivor. I'm in awe of you. I know the statistics. I know how few foster kids manage to pull themselves up and better their lives. You were dealt bad cards to start, but you took everything that was thrown at you and pushed it behind you or marched over it. I don't know many women stronger than you. I love you. I want you in my bed and in my life."

With the exception of the letter she'd received from her mother, no one had ever told her they loved her.

"Do you think we could go on a date?" she asked, while Rick dabbed the tears from her cheeks.

"Excuse me? Did you say a date?"

"A real date. You know? Dinner and a movie? We haven't been on one. I want to go on a date with you—like a normal couple."

"I don't know if we'll ever qualify as normal but, yes, I think that could be arranged. Now let's get out of here before I decide to test how hard the bed of this truck is."

Rick's eyes sparkled and she was grinning so wide, her cheeks hurt. As she leaned in for a kiss, she caught sight of a movement behind Rick. The driver's door jerked open. Rick's head was slammed against the steering wheel.

"Scream and I'll finish the job."

Too stunned to speak, Finch couldn't manage anything other than a nod.

The barrel of a semi-automatic pistol inched a bit closer to Rick's head. "Do you understand me?"

"Yes."

Gonzales didn't resemble the calm, organized woman Finch worked under since the manager's arrival six months ago. Dressed in black from head to toe, she wore a hoodie which covered her hair. Gonzales' expression was cold, hard, and deadly.

"What is it you want?"

"You."

"Why?"

"Because your family has been a pain in my side since your dad stumbled on to my little business."

Finch flicked a quick look at the building they'd just left. The upstairs was dark.

"I wouldn't if I were you," Gonzales warned. "If you call out, I'll kill him."

The look she gave Finch was hard as steel. It telegraphed that Gonzales had meant every word. She'd seen the threatening look in more than one foster parent. Talk. Keep her talking. A trick she'd learned in foster homes when met with that cold, frightening stare. Distraction sometimes took the wind out of their sails. Other times it only delayed the inevitable. And then there were times it didn't work at all. Regardless of the outcome, she wanted Gonzales' attention on her and not Rick. Finch had spotted the slight movement of his right hand as she'd turned to face the bitch.

They could both be dead in a split second. Hell, they should be dead. Gonzales could have easily killed them. Why hadn't she? Focus. At the moment her job was to keep them alive.

"Did you know the FBI has Tony?" Finch caught the split second of surprise before Gonzales recovered.

"Tony won't talk. He knows what happens to those who do. He never suspected his spa manager was pulling the strings. He's stupid. But there's a cure for stupid."

She suspected the cure for stupid was death. Which meant that this organization had ties everywhere. There was no way Finch and Rick would live through this unless she was stopped tonight.

"Why did you kill my father? Was it for the same reason you killed my mother? Did they get too close?" Gonzales' grip on the gun tightened. Finch was making her nervous. She didn't know if that was a good or bad thing, but no one was getting shot at the moment.

Rick flexed his fingers. Thankfully, his large body blocked Gonzales from noticing the movement.

"Your father didn't know who I was, but he was smart. He discovered what was going on and was getting close to me. He was useful in that he taught me a lesson on carelessness. Your mother was an unknown factor. I'd planned to eliminate her to be safe, but she disappeared the day your dad went for a swim in Lake Mead."

Gonzales had admitted she was the head of the organization. Which would not only make her a traitor but a murderer. The information should have scared the shit out of Finch, but there was a sense of closure. Her parents were dead because they tried to stop this bitch.

"You mean *your* boss had to eliminate my parents, don't you?" she responded, intentionally baiting her captor. "You're barely old enough to have been behind this conspiracy from the beginning. Besides, I don't think you're smart enough."

Her insult had its intended effect. The gun was no longer aimed at Rick's skull but was pointed dead center at Finch's chest. Finch willed her breathing to slow. Hyperventilating and passing out wasn't going to help.

Rick's forehead still rested on the steering wheel, but Finch had caught the flutter of his lashes.

"You're just like your parents. Defiant. Look where it got them. Well, surprise. I've been running this game since the start. Initially, I hadn't planned to build an organization. It started out as a small side hustle. My first mark happened to be a government employee. He liked gambling, drinking, and sex. Drinking was the only thing he was good at, unfortunately for him—and me."

"He gave you state secrets for sex?"

"Honey, I was good, but I wasn't that good. No. We worked out a deal to make his losses go away. That kind of information is worth a lot of money. He also continued to gamble and lose. It was a nice set up."

"How? How'd you make it work?" Finch forced a grin. "You can't tell me, can you because you're only one of the cogs in the wheel? Not the hub."

"You're wrong. You have no idea how many clients I have willing to hand over secrets to feed their addiction. You can't imagine the number of governments and powerful people who want that kind of info and how much they're willing to pay."

Finch imagined a lot. "The FBI has enough information to put it together."

"What do they have? Damn it. Tell me."

"How the hell are you capable of running a syndicate you're describing if you can't figure out the obvious? Everything my mother sent is in code. I don't know what's in it except for the names of the people who were sharing government secrets. But the FBI has the skills and tools to break it open and is digging fast." Just a little more time. She watched Rick out of the corner of her eye. He was silently tapping three fingers against this thigh—one at a time. One. Two. Three. One. Two. Three.

"I didn't know a damned thing about this crap until you guys showed up. If you and Tony had left me alone, you and your traitorous scheme may have never risen to the surface." Gonzales obviously didn't know her mother had sent information to the FBI.

"I'd be stupid to take that chance."

"Why don't you take off for parts unknown? Go to a country where you can't be extradited. Leave us alone. You killed my parents, but you can't kill everybody."

"Your parents put me to a lot of trouble and expense. Now you'll get the chance to meet them. If not for you three, I'd have milked this for years, but you're right. It's time to take a little vacation."

"I wouldn't come back if I were you. You'll be arrested the minute you step on U.S. soil."

"You won't be here to find out. Besides, no one will talk. Who would admit to espionage?" Her lip actually curled in a snarl.

"Yet here you are doing just that."

"Because you won't live to repeat it. You're coming with me until I'm safely out of here. We can chat along the way."

"I'll only slow you down. You need to run—and run fast." Gonzales was taking a big chance no one would spot her or look out and notice Rick hadn't left. Was she that cocky?

"You're my ticket out of here. They won't shoot first and ask questions later if you're with me. I might even change my mind and let you go if you do as I say. In the meantime, you can fill me in on what was discussed in that powwow upstairs."

The hell she would. Still, she needed to keep the bitch engaged. Rick's hand, which had stilled, moved again. He raised his index finger, slowly this time. Gonzales' eyes shifted in his direction.

"Why did you take the job at the spa?" Finch asked quickly. "Is it because they'd found my mother's body?"

"Imagine my surprise when I learned of your existence after the death of O'Shea—Anne O'Shea, that is. She'd done a remarkable job of keeping you a secret until then. Clever woman. Gave her points for that.

"After some digging—no pun intended—there was no indication she'd been in contact with you since the day she dumped you at that fire station. Then her body was found. God damn fuckin' idiots. Can't find good help these days.

How hard is it to bury a body?" She shook her head. "Once her body was found, I wasn't taking any chances. My marks might gamble, but I don't. With those damn ancestry sites being used to solve cold cases, there was always the possibility—no matter how slight—the two could be linked together. I decided to go on the offense and find out what you knew then deal with the problem. If I hadn't had a major deal going down, I'd have been here sooner."

The ancestry site had made a connection, but not the way Gonzales had figured. Rick raised a second finger. "Why you? If you're the wizard behind the curtain, why did you come here? Why not send one of you minions?"

"I needed a break after I finished the last project. Besides, I can run my enterprise from anywhere. I arranged for the opening at the spa and took the former manager's place. You appeared harmless enough. You never mentioned family. No one came looking for you, but to be sure, I brought Tony in. He'd been a master at prying secrets from those hooked on gambling, but apparently, not so much, when it came to you. He reverted to searching your place but other than some old documents that told us nothing, he came up empty. The boat ride was his idea. Thought he'd seduce the information out of you. Ha. He blamed the two Neanderthals he'd hired for that disaster. Look where that got us. You landed in the arms of a friggin' army—a very curious one."

The second Rick's finger tapped a third time, his arm arched up, slamming into Gonzales' gun hand. Finch grabbed the door handle and fell to the ground as she scrambled out of the truck. She heard the pfft as a bullet hit the roof of the cab above the passenger seat. She raced around the rear of the vehicle. She wasn't leaving Rick.

Despite Rick's size and strength, Gonzales wasn't

injured—and she wasn't giving up. She swung her fist like a hammer, hitting him on the temple. The blood from the earlier hit, made an easy target. The only positive was that the bitch was so intent on breaking free that she didn't hear Finch's approach. Shoving her foot into the back of Gonzales' knee, the woman's legs buckled, allowing Rick to wrench the gun free of the bitch's hand. He turned it on Gonzales who landed face first on the ground. There had been a satisfying thud as her jaw clipped the running board.

"Are you all right?" Finch started toward him.

"Stay back and away from her," Rick warned.

Finch scurried out of reach. He was right. No point in giving Gonzales the hostage she'd come for in the first place.

The blast from his truck's security alarm made her jump. Hand to her chest, she noticed Rick's fingers on his key fob. Lights almost immediately flooded the area.

"Quicker than a phone call," Rick explained.

"Answer me," she yelled, after catching her breath. "Are you all right?"

"Yeah. What about you?"

"Good. Good. I didn't know how long I'd be able to keep her talking," she started babbling. "I don't understand why she didn't shoot us both." Her whole body was trembling. Finch plopped her ass on the ground as her knees began to wobble, deciding not to trust her legs. "I was scared shitless."

"Finch…"

She recognized the worry in his eyes, but their prisoner's position made it difficult for Rick to get out of the driver's seat.

"I'm fine. I was scared to death I'd say something that would piss her off. I could have gotten us both killed." And now that she had a second to recall what had happened, she was astonished they were both still breathing.

"You were fantastic. You got her to confess the whole damn thing. Hands behind your head!" he yelled at Gonzales who'd begun to move.

Finch heard the doors slam, followed by stampeding feet down the stairs, but she kept her eyes on Rick.

"It's hard to believe she's the mastermind. Why in hell would she expose herself like this?"

"She didn't plan on leaving witnesses. You kept her talking. It gave me the chance I needed to get to her. I should have never let her get the drop on me."

"She was going to shoot you. I'm so…"

"I've warned you not to say that again. None of this is your fault."

"I distracted you."

Rick didn't have a chance to rebut her statement. Colt and Gib appeared.

Gib reached in the passenger side of the truck, grabbed the key fob Rick had tossed onto the seat, and silenced the alarm.

"There are flex cuffs in the console," Rick told him.

As soon as Colt had Gonzales covered, Rick placed her gun on top of the truck, then hurried over to Finch. Crouching in front of her, he caressed her hair, face, and arms. "Are you hurt? You're not hurt, are you?"

"Shaky, but okay." She tenderly touched his temple. "You're the one who's injured."

"I've been hit harder. I'll live. It's my turn to say I'm sorry. If anything had happened to you…" The look in his eyes said it all. She'd never felt so precious.

"Shhhh. We're both fine. A little worse for wear, but we're still here. That's what's important."

"Kevin's on his way along with the real medics," Gib

jested. His eyes widened as he made his way to the driver's side. Gonzales, had been pulled to her knees and was now facing Gib. A look of dismay on her face.

"This is the mastermind?" Gib asked after a noticeable hesitation.

"Looks like it," Rick confirmed.

Kevin beat the police and medical units by seconds. Since he didn't have any gear to unload, he made it to Finch before the paramedics did. She shooed him away, directing him to look at Rick. Her nerves might be shattered, but she wasn't the one who was bleeding.

It took a while, but the initial frenzy abated. Finch took refuge in the rear of a patrol car. She sat sideways on the seat, her legs dangling out the open door. She didn't want to feel trapped again. Nerves had her bouncing her heels against the bottom of the door frame. At one point, she glanced at the rear steps and noted the women had gathered—watching over her. She wished she was with them.

Colt had already placed a call to the FBI. Morgan and Hernandez were once again on their way to Sanibel. After disconnecting, Colt warned Finch not to mention the federal investigation. The warning was unnecessary. Rick's supervisor, Pulaski, had responded with the local units and took over the questioning.

She and Rick had been separated. She'd spent enough time with the police to know they didn't want one witness leading the other. Kevin stopped by to tell her Rick was going to have a hell of a headache, but he had a thick skull. He then insisted on checking her wrists. After he was certain she hadn't pulled out any of the stitches, he'd left to join his friends who had stepped off to the side to let the officers do their work.

Gonzales had been sequestered in the rear seat of another police unit. The woman was tense, maybe even scared. She was bent forward at the waist. Finch assumed the manager's hands would still be secured behind her back. She had to be uncomfortable. Finch didn't give a rat's ass.

Morgan and Hernandez arrived followed by several agents from the local FBI office. The questioning began again, with even more detail this time. Repeating old information and adding new. Adrenaline had kept her moving, but it was waning. She was so tired by the time they'd done questioning her, she fought the urge to crawl across the seat and take a nap. Instead, she adjusted her position so she could rest her head on the back of the seat.

"Finch?"

Damn. She'd zoned out. Who does that in the middle of a clusterfuck? Rick was staring worriedly at her from his position next to the open door.

"What's wrong? Does Kevin need to take a look at you?"

"Huh? No," she said scanning the area. The lot was nearly empty. Apart from the patrol car she was sitting in, all official vehicles were gone. "He already did. I'm just tired, I guess. Are we done?"

"For tonight. There'll be additional questions as they gather information, but we're good for now."

"Where's Gonzales?" Curiosity, not fear, drove the question. She wasn't afraid any longer. She'd spent a good deal of her life afraid and alone. She didn't feel either anymore.

"On her way to Tampa. I have no idea where she'll go to next. She's the Feds' problem now."

"I'm not, but I hope she rots in hell."

"I suspect that's what it will feel like for her. Even felons hate traitors and she's not getting out on bond. Death penalty will definitely be on the table."

Rick took her elbow and guided her out of the police unit, placing a hand on the top of her head so she didn't bump it on the door frame. He then steered her toward the stairs leading to Colt and Cat's place.

"Please don't tell me there are more questions. Not tonight, at least."

"No. No questions. We're spending the evening in Colt and Cat's guestroom. Kevin insisted on additional eyes on me for the night. I didn't feel up to arguing with him. And as much as I'd like to, neither of us has the energy for tearing up the sheets." His blue eyes sparkled in the light from the back porch.

"I'd feel better if you went to the hospital." A bandage had been placed over his temple.

"The medics and Kevin have cleared me. Some aspirin and I'll be good."

Finch stood beside Rick at the bottom of the steps, gazing at the deck above. Her body was screaming for rest, making the stairs appear insurmountable. Inhaling deeply, she took the first step using the railing for support. Her legs were less than steady, but they'd hold.

The women rushed to her side as they entered the living room, immediately hustling Finch into the master bath. The large Jacuzzi tub was filled. Bubbles covered the surface of the water, glistening in the light and making little snapping sounds as they burst. She wasn't able to raise an objection before she was stripped and instructed to get into the bath. Her protests were overridden and then went silent as warm water was forced through the tub's jets. Oh my God, she had no idea this was precisely what she needed. Her tension and aches began to slip away. A glass of wine was placed on the bathtub tray where she'd been told to rest her arms to keep her wrists dry.

These women were amazing. They chattered, laughed,

and comforted her. They cared about her—and for her. The knowledge forced a tear from her eye.

"What's wrong?" Shayne asked. Grabbing a tissue, she dabbed her cheek. "Are you hurting?"

"I've never had friends. Not real friends." She didn't try to stop another tear from falling.

"You do now," Josie stated firmly. "And you'd best stop crying or Rick will be convinced we tortured you in here."

"He said he loved me," Finch told them, a bit timidly.

"Oh, honey," River said, her North Carolina drawl coming through. "There's no doubting it. That man has fallen hard and it's about damn time."

There was a knock on the door. "Everything okay in there?" Rick asked.

The room broke out in laughter. "Everything is fine," Cat answered, still smiling. "Go next door and take a shower at Gib's. You're not crawling into bed stinking of sweat with this lovely lady."

"I've already done that. You guys need to finish up. She needs her rest."

Josie rolled her eyes. "She hasn't been out of his sight for thirty minutes and he's already mooning over her absence."

"She'll be ready when she's ready," Cat ordered. "Go sit down."

Between the warm bath and the wine, Finch found herself laughing with her new friends.

47

———————

*A*s the women started to filter out of the bathroom, Rick said good night to his friends. He pulled the Murphy bed from the wall of Colt's office which doubled as a guest room. The linens were already on the bed so all he had to do was grab the pillows and blanket from the closet. The mattress was a double, so it would be a tight fit for both of them, but he didn't care. The closer he was to her, the better.

The door opened. Finch quickly stepped inside, shutting it firmly behind her. The smile she wore lit up the room. She glowed—and he thanked God she was safe and with him.

Pulling her into his arms, he kissed the top of her head. "Why the big grin?"

She brushed a kiss against his neck before pulling away. "First, I look absolutely ridiculous."

He hadn't missed the baggy t-shirt or the leggings that were way too short for her height, but he was focused on the sparkling flecks in her copper eyes and her dazzling smile. "You look beautiful."

"You're blind, but I'll take it." She went up on her tiptoes and gave him a peck on the cheek.

"You said 'first'. What else has you grinning like the cat that ate the canary?" Once again, he tucked a loose strand of hair behind her ear.

"I have friends. I have real friends."

She sounded so astonished his heart hurt for her. He'd never known what it was like not to have family, friends, or teammates to call on for help or to simply share a beer. That she had to wait almost thirty years to claim any true friends was sad. He was grateful that his teammates and their spouses had taken her into their circle, and that she understood the depth of that friendship.

"And I have you," she added, her grin growing wider.

"That you do." He cupped her head between his hands and kissed her, long and deep. His large hands encircled her wrists, lightly running his thumb over fresh bandages. "I can't tell you how much I'd like to press you against that mattress and devour every inch of you, but Colt or Cat will be checking on me periodically. SOP for head injury."

"SOP?"

"Standard Operating Procedure."

"I repeat. You should have gone to the hospital."

"I'd rather beat myself over the head with a baseball bat. I'm good. I promise you." He guided her to the bed. "I wouldn't risk anything that would keep me from spending a very long life with you."

"I love you," she whispered.

"That goes both ways," he said, brushing his lips against hers. "Now," he said, patting the mattress. "Let's settle in. I've got a few things to tell you."

"Good or bad?" she asked, slipping under the covers.

"Nothing bad." He tugged her closer, then pressed her head to his bare chest. "While you were lounging in the tub and being plied with wine—Ouch!" He flinched when she pinched his side. He smiled. Damn. She was amazing. Not only had she fought off a man with her hands literally tied, but she'd also been able to distract the woman who had them at gunpoint until he was able to disarm her.

"As I was saying," he continued, covering her hand with his. "While you were busy being pampered and plied with alcohol, we were putting our heads together and trying to connect the dots. Do you want to hear our theories?"

"Duh."

"There are a lot of gaps, and we may never know everything considering the subject matter."

"Because the subject matter is too sensitive?"

"Yeah. I don't think we'll get the details of Gonzales' operation, but I think we can make some educated guesses as to what happened. We may learn more from your mother's notebook. Nothing specifically related to the scheme as the government will redact it. Still, we may be able to get a better feel for what was going on."

"Do you think I'll ever see it again?"

He tightened his clasp on her shoulder. Part of what he was going to share would be hard for her to hear. All he could offer her was support and his love.

"I trust Morgan and Hernandez to do what they can to get it back to you. If there is anything classified in it, there's going to be some dancing around."

"Which is understandable," she muttered. He felt her moist breath against his chest.

"So, what do you know—or think you know?"

"If Gonzales was telling the truth about starting this whole dollars-for-secrets plot, we suspect this whole scenario started close to thirty years ago. She would have been in her early twenties then. Remember this is all guesswork, but it's likely she was working for one of the casinos when she found her first mark. Whether she was looking, or the opportunity had simply presented itself, we may never know even if the government unearths the truth."

"Is it possible she was a plant by another government?"

"It crossed our minds, but if another country was involved, their intelligence people would have dealt with your mother a long time ago. Gonzales was sloppy toward the end—even cocky. Tony and the men he hired were dumbasses. Foreign intel would have found you long before Gonzales did. No. I'm pretty certain she was a freelancer selling to the highest bidder."

"Bitch."

"She's that and more," he agreed. "Josie touched base with Mr. Woodward again, the reporter that worked with your dad. As it turns out, your mother was also a journalist at the Las Vegas Review-Journal. She covered breaking news for the most part. Your dad had balls of brass, to quote Woodward, so it was out of character for him to be nervous about a story, but he was edgy about this one. Woodward said O'Shea felt unsettled when he left for the FBI office—like he was questioning whether he was making the right move. Woodward doesn't know if he ever made it there. The FBI will be digging deep on that part. If anyone at the FBI is, or was, compromised, they want to know about it.

"After your parents weren't heard from for several days, Woodward said the editor was the one that called in a missing person report. Several members of the paper's staff went over to the O'Shea's apartment, but there was no sign of them. Both cars were gone. Based on Gonzales' ramblings, we can guess Gonzales killed your father, or had him killed. Your mother took off and kept running."

"Why wouldn't she have called the police? I would in a heartbeat if something happened to you."

He kissed the top of her head. "She may have had good reason not to trust them. I'd bet your parents had a plan in place if your dad didn't return from the FBI. Woodward said your dad was nervous but he was also smart, so that would make sense. What happened between the night your dad and mom disappeared and the time you landed on the steps of a fire station would be pure speculation without further information. If we don't get the answers from your diary, we can try to put the puzzle pieces together ourselves. It will take time, but we'll get there."

"It doesn't matter. Honestly. I'm curious, but knowing they cared about me is all I need to know." She nuzzled against him. "What else did you figure out?"

"She was constantly on the move, as the postmarks on your packages showed. We don't know what she was thinking, or how she reasoned things out when it came to you. I'm convinced she did what she believed was best."

"What's your consensus on how Gonzales pulled off her scheme?" She let out a sigh. She sounded weary. Who could blame her?

"Gonzales' first mark would have been her hardest but once she found a buyer for the information, she would have had a bankroll that allowed her to pay off the gambler's debts with plenty of money to spare. After a few more successful transactions she'd be in business. There is always a foreign government seeking state secrets, even friendly ones, for huge sums of money.

"It's hard to believe based on the way she acted tonight, but she had to be smart and slick. Finding targets, contacting interested parties, and not a whiff of it hitting the intel world.

"Over time, she stopped trolling for marks herself. From what Gib was able to gather while in Vegas, Tony was skimming for new marks and touching base with old ones. Addicted gamblers almost always wind up owing the house again and Tony was there to give them relief in exchange for information."

"Why was Tony at the Tampa casino?"

"Gonzales may have had him on a fishing expedition for new targets outside of Vegas. U.S. Army Central Command is based in Tampa. Lots of classified information passes through there."

"How was it so easy for him to get a job as a manager there?"

"Probably a favor to another casino. Despite the Tampa casino being tribal owned, I've learned they are all tight with one another. *You scratch my back. I'll scratch yours.*"

"Any idea how deep Tony was involved?" Finch yawned and snuggled closer.

"Hard to say. The Feds have Gambino. He'll talk. Considering the seriousness of this crime, he'll want a deal. This is death penalty level shit."

"I can't figure out why my mother sent me those charms? I'm not a cryptologist. I had no idea who they were from or what they meant. What made her think I'd keep them?"

"I don't know. It may be as simple as a mother's instinct." His hand glided over the length of her arm.

"I don't think she realized how bad foster care would be."

"Taking you with her would have endangered you, as well. If she left you with a relative, she may have put them in danger, too. I wouldn't be surprised to find out there were inquiries made to family members."

"I have family?" She propped her upper body on her

forearm and gaze down at him. "Real family? Blood relatives?"

"The FBI mentioned a maternal grandmother who was still alive." He was grinning at her stunned expression. "I'm sure she'd love to meet the granddaughter she never knew existed."

"I wonder if I have other family?"

"It stands to reason. We'll talk to your grandmother. We may also learn of others from the results of your ancestry test."

"It would be nice to know I have family." She rested her head on his shoulder again. "It would be even nicer if they were good people who wanted me as part of their clan. If not, I have all the family I need here."

"What about your name? Will you be changing it to O'Shea?"

She was silent for a minute. "I don't think so. I became Savannah Finch on my own. I earned my name. Maybe one day I can name a child after them, but I'm going to stay Savannah."

She was Savannah, but he had every intention of asking her if she was willing to change her last name.

EPILOGUE

*T**hree weeks later – Sanibel Island*

FINCH HAD SNUCK onto the private beach where she'd come ashore after her swim across San Carlos Bay. She'd wanted to return to where it all started. Coming here was akin to opening a book she'd already read. She needed some time alone to sort through it, skip over the bad chapters and focus on the good.

She'd been living in a hurricane for the last few weeks. If not for Rick and company, she'd be nothing but tattered debris, pushed to the curb or pulled out to sea. As wild as things had been, they went into overdrive after the night of Gonzales' arrest. A new team of FBI agents along with investigators from Homeland Security arrived the next day. They didn't waste any time dividing and conquering. While she and Rick were their main focus, everyone was questioned at one time or another during the first two days. It had been intense. Fortunately, each night she was able to lay with Rick. When they weren't burning off the stress of the day, they were talking about her future.

She had options and relatives. The FBI had contacted her maternal grandmother and informed her of her daughter's murder, although not the full story behind it. Many of the details surrounding her mother and father's deaths would remain classified. Finch was okay with that. What her parents had set out to expose had been uncovered. Finch wanted to believe they rested in peace now —together.

She'd flown to Nevada to meet her grandmother. Her grandmom wanted her to stay. But Finch had a new family here. She'd known the minute she'd gotten off the plane in Las Vegas, that it would never be her home. A big event was being planned in Vegas so that both sides of her family could meet the secret daughter. Her spitfire of a grandmother had insisted and was taking care of those details.

She'd also spent a few days in Washington, D.C. answering questions from individuals a few steps higher up the ladder than her previous interrogators. Rick had already been debriefed and was needed at work, so Gib had accompanied her on his mysterious friend's private jet. As stressful as those days were, he was always waiting for her as she exited the FBI offices. He'd take the weight of the day off her shoulders with laughter and light-hearted conversation. The other positive of the trip was the charms her mother had wanted her to keep were returned along with a copy of the notebook. As Rick had suspected, a portion of it had been redacted, but not as much as she'd feared.

She'd started to read it on the return flight. Gib had been unusually quiet, only interrupting her to see she ate and drank something. She'd finished it last night tucked in bed next to Rick. He'd held her while she read the sad and horrifying tale that was her mother's life. Anne O'Shea had been running and searching for information for almost thirty years. Finch had to admit she'd become obsessed with finding who was responsible for her husband's death and bringing him to justice. That obsession, in Finch's opinion, had led to several bad decisions on her mother's part.

The notebook, unfortunately, didn't fill in all the holes they'd hoped it would, particularly how Finch landed on a Tampa fire station's doorstep. Despite knowing her parents' names, Steve's search for a record of her birth hadn't been successful. There were also gaps in time and location, as if they weren't important to what her mother had wanted to convey—that she'd loved her husband and daughter very much. Each entry ended with a heart drawn around their names. Every year on Finch's birthday, she'd tell her daughter how much she was loved and how proud she was of her.

Despite the sobs, Rick never suggested she put the diary away. Instead, he held her tighter. She'd cried herself to sleep in his arms. The next morning, she felt as if she'd been given a new beginning. She knew she'd been loved. Knowing the truth of the matter and reading her mother's words of love, all her years of resentment slipped away. She'd shed her past, along with a lot of tears, and now had a future open to her.

Pulling her knees to her chin, she watched the sun dart in and out of the clouds in the afternoon sky. At the sound of tires crunching the crushed shell drive that led up to the beach, she smiled. She'd texted Rick so he wouldn't worry when he didn't find her at home.

"Hi," she said, not looking over her shoulder. "Playing hooky?"

"Took off a little early today. I have plans for this

evening," he said, crouching in front of her, similar to the day he'd found her.

"Would those plans include me?"

"If you'll have dinner with me tonight. I have reservations for two at a waterside restaurant."

"Are you asking me on a date?"

"A date. A celebration. Whatever you want to call it."

"What are we celebrating? My new car?" Gib had taken her to a dealership owned by a man who was a huge fan of Colt and Gib's photography. He was also a client of Steve and Troy's security business. She got a sweet deal on a slightly used Camaro. Used or not, it beat the hell out of her ancient Toyota.

"I like your wheels."

"Thanks. I do, too. How about we celebrate them and my new job."

"You have a job?"

"Eh, maybe. The owners of Spa Terra contacted me. They asked if I'd be interested in managing the place when they reopen."

"You know you don't have to work."

They'd discovered both her parents had large insurance policies and had also set up an investment fund for her which had grown sizably over the years. Then there was the substantial reward from the government. She'd be comfortable if she decided not to work again. "I know, but I'm not good at doing nothing."

"Have you considered opening up your own business here on Sanibel? You'd have plenty of clients, especially in season. It would mean more work than just managing, but on the upside you can make your own hours and be your own boss. Plus, you wouldn't have to travel."

"Hmmm. Hmmm. It never occurred to me I'd have the means to do that."

"We can talk about it over dinner."

She clasped the hand he held out to her and let him pull her to her feet. "If we're not celebrating my new car, what are we celebrating?"

"Us," he said. "If you'll have me." He slipped a ring out of his pocket. "I hope this is okay," he said, holding the bright, warm amber stone up to the light. "It reminded me of your eyes. If you'd prefer a diamond…"

"It's perfect." It wasn't a traditional ring. He'd obviously put a lot of thought into it, making it all the more special. "How about we skip dinner?" she asked before kissing him deeply, lovingly—hungrily.

"I owe you a dinner date and tonight is the night. I want to watch your eyes sparkle in the moonlight. I want to hear you laugh as the bubbles from the champagne tickle your nose. Then I want to go home and make love to my future wife."

She had a future—a future she'd never believed she'd have. One filled with love. She threw her arms around his neck. "I love you. I've never said that to another person. I didn't know what it was like to be loved."

"I'm going to make sure you know what it feels like every day for the rest of our lives," he said, lifting her into his arms.

AFTERWORD

Secrets Unlocked was completed just days before Hurricane Ian roared onto Sanibel Island and the surrounding communities. After the storm passed, I hesitated to send the story to my editor. The place I wrote about was gone. The causeway had collapsed, businesses destroyed and, most sadly, lives were lost. But Sanibel Island and the rest of Southwest Florida are healing. Organizations like Team Rubicon, World Central Kitchen and others have done a tremendous job lending a hand. Smaller, local organizations like Captains for Clean Water https://captainsforcleanwater.org are working to clean up the waterways and help small businesses along the coast get back on their feet. If you're so inclined, please consider a donation.

ACKNOWLEDGMENTS

Books are not the sole result of a writer searching for the right words and a plot that will hold your interest. They are the result of family, friends and others who step in and give the author support, ideas, critiques, and answer research questions. You know who you are, and I thank you for all your help. A special thank you to Victor H. Royer for lending me his expertise on the workings of Las Vegas. I would have made some serious missteps without his advice.

Sue-Ellen Welfonder is a USA Today Bestselling author, and I am lucky to know her. She has given freely of her time and expertise. I can't thank her enough.

Once again, Elizabeth Turner Stokes of estokescreative.com has created the awesome cover.

And, finally, to all of you who read my stories and leave reviews. They are, quite frankly, the biggest boost you can give a writer. Please take the time to review this and other writers' efforts so that we may continue to entertain you.

ALSO BY C. F. FRANCIS

Sanctuary Island

Lovers Key

Explosive Touch

Run, River, Run

ABOUT THE AUTHOR

C. F. Francis is a native Floridian who loves mystery, suspense and romance. Her favorite pastimes are reading (of course) and traveling. Her diverse background includes working in law, insurance, tourism and a stint with the Florida Legislature's Organized Crime Committee. She is honored to have friends who have served in the Special Forces and Military Intelligence, who have generously shared their expertise when asked. Ms. Francis lives in Southwest Florida near the areas where her novels take place.

If you enjoyed this story, please consider leaving a review on BookBub, Goodreads, or your retailer's site.

You can follow C. F. Francis at:

www.cffrancis.com